Jessica Andrews writes fiction. Her debut novel, *Saltwater*, was published in 2019 and won the Portico Prize in 2020 and her second novel, *Milk Teeth*, was published in 2022. She is a Contributing Editor for *ELLE* magazine and she writes for the *Guardian*, the *Independent*, BBC Radio 4 and *Stylist*, among others. She was nominated for the *ELLE* List in 2020 and shortlisted for the Women's Prize for Fiction Futures in 2022. She co-runs literary and arts magazine *The Grapevine*, and co-presents literary podcast *Tender Buttons*. She is a Lecturer in Creative Writing at City University, London.

~

'Languid, elegantly written and dripping with a rich
emotional humidity'
Martin Chilton, *Independent*

'Andrews's lyrical prose overflows with sweet metaphors
and sensuous imagery'
Ellys Woodhouse, *New Statesman*

'Across its blissfully sprawling passages detailing
scenes from different cities, what anchors the novel is
its exploration of how hunger, class, desire and gender
are interlaced . . . the writing is gilded with a vulnerable
immediacy, blisteringly honest and visceral'
Miriam Balanescu, *Irish Times*

'In lyric dispatches, with the condensed cadences of
poetry, Andrews's novel brilliantly explores the ways we
grow into and beyond the limits of ourselves'
Andrew McMillan

'A sensual and languid love story'
Sadhbh O'Sullivan, *Refinery29*

'Andrews's prose is distinctly stylised. It possesses a heightened sensuality which reflects the protagonist's aspiration to live fiercely, "like lightning" – free of restraint'
Michael Donkor, *i*

'Electrifying . . . An intimate exploration of class, precarity, sex, power and, above all, of the fragility and exuberance of love. The prose is vivid, gorgeous and supple. It's immediate and ultra-sensual and has the emotional pitch and intensity of the best gig you've ever been to. A thunderbolt of a book'
Francesca Reece

'*Milk Teeth* is true and I am so grateful it exists. What a relief it is, finally, to step off the ledge: to choose to adventure, to give and take care'
Livia Franchini

'Sharply sensuous . . . Andrews takes aim at the cultural pressures shaping unhealthy ideals of femininity without ever seeming to preach'
Anthony Cummins, *Daily Mail*

'A transporting, visceral second novel . . . a sizzling novel to read in the heat, when you're hungry for life'
Lucy Writers Platform

'Heady, sweaty, sexy, salient. I devoured it'
Abigail Tarttelin

MILK TEETH

Jessica Andrews

sceptre

First published in Great Britain in 2022 by Sceptre
An imprint of Hodder & Stoughton
An Hachette UK company

This paperback edition published in 2023

8

A CIP catalogue record for this title is available from the British Library

Paperback ISBN 9781473682825
eBook ISBN 9781473682832

Typeset in Sabon MT by Palimpsest Book Production Ltd,
Falkirk, Stirlingshire

Printed and bound in Great Britain by Clays Ltd, Elcograf S.p.A.

Hodder & Stoughton policy is to use papers that are natural,
renewable and recyclable products and made from wood grown in
sustainable forests. The logging and manufacturing processes are expected
to conform to the environmental regulations of the country of origin.

Hodder & Stoughton Ltd
Carmelite House
50 Victoria Embankment
London EC4Y 0DZ

www.sceptrebooks.co.uk

For Nancy

You're so young. You can eat the whole world,
if you want to.

Taxi driver, London, May 2019

Part One

Part One

I

I kiss you for the first time on my birthday. I am sweating in gold sequins in a basement in Peckham. You are wearing a mask in the shape of a cat's face and you take it off as we walk into the smoke. Your lips are wet and your tongue tastes of blood. We go outside for some air and watch the sky begin to lighten. A cigarette burns between your painted fingernails and you ask if I have any resolutions for my twenty-eighth year. I focus on the silver curling from your lips and say,

'To be unashamedly myself.'

We walk to your house through the park, tower blocks purple in the dawn. I swing your hand between us in the half-light. You disappear into a dark crop of bushes and your earring glints beneath the fading moon.

'Just having a piss,' you call through the darkness. 'Don't go anywhere.'

'I might be gone by the time you get back.' I twirl beneath an orange streetlamp. 'And then you'll never see me again.' You emerge from the grass, zipping up your fly, your black denim jacket torn at the cuffs.

'That would be a shame,' you whisper into my neck and your voice breaks around my shoulders like a wave.

Later, in the warmth of your bedroom, beneath a string of red lights, you ask me,

'What do you want?' You trace the outline of my hips with your fingers. 'Tell me what you want me to do to you, and whatever it is, I'll do it.'

'I'll have to think about it,' I say too quickly, flushed with panic.

2

I have a skin tag on the underside of my left wrist, fleshy and raised, like a pink mushroom. When I was a child, I stole a needle from my mother's sewing box and poked it until it bled.

'It means you're special,' my mother said, wiping the red away. 'You might have magic powers.'

'What kind of powers?' I asked her.

'You'll have to wait until you're older. That's when your powers will start.'

'But I don't want to wait.'

'No.' She traced a lipstick across her mouth, looking past me at her reflection in the mirror. 'But you have to.'

I sucked fizzy cola bottles and sherbet flying saucers, gummy rings jammed onto every finger.

'I'm married,' I declared.

'Who to?' my mother frowned, serving crinkle-cut chips and crispy chicken dippers doused in ketchup, squirting cream straight from the can into my mouth afterwards.

I wore long denim shorts from the boys' section or dungarees with a red crew-neck T-shirt. I played football at lunchtime, tossing my ponytail when the boys rolled their eyes as I missed the ball, ignoring the stares of my friends in their checked summer dresses, grass stains smeared across my white ankle socks.

I sped down the street in my light-up roller blades, fast and fearless as the wind tore at my T-shirt and my hair streamed behind me in ribbons. I sat in the long grass, pulling daisies from the soil and tearing off their petals chanting,

'He loves me, he loves me not,' not sure which answer I should be hoping for.

'I'll never wear one of those,' I said to my mother, wrinkling my nose at the sun-bleached pair of breasts nestled in a white lace bra on a peeling billboard, as we sped past it in the car.

'But you'll need one.' My mother turned up the heating. 'When your boobs start to grow.'

'Maybe I won't have them.' My bare nipples prickled inside my T-shirt.

'Oh, love,' my mother said, sadly. 'You will.'

3

I walk from my house to yours, kicking up leaves in my shiny leather shoes. My veins are laced with silver and my hair almost crackles. I skip up the steps and stand too close to your blue front door, waiting for you to answer. Your body looms behind the frosted glass like something underwater. The door swings open and we teeter uncertainly for a moment, then you give me a soft look and I fall into it.

'Do you want something to drink?' You lead me to the kitchen. 'Tea? Water? A tinny?' Your worn jacket is hung on the back of the door, scuffed Dr. Martens kicked off in the hall. Your kitchen smells of damp wood and rotting fruit and I drink it in. You swing yourself up onto the kitchen counter and for a moment you seem nervous beneath the electric light.

I start to say 'tinny' but it comes out as 'tea'.

'Alright. Got this herbal stuff. It's got dandelions or something in it. Picked them from the mountains myself.' You open the cupboard and pinch a handful of herbs from a fingerprinted jar.

'Which mountains?' I raise my eyebrows.

'Good question.' You hand me a chipped yellow mug and I drink too quickly and burn my lips. My mouth is flooded with buds and leaves and you brush them away with your tongue.

The thin chain around your neck grazes my soft stomach. Your skin smells animal, like meat and fur. You touch every part of my body with urgent hands and I turn gold all over.

My mouth says, 'I want you,' before I can stop it. You kiss my ankles, my collarbone, the spaces behind my knees. I cling to you like a burr.

When I wake, it is dark and you are leaving.

'Morning,' you whisper. 'I've got a meeting with my supervisor.' I cast around the room for my tights and pull them on over clammy skin. 'Stay, if you like.'

'It's okay.' I rub my eyes. 'I should go. I've got things to do.'

We stand in the street and the white light hardens our

edges. Your big black overcoat is covered in bits of fluff and I want to reach out and touch it.

'Have a nice day,' you wink, swinging your leg over your bike.

'See you later,' I reply, all moons and stars and fear.

I walk back home through the morning rush, my lips chafed and swollen, the smell of your sweat in my hair. The air is sharp on my tingling skin and I unbutton my coat and let it sting me awake. I carry the thrill of you inside me like something dangerous; a pan of boiling water, threatening to spill. I think of the light splitting your bedroom curtains, your face smudged with sleep on the pillow. In the past, I would never have allowed myself to reach out and take any part of you but I am trying to live more easily, to become someone softer.

People hurry past me carrying cardboard coffee cups and paper pastry bags, laptop cases, newspapers and mobile phones. I walk slowly, pushing against the current. There are clementines lined up outside the fruit shop in a string of orange beads, sunflowers shedding their petals onto the pavement. There are figs laid out like a tray of soft bruises and I reach for one without thinking.

'Two for a pound,' the fruit seller says to me and I press a gold coin into his palm, his fingernails rimmed with soil. 'Very good ones this year.' He nods his approval as I select another, weighing it in my hand. I thank him and walk back into the day, biting into the purple fruit. Sticky pink strings get caught between my teeth. I feel the shadow of your lips on my neck and go dizzy with it.

4

When I was at school, my teacher kept a statue of the Virgin Mary on a wooden shelf above the whiteboard. I was entranced by the blue of the sky caught in her veil and the band of gold leaf that settled in her hair. I stared up at the silver Swords of Sorrow driven into her bleeding heart.

'Mary never committed a sin in her whole life,' my teacher said. 'And that's why she was chosen to be the mother of God.' I held my breath and tried to count all of the sins I had already committed. I would never be chosen and I had barely even begun.

I counted the ribs etched in Jesus' skin and watched garnets of blood drip down his concave stomach. I sang,

'They whipped and they stripped and they hung me on high,' along with the choir as I pressed a sharp pencil into the soft centre of my palm, gritting my teeth as I tried to imagine how it would feel to have nails driven through my hands. I read about Jesus starving in the desert, John the Baptist in his camel-hair shirt and Mary Magdalene on her knees, repenting for the sins of her body, rubbing oil into the soles of Jesus' callused feet.

'I'm going to be a nun,' I told my mother on our way home from church one Sunday, my white leather bible tucked beneath my arm.

'Really?' My mother raised her eyebrows. 'Why do you want to be a nun?'

'So I can get into heaven.'

My mother stifled a smile. 'There are other ways to get into heaven.'

'How?'

'By being a good person.'

'But what about sin?' My mother was quiet. 'Will you get into heaven?'

'No.' She avoided my gaze. 'Probably not.'

I've been cheeky to my mam, I scrawled across a piece of paper to take to confession. *I forgot to do my homework.* The priest placed his warm hand on my head and muttered a prayer, the soft cadence of his whisper curling around my body like a spell.

'Go in peace,' he said, as I skipped down the aisle to join my classmates, nervously chewing their sleeves as they waited to be absolved of eating too many sweets and staying up late watching telly.

'It's beautiful, isn't it?' My teacher smiled down at me. 'To feel pure and clean again.'

5

We meet outside the South London Gallery. You have been working on your dissertation in the library and your eyes are glazed from a day of screens and strip lights. I feel shy around you in public, our faces pink against the darkening sky. The exhibition is closing and you lock your bike to the railings with a jangle of keys then we hurry inside. Your hand brushes my waist on the stairs.

'Sorry,' you murmur, in a voice that drips. We sit on a box in a shadowy room and watch a projection of shifting colours. There is a voice recording and I try very hard to listen but I am distracted by your body beside me; your movements strobe-like, struck by light.

'The gallery will be closing in ten minutes,' says a voice over a loudspeaker.

'Thank god,' you whisper. 'Couldn't concentrate on a single word.'

'Really?' I try to sound disapproving.

'Really,' you say into my ear. I can smell the power in my own skin, creamy and bitter, like burnt milk.

We go to a nearby pub and I can't focus on anything. The polished rows of glasses on dark wood and the red buses rattling by outside feel flimsy, as though I am in a play about London, as if the vodka bottles are props filled with water and everything could topple at any minute. You rest your hand on my thigh beneath the table and it seems inconceivable that I could want something and have it so easily.

'Do you want to come back to mine?' you ask softly, pushing away your half-drunk pint of muddy bitter.

'Yes,' I say, breathlessly. You stand up and shrug on your jacket, taking my hand and pulling me out onto the street. We stop at a newsagents for a bottle of wine.

'I only like rosé,' you confess. 'Is that alright?' I take in your long limbs in the doorway, washed-out T-shirt belted into black jeans, all tangled curls and trailing laces.

'Okay,' I smile. 'Very teenage.' You flush and disappear into the shop and I lean against the wall, trying to get a grip on myself. You emerge a few moments later, a blue plastic bag swinging from your fingers.

'I feel a bit like a teenager,' you say, pushing me up against the wall and kissing me. I laugh uneasily, rough brick grazing the back of my neck.

'I don't want to be a teenager,' I murmur.

You move your hands through my hair. 'I think we're all

teenagers, really. Inside.' I consider my teenage self and feel relieved to be here, far away from her sweet perfume and cloying secrets.

'I'm glad I'm not a teenager.'

'Yeah,' you take my hand as we cut across the green. 'I mean, I'm glad I'm not a teenager, either.' Your eyes glitter in the purpling dark. 'Teenagers would never do the kinds of things that we do.'

'What kinds of things?'

You pull me along the pavement. 'Just wait and see.'

We learn all the soft parts of each other. A scar on a thigh, torn by a screw. A freckle on the sole of a foot. Flakes of eyelid eczema, a bobbled shaving rash in the pit of a groin. A childhood chickenpox mark. A smudged tattoo from a hot tarmac summer. We are almost young and although our bodies hold many things, they do not show up on our skin yet. It would be easier somehow, if they did.

6

I turned thirteen and my mother took me to Marks and Spencer to get a bra properly fitted.

'No one ever took me to get measured,' she said. 'I just wore your auntie's old ones.'

'Were you the same size?'

'No.' She shook her head, sadly. 'Not even close.'

I pulled off my T-shirt in the changing room, avoiding the mirror, as a woman with cold hands wrapped a tape measure around my breasts.

'We'll have to look in the D cup section,' she winked over my head at my mother. 'You lucky thing.' I crossed my arms over my chest as she disappeared through the curtain. I hated my breasts. They were soft and ungainly, bulging beneath my T-shirts, weighing me down. I envied my friends as they mocked their own 'bee stings' and went bra-less beneath halterneck tops or wore pretty, flimsy triangles with thin straps. The bra-fitter returned with armfuls of lace, fitted with clasps and adjusters, side supports and mesh. She frowned as I spilled out of a pair of pastel-pink cups.

'Can you do a little jiggle?' she asked me and I stared at her blankly. 'Come on,' she said, bouncing on her tiptoes. 'Just so I can check the support.' I wiggled my shoulders reluctantly, my face burning red.

'No, that one's not right.' She looked at my mother again. 'All the young girls have big boobs, these days.' She covered her mouth and whispered, 'It's the hormones in the meat.'

My friend Emma's dad worked in an abattoir and brought home huge bags of meat dripping in plastic. When I went to her house for tea, we sat at the table piled with beef steaks and chicken wings, a jug of homemade peppercorn sauce on the side. Her dad sat at the head of the table in his bloodstained shirt, shaking his head at our blackened steaks.

'You lot are soft,' he said, mopping up a pool of blood with a slice of white bread.

Emma had thick, glossy hair and long fingernails filed to sharp points, painted neon pink. I envied her clear skin and her fat ponytail as I picked the skin around my own bitten cuticles.

'My mam says it's all the protein,' she said, applying a layer of glittery lip gloss and tossing her hair in the mirror. 'It makes you strong.' I crossed my arms over my breasts, imagining chemicals coursing through hooves and fur then splitting on my tongue.

'I'm becoming a vegetarian,' I told my mother later, pushing away my plate of chicken nuggets.

'That's your decision.' She speared one of my chips with her fork. 'But you need to make sure you eat properly. You need to get all of your vitamins.'

'Don't worry.' I took a sip of orange cordial. 'I will.'

7

I go for a drink with my friend Rosa. She pulls off her black beret and hangs it on the back of her chair. I carry over half-pints of lager and a packet of dry-roasted peanuts. I tell her about the cat-shaped mask and the dandelion tea, the books on your shelf arranged in Poetry, Plays and Prose.

'You like him,' she says, accusingly.

'I don't know.' I tear open the silver packet with my teeth. 'It feels weird. I'm good on my own.' Rosa takes a sip of her beer and her lips leave a purple smudge on the glass. She crunches a peanut and gives me a knowing look. 'What?' I ask her.

'You never let yourself have the things you want.' We watch a group of men playing pool in the corner, coloured balls skittering across green felt.

'That's not true. I don't know what I want.'

'Really?'

I drink a mouthful of beer, avoiding her gaze.

'Are you hungry?' asks Rosa. 'Shall we get some food?' She tosses a menu across the table and I pretend to read it.

8

When I was in primary school, my mother had a miscarriage. She woke up one morning with a pain in her stomach and I watched as she threw her silky nightie straight into the washing machine, her pale hands stained with blood.

'I'm okay,' she said as I reached for them in horror. 'It's just a women's thing. I'll explain properly later.'

My dad left work to come and take me to school so my mother could go to the hospital. He was twitchy and distracted, blue shadows beneath his eyes.

'I don't know how to plait hair,' he said, flummoxed by the glittery butterfly clips nestled in his oil-stained palm. 'Can you not just wear it down?'

At lunchtime, I unwrapped my sandwiches to find slices of ham pressed between thick wedges of yellow. I hated butter and the smell rushed vomit up the back of my throat.

'You've got to eat them, love,' the dinner lady sighed. 'I'm going to sit here and watch until you're finished.' I chewed my crusts reluctantly but there was something hard lodged in my throat that throbbed when I tried to swallow. 'There are starving children in Africa,' the dinner lady scolded. 'And you won't eat your lovely dinner.' My tears dripped into the tin foil and the dinner lady's cheeks were mottled pink. 'What's the matter?' she asked but I couldn't tell her about the feeling in my throat or the blood in the washing machine or that my dad didn't know what I liked.

'My mam's in hospital,' I choked and the dinner lady relented and helped me pack my lunch away.

A metallic edge separated me from my classmates for the rest of the day. I felt different from them, as though I was carrying a careful secret that stopped me joining in with their chewing and slurping and playground clamour. My hunger held my worry and my fear like a dam, so I didn't have to feel it any more.

9

You invite me to your house for tea and the day passes in a jittering blur. I finish my shift at the café and then cycle between my students' houses, checking my phone for your name in light. I am worried about what you will cook and whether I will be able to eat it.

'Shall I bring anything?' I text you, hoping for a hint. Your reply blooms green across my screen and my stomach bucks.

'So sorry. Don't think I can do tonight. Got a deadline in the morning and it's gonna be a late one. Really want to see you! Lemme know when you're free?' My breath catches in my chest and I hate it. I have been strong and self-contained for a long time now. I don't rely on anyone else. But now you are in me and just like that, you hold the soft, wet muscle of my exposed heart in your hand.

'No *worries,*' I reply, breezily. '*Not sure when I'm free. I'll let you know?*' You send me a broken heart and I shove my phone into the bottom of my bag without a reply.

My mother quit her job as a teaching assistant when I was born, so she could take care of me. My father earned good money working in a pharmaceutical factory, but he controlled their bank account and my mother had to beg him for food money every week.

'I've only got two pounds left in my purse,' she pleaded as he left for work in the pale dawn. 'We've got no milk or bread and I need to put some petrol in the car.' My dad left a smattering of coins on the kitchen table and my mother scraped the linings of coat pockets for extra pennies, digging her fingers behind the cushions on the settee, pulling out lint and fluff.

Our small terraced house was bursting at the seams with plastic toys and piles of washing and my mam was always asking my dad if we could move somewhere bigger but he told her that he couldn't afford it. He bought a house to rent out in secret and my mother found a letter from the estate agent in the glove compartment of his car.

'Look,' she showed me, her hands shaking in fury. 'He lied to us.'

Sometimes, my mother and I drove to the shopping centre after school and trailed around the shops, sighing over silky blouses and floral dresses that promised to make us into better versions of ourselves, if only we could afford them. My mother found a pair of long leather boots that hugged her calves and made her look like Kylie Minogue. I zipped them up for her as she stood in front of a long mirror, the leather supple and waxy beneath my fingers.

'You look amazing,' I said, as she fluffed her hair anxiously.

'Do you think so?' She checked the price tag and her face fell. 'They're expensive.' She looked at her reflection, pulling at her short black skirt and straightening her denim jacket.

'I think you should buy them,' I breathed, seeing the power rippling beneath her skin.

'But I can't afford them,' she frowned, bending down to pull them off.

'Just put them on your credit card.'

'You're a bad influence.' She straightened up and checked the mirror again. 'Do you really think I should?'

When we got home, we bundled our glossy carrier bags into the house while my dad was smoking in the garden, burying the boots at the back of the wardrobe where he wouldn't find them.

'Quick!' My mother flushed at the sound of him opening the back door. 'Don't tell him we went shopping. It's our secret, alright?' I mimed zipping my lips and throwing away the key, thrilled that we had a secret to share. I didn't wonder why my dad might be angry. I just knew we wanted things that were not meant for us, expensive things that we did not deserve.

I go swimming in the local pool, slipping into the blue and stretching my body as far as it will go, my muscles expanding as my arms part the water like silk. The evening sun falls through the window, scattering silver droplets as I swim through the rays, dappling my arms in ghostly waves. I am powerful in the water, propelling myself forward, kicking lengths until I am no longer thinking about my body; its weight, mass and density hidden beneath the surface. I think of you as I push through the ripples; your messy room and your soft, curling consonants, the whorls of hair on the back of your neck.

I told you that I liked swimming and you said,

'It's nice to think of your body in the water, held by all that blue.'

I wish it was like that. I wish I swam just to be held by something bigger than myself but there is a sharp, biting feeling that always pushes me further, faster and harder to the point of cruelty, my body hungry and sore. Sometimes my thoughts feel so fractious and my body so heavy that I am razed with a hot, red panic until I get in the water, desperate to forget myself in breath and lengths and rhythm. I think about my body beneath your fingers, how a want rises up in me I cannot contain. I don't want to deny myself living but traces of the girl I once was are still caught in my blood, pushing me to seal up and run away. I wonder where you are and what you are doing. I imagine you cycling home without your bike lights, your face flushed in the silver air. I swim faster, until my legs are shaking. I push harder, to try and gain control.

There were some girls in my class at school who were swimmers. They woke in the dark each morning to cut lengths across a glassy pool, their voices bouncing across the white tiles. They came to class stinging with chlorine, their damp hair making wet patches on the collars of their shirts. They ate little tubs of carrots with cottage cheese, hummus and celery, handfuls of almonds. They wrinkled their noses at my Dairylea Lunchables and my packet of Hula Hoops, the purple Twirl my mother packed carefully into my lunchbox.

'You eat a lot of chocolate,' they smirked as I bit into the sweetness, leaving flakes across my lips.

I told my mother what they said when I got home from school.

'Just ignore them, pet.' She shook her head. The next day I packed an entire multipack of KitKats in my school bag and solemnly lined them up on the table at lunchtime, one after the other, delighting in the horrified whispers that hissed over apples and oranges towards me. I laughed the girls' sharp words away but I still felt that they were good and pure while I was dirty and weak, giving in to my desires while they abstained.

I became friends with one of the swimmers and she stayed at my house one Saturday. She arrived with a plastic water bottle filled with ice and lemon, her pyjamas neatly folded in her pink gym bag. My mother made us jacket potatoes with beans and salad. She grated cheddar cheese into a plastic bowl and I grabbed a large handful and heaped it over the top. We ate in the sitting-room on our knees, watching the telly. I ran my finger along the rim of my plate and sucked the salt and tomato sauce from my fingers, then went back into the kitchen to get a second helping. The swimmer watched me as I chewed defiantly, refusing to meet her gaze.

'It's weird,' she said later, as we changed into our pyjamas, turning to face the wall, hiding our bodies from each other. 'You're so skinny but you eat so much.'

13

I meet you outside the grocery shop on your road. You are wearing a rumpled shirt beneath your coat, a dirty tote bag slung over your shoulder. I notice the single silver hoop that cups your earlobe and reach for it before I can stop myself. You kiss me on the lips and say,

'Fancy seeing you around here.'

'Likewise,' I smile and push you gently through the door.

There are squashes wrapped in plastic, cleaved in two, their mouths wide open. I sink my hands into a bucket of brown potatoes and trace the silt they leave on my fingers.

'What do we need?' I ask you.

'Broad beans,' you say. 'Leeks. Basil. Courgette. Crème fraîche, if they have it.' I rub the skin of a shiny tomato and sniff a lemony shock of coriander. I scan the rows of tins for broad beans and come back empty-handed.

'I don't think they have the beans,' I start, but you pull a green pod from right in front of me.

'They're here.' You look at me strangely. I have never seen them in their leaves before and my face heats up.

'Right.' I tear a paper bag and begin to fill it. We find

a long, frilly leek and I cradle it in my arms all the way to your house.

'Like a baby,' I declare, and you laugh.

Your kitchen is stacked with crusty plates and curls of orange peel. Tea bags bulge from their boxes and coffee grains have thickened in a half-drunk cafetière.

'Animals.' You point upstairs in the direction of your housemates.

'It's not that bad.' I sponge congealed butter from a knife. You shrug and take off your coat, rolling up your shirtsleeves. There is a fern tattooed on your forearm and it flashes like a dare.

'Wait.' You lift the lid from a big orange pot on the stove. 'Taste this.' You cast around for a spoon. Worry settles in my stomach like sand.

'What is it?'

'It's a soup I made earlier.'

I take the spoon from you and taste it, tentatively. 'Delicious.'

'Can you guess what I put in it?'

'Um, tomatoes? Maybe garlic?' I close my eyes, desperately trying to think of ingredients. 'I don't know what else,' I mumble.

'Just focus on the flavour.' I let myself sink into it, trying to settle my thoughts, raised like hackles. An acidic aftertaste prickles my gums. I open my eyes.

'Did you put lemon in it?'

'Yes!' Your face breaks into a smile. 'Excellent tastebuds. Very glad to have you on board.' I turn on the tap and begin to rinse the vegetables. The cold water soothes my warm skin and I feel relieved, as though I have passed a test confirming I know how to recognise pleasure.

You put on the Temptations and start chopping and

slicing. I break a bulb of smoked garlic into cloves and prise the broad beans from their shells. You flatten pastry with the heel of your hand and mix thick ricotta with fresh basil and Parmesan. I watch your careful fingers sprinkling and stirring, a red ache twisting in my stomach. I am hungry smelling the herbs and butter as I grease a baking dish and I let it ripple through me, thinking of your hand on the back of my neck as you told me to focus on flavour. You grate a lemon rind and the tang of its skin fills the kitchen. I crack an egg on the side of a glass bowl and slice a courgette into pale coins. The front door slams as your housemate goes out and then your hand is on my thigh beneath my dress.

'Do you like that?' you whisper and I kiss you in reply. You push me up against the fridge and I am drenched in want. A shopping list floats to the ground. I slip my hands beneath your shirt and dig my nails into the soft of your back. You bite my shoulder so hard it bruises black. We are breathless by the eggshells and the onion skins. Your eyes are grey and you look at me softly.

'Want to go for a walk while it's in the oven?' I hold your gaze, heat rising in me like a gathering storm. We put the tart in the oven and leave it to brown. The leaves on the street are curling yellow. I have always liked the days between seasons best; the point at which things begin to change.

14

I had a science teacher at school whose eyes traced my thighs whenever I walked into his classroom. His bright pink stare made me feel breathless and sweat dampened my armpits when I sat at the bench in front of him. He liked seeing me squirm, the way that worry coloured my face and plumped my lips.

'Everyone look over here,' he said, drawing the room of eyes towards me. 'Let's watch.' He scrubbed a green chopping board in preparation for dissection. 'If we stare at her for long enough, her face will turn bright red. A curious quality of the teenage human.'

One afternoon, he made us all step on a pair of scales at the front of the classroom, to prove an experiment about mass and weight. We each had to write our name on the board and chalk our weight in kilograms next to it. A current sparked through the classroom. The boys swaggered over to the scales, keen to prove their solidity, but we girls buried our faces in our textbooks, refusing to join in.

The teacher rolled his eyes. 'Come on, girls. It doesn't mean anything. It's just a number.' I stood on the scales carefully and wrote my number next to my name. Some of my friends refused to take part but I felt like I had to do it, to be brave enough to calculate weight and mass to find my density, which, our teacher reminded us,

'Proves the existence of something.'

15

We go out dancing in a disco-lit Deptford bar. The walls are sweating and the gin is bitter. The glitter smudged around my eyes leaves trails in my vision as I look for you in the crowd. I find you in a blood-red silky shirt, your eyes closed and the lids painted silver. You are snake-hipped and electric as you raise your arms above your head and look straight at me. We lock eyes, moving around the room, spinning in circles, your feet sliding towards me and away. You are asking me a question with your body, leading me to an edge and daring me to fall. We come so close our lips are almost touching. I can smell dark rum on your breath. The music is elastic and we throw ourselves at it. We are boundless and mercurial, a shifting silver joy.

'Do you want to get out of here?' you breathe into my ear. I nod and we grab our coats and stagger outside.

We get a taxi to your house and the streets are smudged through the window. You rest your head on my shoulder and mumble something I can't hear. Traffic lights leak across your face turning you emerald, ruby and gold.

In the darkness of your room, we shed our clothes like skin. Your body is a danger and I want to climb into it. I want to strip away your muscle and your fragile cage of bone.

'I feel very close to you,' you whisper in my ear. I am close to you but I want to be closer, to feel the friction of our lungs rub together, but there are things inside me you do not know about. There is a sharp, dark splinter in my chest and I am scared of the rush and spill of my blood, the hole it will leave, if I reach down and pull it out.

I wake with my limbs stuck to yours. My legs are streaked with black dirt and the balls of my feet ache. I bury my face in the morning cling of you; stale sweat and warm breath. You stir and dig your fingernails into my back, run your hands across my breasts. Daylight splits the curtains like something cracked open. We are hot and sticky beneath the sheets. You groan and roll over.

'My head hurts.'

'Poor baby,' I tease. You laugh and then move away, suddenly falling quiet. 'Are you okay?' I murmur, reaching for you. You turn to face me and a sadness I cannot grasp falls across your eyes before you quickly blink it away.

'I'm fine,' you whisper into my ear, pressing your body close to mine until I am molten.

You make pancakes while I am in the shower, beating eggs and rinsing blueberries, drizzling honey from a jar. I watch you from the doorway, my wet hair soaking into a borrowed T-shirt, your hips wiggling to Talking Heads. I want to ask about the sadness I saw curled beneath your skin but I don't know how to begin. Your face has a sheen of glitter and I move forward and reach out a finger to brush it away.

'God!' You jump. 'How long have you been standing there?'

'Just a minute.' I feel translucent in the daylight, as though the night exposed something about me that I can't take back.

'Are you hungry?' You put a stack of pancakes on the wooden table, filling a glass with orange juice, boiling the kettle. I sit down opposite you and sprinkle a pinch of cinnamon over my plate.

'They're perfect,' I say and you wink. I eat so many pancakes that you raise your eyebrows in disbelief and I am pleased. I want to impress you with my appetite, my capacity for pleasure.

When I was a young teenager, my friends and I spent Saturday afternoons piled into someone's parents' sitting-room. The windows steamed up with hot breath and hormones as we pulled the cushions from the settee and lay in a heap on the floor, listening to the Red Hot Chili Peppers and dreaming of the future. We talked for hours in the darkness, our bodies close together, passing around bowls of crisps and jumbo bottles of Coke, the rim slippery with saliva. We were on the cusp of something we could not name, a thick, white heat settling between us.

Sometimes we all slept over, sipping slugs of vodka pinched from a cupboard, wriggling into sweaty sleeping bags wearing all of our clothes. Someone put Babestation on the Freeview channel and women in underwear nestled phones between their breasts and ran their fingers along the waistbands of their knickers in the background, while we pretended not to be interested, each of us drenched in our own damp heat. The boys always wanted to play Spin the Bottle and we girls obliged because we didn't want to seem uptight. I often ended up having to kiss Jamie, who shoved his tongue between my lips and wiggled it vigor-ously, while everyone else watched in loaded silence, judging our technique.

Afterwards, I decamped to the kitchen with my friends Emma and Katie, nursing mugs of vodka and running our tongues over our teeth.

'That was so gross,' Emma groaned, leaning over the sink and rinsing her mouth with water straight from the tap.

'I actually can't think about it,' I said, taking a swig of

my drink. Katie fluffed up her hair, checking her reflection in the window.

'I kind of liked it.' She smiled at us uneasily.

'Oh my god,' we spluttered. 'You did not!'

Sometimes the boys nestled into us when we settled down to watch a film, their hands straying across our hips and waists. Their desire coated our bodies like oil and I sensed the power in my own flesh but it felt like it came from them somehow, as though they could cast their gaze elsewhere and turn it off at any time.

I couldn't sleep one night, sticky with spilled Coke and tingling with the horror film we had just watched. I wriggled around in my staticky sleeping bag until Jamie came over and lay down next to me.

'Are you okay?' His breath was sour.

'Yeah. Just can't sleep.'

He pressed his body close to mine. 'Me neither.' I turned away from him and closed my eyes but his hands came creeping into my sleeping bag and inside my clothes, touching my clammy skin. I wanted to tell him to stop as he slipped his hand between my legs but I was frozen somehow, static and unable to speak. I squeezed my eyes tightly shut until he lay back, his hand loose around my waist. I felt pinned to the carpet, as though something impossibly heavy was pressing down on me.

'Sweet dreams,' he whispered in my ear. I lay awake for hours, staring at the wall. I wanted to get up and leave but there was nowhere to go, just the dark streets outside, the dank blue alleyways and the open fields.

In the morning, Katie and I squeezed toothpaste onto our fingers and rubbed it across our gums in the poky bathroom, running our hands through our hair and sniffing our clothes. I told her about Jamie.

'Yeah?' She sat on the toilet and started to wee. 'He did that to me once, too.'

'What? When?'

'A couple of months ago, maybe.'

'Oh.' I was crushed by her words. I didn't want Jamie but I wanted to be wanted, to be chosen and marked out as special.

'I don't know if I really liked it,' I confessed.

'No?' She wiped herself and checked the toilet roll. 'Why not?'

'I don't know.' I fumbled for words. 'He smelled kind of weird.' Katie pursed her lips in the mirror.

'I always think he smells nice.' She smoothed down her vest top, sucking in her stomach and pushing out her breasts. She caught my eyes in the mirror and I looked away.

17

We walk arm-in-arm along Peckham Rye. Saltfish hang from shop doorways in silver streaks and plantains cling together in yellow crescents. The sky begins to darken and bars and restaurants spit pools of gold onto dirty pavements.

'This way,' you say, pulling me into a small tapas bar, your scarf trailing along the floor. I bend to pick it up as you say something to the waiter in Spanish and he smiles and beckons us to a table. Garlic hangs from the ceiling in smoky clumps. Women clutch large glasses of red wine, laughing loudly with their heads thrown back, showing all

28

of their teeth. I watch your chapped lips in the sticky light and feel as though I have fallen into someone else's life. You squint at the chalkboards hung above the bar.

'Shall we get croquetas? And arancini balls? What about tortilla?'

I nod, feeling dazed, watching olive oil shimmer through green glass. 'What do you fancy? You have to choose something, too.'

I glance at the menu. 'Olives?'

'Is that all? You can have anything you want,' you say, but I know that is not true.

I nod. 'You choose the rest.'

I look around, noting the dishes sweating on the service bar in the open kitchen, steam hissing from the dishwasher, boxes of wine stacked on the floor. I know how to carry plates, how to change a beer keg, how to make a latte in a perfect swirl, how to pour a pint with just enough head, how to carve candles to fit wine bottles, how to get people to leave at the end of the night. I don't know the names of all the herbs and spices. I don't know about flavour, texture and nuance. I don't know how to choose because that is not something I have been asked to do very often. The air is thick with chili and pepper as people unfold around us, unwinding and unpeeling their coats.

'Are you happy with this?' you ask, counting the dishes on your fingers. The waiter brings a small dish of salty olives and I nod and take a sip of my wine. It is thick and dark like liquorice and it smooths my nagging edges. I feel like a whole person sitting here with you, eating and drinking, spending money, doing things that other people do.

'Do you come here a lot?' I ask you.

'God, no. I cook at home, mostly. Can't afford to go

out, really.' You look nervous. 'But it's sort of a special occasion.'

'Oh?'

'I handed in my dissertation yesterday.'

'What? Why didn't you tell me?'

You shrug. 'I don't know. It didn't seem real.'

'Congratulations!' I clink my glass with yours. 'That's huge.' You brush your hair out of your eyes. You are wearing a wrinkled gold shirt with three buttons missing.

'There's something else.'

'What?'

'I've been offered a research job through the university. In migration and linguistics.'

I feel a sharp flicker of resentment at the world unfolding for you in ways it could not for me but I swallow it. 'What? Amazing! Why didn't you tell me any of this?'

'Well.' You fiddle with your fork. 'It's in Barcelona.'

'Oh.' I feel a falling sensation, as though the ground is rushing up to meet me. 'Well. That's great. You should definitely go.' Your eyes are light with the possibility of it, as though you are already standing beneath a hotter sun. You look at me guiltily and I blink too fast.

'I've been wanting to leave London for ages,' you say, gently. 'Since my dad died.' You press your finger into the candle wax, dripping red across the table. 'It just feels like there's too much history here, weighing me down.'

I tense my legs.

'I spent my whole childhood here. Do you know what I mean?'

I know about weight and what it's like to feel your past pressing down on you, to drag it through the days. I know about space; how to hide and shrink from it. I know about reinventing yourself and I know about running away.

30

I reach out and touch your hand. 'I think so.'

You squeeze my fingers. 'I wasn't expecting you.'

'No.' My face is hot. 'Me neither.'

Our food arrives and you eat hungrily, peeling peach-coloured prawns from their shells. I pick at the croquetas with my fork, forcing myself to eat more than I really want, so that you will not notice my flatness. We talk about the books we are reading and our plans for the weekend, but something has hardened in me. I don't want to think about the future because it is closer to you going away.

'When are you leaving?' I ask, fiddling with a button on my blouse.

'Probably next month. I need to find someone for my room.'

'That's soon,' I say, softly.

'Yes.' Your leg finds mine beneath the table. 'But we still have some time.'

Later, in your bedroom, I lie awake with my arm across your chest as you slip into dreams, sighing and shifting in the cool sheets. I feel your pulse beneath my wrist and I am afraid of how fragile it seems, of how careless we are, of how quickly everything changes.

18

When I was a child, my dad used to lock himself in the bathroom and drink cans of lager. He poured my bubble bath into the water and submerged himself for hours, until the suds turned cold and his empties were piled high in the wicker bin.

'Go and check on your dad,' my mother said and I lay on my belly in the hallway, listening for splashes, straining to see him through the thin gap beneath the door. Sometimes he fell asleep and we worried he would slip beneath the surface and drown.

One night, my parents had an argument and my dad locked himself in the bathroom and refused to come out. My mother banged her fist on the wooden door.

'Please,' her voice splintered. 'Come out and talk to me.' I pressed my face to the whorls in the wood, wondering what they could see with their blackened eyes.

'Dad?' I called, trying the gold handle with my small fingers.

'Go and get a coin,' my mother whispered to me. 'My purse is in the kitchen.' I prised open her red patent purse, rolling a dirty pound coin between my fingers. The lock could be opened from the outside by pressing a coin into a metal groove and twisting it. My mother's hands shook and the lock rattled. The thin strap of her nightie fell from her shoulder, leaving her freckles exposed. We heard a creak and a thud from inside.

'Oh,' my mother gasped. 'He's opening the window.' She jiggled the lock but the door wouldn't budge. Cold air rushed through the cracks. 'Don't you dare leave us,' my mother cried.

'Dad,' I joined in. 'Don't go.' We heard a thudding noise, just as the lock burst open with a click. My mother pushed open the door to find the window wobbling on its hinges where my dad had forced it open. We saw him scramble over the back fence and jump down into the alleyway behind our house. We stood in the cold for a moment, shivering in our thin nighties, the moon casting silver across our faces. My mother squeezed my hand.

'I told him not to go,' I said to her, a blackness in my belly. Her eyes were dark and faraway.

'He'll always go.'

I leaned over the sink and looked out of the window, cold porcelain goosepimpling my skin. 'Will you go?'

'No.' She reached over me to close the window. 'I have to stay.'

19

Your housemate works on reception at the ICA and he gives us free tickets for a documentary about John Coltrane. We ride the top deck of the bus into the city centre and look up at the glassy buildings cutting into the sky like knives.

'Do you ever wonder who London is for?' I ask you as we sit at the front with our feet pressed against the window.

'What do you mean?'

'Like, do you feel like London is for you?'

You fiddle with a packet of tobacco in your coat pocket. 'My life has always been here.' We cross the river and the lights are reflected in the water like drowned stars. 'So I suppose I do, in a way.' It seems unfair to me that you belong in London and yet you are leaving for somewhere new.

'I sometimes have this feeling,' I say, as we approach Trafalgar Square, the fountains spitting pink light. 'That

I'm just playing at living here. Like, I go to a café or a pub or something, but it doesn't feel real.'

'Yeah?' You twist in your seat and ring the bell.

'Yeah.' I struggle for words. 'I don't know. It's hard to explain.'

You light a cigarette as we walk along the Mall, a row of Union Jacks looking down on us.

'Where does feel like yours?' you ask, buttoning up your coat. I think about it, listening to our shoes hit the pavement. I have lived in so many different places and none of them ever really felt like mine. I have always felt like other people have more right to a space than I do, as though I am not quite the right shape, as though none of it rightfully belongs to me.

'I don't know,' I say, then change the subject.

We settle into our chairs in the darkness. I try to focus on the screen but the places where our bodies touch feel charged with static. I close my eyes as the music unspools around us. I wonder whether anything will ever truly belong to me. I wonder if I could find the end of the cruelty that runs through my life like a silver thread and pull it out. I reach for your arm in the darkness, feeling your woollen coat beneath my fingers. I wonder if it is better to hold on to things, instead of just opening my palms and letting them drift away.

We walk through the park afterwards, our breath making shapes in the night.

'What did you think of the film, then?' You slip your arm through mine. A car drives past and drenches us in light.

'It was alright.' I try to think of something interesting to say. 'What about you?'

You shrug. 'I always preferred Alice Coltrane, to be honest.' We reach the bus stop and I feel restless.

'Shall we go somewhere?' I ask you, scanning the bus route.

'Where do you want to go?'

'I don't know. We could go anywhere. We could just get on a bus and see where we end up.'

You raise your eyebrows. 'That doesn't sound very fun. It's cold. And late.' You pull me close. 'Why don't we just go home? You can stay over, if you like.'

'Okay.' I feel silly as the bus pulls up. We tap our Oyster cards and you rest your head on my shoulder as I watch the city slide through my reflection in the window, as though I barely exist within it. I turn the word 'home' over and over in my mouth, heavy and solid, like a precious stone.

When we get back to your house, we take off all our clothes and climb beneath your duvet. You touch my breasts and I reach for you while my body curls in pleasure, but all I can think of is the fact that you are leaving and then everything will change.

'I want you to fuck me really hard,' I breathe and you do and it almost hurts but the edge of pain feels real in a way that cannot be questioned, something solid to hold onto in this world of shifting things.

20

My parents' relationship disintegrated and my mother and I went to stay with my auntie for a few months. I had to share a room with my cousin, who was a few years

35

younger than me and sometimes I looked after him, making him fish fingers and helping him with his homework while our mothers were at work. I looked around my cousin's bedroom at his teddy bears and toy cars stacked on the shelves and I felt afraid, as though my own room had crumbled to dust, meaning that I could never go back and there were no markers of who I was any more. I heard my mother crying late at night and I buried my fears in my borrowed pillow. I knew I had to be strong and responsible. My own churning worries were small in comparison to hers.

I stepped carefully over my cousin's train track and inched around his Playmobil pirate ship, but I kept tripping over pieces of Lego and standing on plastic parrots, hopping and clutching my foot.

'You're breaking all my stuff!' he shouted with his cheeks puffed up.

'Stop leaving it all over the floor, then.'

'It's my floor. I can do what I want.'

My cousin went to bed earlier than me and I tried to sneak in quietly at night, reading under the covers with a head torch.

'Turn the light off,' he groaned, his voice muffled beneath blankets. 'I can't sleep.' I drew pictures of houses in my journal with my blueberry-scented gel pen; castles with spiralling turrets and sunflowers growing up the walls. I drew horse-drawn caravans and overgrown treehouses, canal boats and cosy terraces, colouring all of the windows in gold. I decided that if I had my own house, I would build a slide and a blue-spangled swimming pool. All the doors would have little round keyholes with special silver keys that I would thread onto a chain and wear like a diamond necklace, so they would never get lost.

When I first moved to London at twenty, I rented a room in a house share in Turnpike Lane. I walked along Green Lanes, past the Turkish bakeries with their barrels of pistachios and dried apricots, the strip-lit betting shops and the newsagent's windows crammed with jewel-coloured bottles.

A man in his thirties with a thick beard answered the door in a Nirvana hoodie.

'I hope the room's alright.' He ushered me along the hallway and up the dark stairs. 'It's pretty small. No one else really wanted it.' I looked through the doorway at the single bed pushed up against chintzy wallpaper, the brown, swirling carpet and the cheap white wardrobe. I had been going to viewings all week and it was the only room I could afford that had a door and a window and didn't involve sharing a bunk bed with anyone else.

'It's perfect for me.' I perched on the edge of the bed, giddy with luck. The man glanced at my heavy backpack, bursting with my belongings and then he looked me up and down.

'Yeah,' he yawned. 'Well. You're pretty small yourself.'

21

You find someone to fill your room and you begin to pack, putting books into cardboard boxes and filling bin-liners with used train tickets, leaky pens and scrunched-up tissues. I offer to help but you say, 'No, it's okay. You don't need to sort through all my junk.' You send me a picture of your empty room, a layer of dust casting silver over everything. I already miss our velvet mornings behind your heavy curtains, my body turning liquid beneath your hands.

'How do you feel about him leaving?' asks Rosa, as we sit on a blanket spread across the roof of the chicken shop below her bedroom window, drinking coffee in the cold autumn sun.

'Okay.' I look at the trees on the street below us.

'Okay?' She smirks.

'Well,' I stall. 'Maybe it's better this way.'

'What do you mean?'

'It's intense. And kind of serious. This way we have a bit of distance, to work out what we want.'

Rosa rolls a cigarette. 'And what do you want?'

'God, Rosa. I don't know. It's early days.'

'How will you know what you want if you're hundreds of miles away?'

I laugh and take a sip of my coffee, stretching out my legs in the afternoon light. I wonder if part of me will feel safer with you far away from me, whether it will calm my trembling hands and my gasping, aching need.

'I don't know,' I admit, fiddling with the cuffs of my jumper.

'I've never seen you like this before.' She presses her thumb down on her lighter but there is no flame.

'Like what?'

The lighter sputters and she inhales gratefully. I wonder if anyone actually knows what they want, truly and deeply, without people or situations clouding their judgement. I wonder if we ever truly want anything, or whether we just respond to the world around us, if our feelings are reactive or whether they come from somewhere deeper. 'What do you want, Rosa?' I ask her, quietly.

'I just want to be loved,' she replies, taking me by surprise. 'That's what most people want.' She looks at me. 'Isn't it?'

22

I grew up in Bishop Auckland, an old market town in County Durham. It looks onto the Wear Valley; green, brown and ribboned with a silver river. There is a high street crammed with rowdy pubs, charity shops and neon-lit takeaways dripping fluorescence onto the cobbles.

My best friend Tara and me sometimes blagged our way into Lacey's after school, ordering pints of Kronenbourg because we thought the French name sounded sophisticated, making us seem older than we really were. We drank them with straws and I loved the way the first pint blurred the boundaries of the world, making the day glow around the rim, as though anything could happen. Drinking made me feel inside and outside my body at the same time. I was aware of my blood thinning in my veins as the alcohol coursed through it and I also felt detached from my body, as though I was floating above it, forgetting the weight of my flesh on my bones.

I craved extremes because they seemed like the opposite of Bishop, although it is an extreme place, in its own way. It is known as Bish Vegas, on account of the women spilling out of the pubs in their sequined dresses and stilettos, and the men with their short-sleeved shirts and football tattoos, swaying beneath the castle that was once home to the Prince Bishops, a tacky rush of saturated glamour, lacking the money and the desert sun.

It felt miles away from anywhere, separated from nearby cities by run-down colliery villages bordered by endless fields. I spent hours on the bus, resting my head against the dirty window, watching the roads flash by and waiting for my life to begin. I spent long, empty Sundays in bed, flicking through the pages of magazines and touching myself beneath my old pink nightie, my toes curling in desire. My thoughts writhed behind my eyelids, hungry and restless, aching for something I couldn't name. I didn't want a particular job or a house or a car, anything that could be easily quantified. I wanted abstractions; a cut-glass sea with light leaking into it, burnt summer tarmac on a motorway at night. I wanted sensation, to go out in the world and let it rip through me, to learn the shape of my coastline, to see if I had any edges. I didn't know what to do with all that want as it swelled in me like a river, rushing and churning, soaking everything in its path.

'Why don't you go for a walk or something?' my mother said, catching me squeezing spots in the bathroom mirror with glazed eyes and matted hair. 'Stop all that preening and moping around.'

23

I rinse your smell from my skin in the shower, trying to pull myself together where my tough outer layer has softened beneath your hands. I brush my teeth so hard that my gums bleed and I spit blood onto white porcelain, pushing thoughts of you away.

I fiddle with my phone nervously the day before you are due to leave, wondering whether to try and meet you, or if it is better to leave things as they are. My screen lights up and my stomach contracts.

'*Change of plan,*' you write. '*My new flat's not ready yet. I'm going to be in town for an extra week.*' I bite the skin around my fingers, watching the dots that mean you are typing. I was ready to forget you and leave this all behind but the glimmer of you so close to me flickers in my chest with a force that takes me by surprise.

'*I'm housesitting in Highgate,*' you send. '*Want to come and stay?*'

I shove some tights and spare knickers in a bag and head for the tube before I have time to think about it.

You are looking after a rambling terraced house belonging to your mam's friend, who bought it for cheap in the eighties, before the city hardened with money and glass. She is away for a couple of weeks and says you can stay there until you leave, as long as you look after the garden and feed her cat.

'You're here,' you say awkwardly when I arrive, your feet bare on the cold kitchen tiles. My hands make anxious fists inside my pockets, then you lean in to kiss me and I give into you.

My own house is chilly and damp-riddled, paint flaking from the ceiling, hungover housemates pounding up and down the stairs in dirty trainers. Highgate is quiet and cream-coloured, bedsheets ironed and neatly folded. The blinds are drawn in the afternoons, to stop the sun slipping inside and staining the furniture. There is a plastic wiper in the shower to whisk wet beads from the glass.

I slop coffee across the table as we read the newspapers, pretending to be different kinds of people. We leave half-read books and jumpers draped over chairs, without worrying they will go missing. Bananas rot in the fruit bowl and we bake them into warm bread, vanilla and sex caught beneath our fingernails. At night we fill the kitchen with candles and I sip plum-coloured wine from a crystal sherry glass, staining the counters with turmeric, filling the air with cloves and cardamom. I look at your toothbrush in the bathroom, your rucksack spilling socks and T-shirts across the carpet, your stack of books on the bedside table. I drink it all in, desperate to remember the precise flavour of you, like smoke and liquorice, before you are gone and your edges begin to blur in my memory, losing their definition.

We take long, slippery baths together beneath a skylight, straining for stars between the chimney pots and rusty television aerials. We lie damp on the sitting-room floor, giggling and touching, our wet hair soaking into the carpet. We prune the roses in our bare feet and pull thick sticks of rhubarb from the soil to make a crumble, simmering sugar in ceramic. I cut lavender and cornflowers and arrange them in vases on the kitchen table. We prise scratched CDs from their cases and dance in the kitchen, naked beneath borrowed dressing gowns as the sky drips charcoal. Our lives seem gentler, blurred in soft focus.

I decide to make a potato curry, browning onions and heaping rust-coloured spoonfuls of garam masala into the pan. I play jazz on the radio and you read a book at the kitchen table, drinking wine from a bottle you pinched from the rack. The kitchen fills with condensation and we laugh at the lives we are playing, far away from the reality of ourselves. I want to preserve the heat and spices because I know all of this will pass but there's nothing I can do and the steam begins to evaporate as soon as it hits cold glass.

You are twitchy and restless as I open a can of coconut milk, jumping whenever I clatter a pan or drop a spoon.

'Are you sure you don't need any help?' you ask for the third time, putting your book face down on the table.

'I'm sure,' I snap and then soften. 'It'll be good, I promise. You don't need to worry.'

'I know,' you say, guiltily. 'That's not what I mean.'

'What is it, then?'

'I'm just not used to this,' you gesture towards me. 'Being cooked for. I usually do the cooking for other people.'

'Always?'

'I suppose so. It feels strange, being looked after. I don't know what to do.'

I put the lid on the pan gently. 'Don't people look after you?'

'They do. In other ways. I don't know. It's kind of what I was saying about my dad, in the restaurant. When he died, I got into the habit of looking after people, like my mum and my brother. Being reliable. Making myself useful.' I refill our wine glasses and sit down opposite you, watching your face in the candlelight. 'That's kind of why I need to go to Spain. To choose something, instead of just falling into it.'

I think about the way I have been living, moving from place to place. I wonder if I have been making choices and testing my agency in the world, but there are lots of things I haven't been able to choose, because I have never had enough money or a proper place to live, because I have been outrunning something which is maybe not a choice at all. I wonder if we are choosing love, or if we are just falling into it, whether it is possible to choose love or if it just happens to you, bright white and blind-siding, shattering everything in its path.

'Choosing is important,' I say, swirling dark wine in my glass. I feel envious of you, on the verge of a new life and then I feel guilty for being envious, because it stems from the loss of your dad.

You look out of the window, avoiding my eyes. 'Yeah. It is.'

The potatoes take too long to cook and by the time they are soft the rice is cold and we are both drunk. I ladle curry into deep bowls and slop it on the stove. We eat too quickly, burning our tongues.

'It's really good,' you say and I am pleased that I can cut and slice and care for you, that I am learning how to care for myself, although maybe if I truly cared for myself then I wouldn't be here at all, where I am vulnerable and open to breaking.

We push our dirty bowls to one side and you reach for my hand across the table. There is something hard behind your eyes, closed up and distant, already moving away from me and unfurling somewhere new.

'Thank you,' you say, kissing the inside of my wrist.

'What for?' I can't read your expression and it makes me uneasy.

'For dinner.' You trace the creases on my palm with your finger. 'And for being understanding.' Anger swells inside me, but I cannot tell if I am angry at you for acting like I have a choice in it, or angry at myself, for being unable to acknowledge how much I want you to stay.

'You're welcome,' I say sarcastically and you frown and drop my hand.

'Why are you being like that?'

'Like what?'

You close your eyes without answering. The air is heavy and dense. I want you to go and find more space for yourself, but you have torn open something that cannot be closed. A part of me resents you for going off into a new life and leaving me here, skirting the edges of your absence.

'I'm pleased that you're going,' I say and you look hurt.

'Are you really?'

'I'm pleased for you.'

'And what about you?'

I shake my head. The space between us feels taut, as though it could snap. I finish the rest of my wine and my gums tingle.

'Come here,' you say softly and my body tenses. 'Please.' You reach for me across the table. I stand up and move towards you, searching for you in the static. You press yourself against me and my breath leaves my mouth in a crumple. You slip your hand beneath my dress and I give into it, offering my body like a prayer. I close my eyes, trying to memorise the roughness of your cheek and the curl of your tongue, the way my thoughts dissolve to sugar in your mouth. We fall into each other's bodies, clawing welts into ribs on the cold kitchen tiles. I touch the hand-shaped bruises bleeding beneath your skin. You look at me and breathe,

'What are we going to do?'

'I don't know,' I say, trying to think clearly. Our want fills the house with a crimson smell, raw with blood and salt.

I had a twin who died during my mother's pregnancy. I overheard my auntie mention it once when she came round for a cup of tea, her lips leaving a coral lipstick print on the edge of her mug. My mother glanced at me and then looked at my auntie meaningfully and changed the subject.

'It wasn't meant to be,' she said softly, stroking my hair, when I asked her about it later. I tried to imagine my twin sister next to me, twirling my skipping rope and pushing me on the swing. I became obsessed with the idea that she was part of me, that her thoughts and feelings had seeped into my body when we shared a womb and that I might be able to communicate with her, if I learned how to listen hard enough. I lay in bed at night, trying to understand the texture of her thoughts, deciphering which of my feelings came from her and which were my own. I talked to her as I played in the garden and splashed around in the bath. I started setting an extra place for her at the dining table and my mother sat me down.

'She was very small when she died,' my mother explained. 'She was poorly and she wouldn't have survived.'

'Were you very sad?'

'Yes.' My mother stroked my cheek. 'But I had you and you made me very happy.'

I looked at the knife and fork I had set out on the table. 'Was it my fault?'

'Oh, love. Of course not. It wasn't anyone's fault.' She kissed the top of my head and took away the spare cutlery. I looked at the empty seat next to me feeling guilty, as though I was taking up my twin sister's space. I couldn't shake the feeling that I had been given too much and my sister too little, as if I had swallowed all of the goodness in my mother's womb, so there wasn't anything left for her.

25

We lie in bed with our hair splayed across the pillow, my fingers tracing the outline of the fern on your forearm, a stained-glass lamp casting the room in a pink glow.

'What do you want to do?' you ask me, tentatively.

'What do you mean?'

'About us.'

I am quiet for a moment, trying to work it out. I want to be with you but I am afraid of saying the words aloud, of admitting that I might want anything at all. I pull the covers tighter around my body. 'Maybe we should leave things open,' I say softly. 'There's less pressure that way.'

You bury your face in my shoulder. 'Okay.'

'I mean, is that what you want?' I ask, turning to look at your face.

'What do *you* want?'

I close my eyes. I am afraid of the maw you have opened up inside me, choking with hunger and need, yet the thought of strange lips grazing your belly gives me vertigo, as though the ground has opened beneath us. 'I don't know.'

You open your mouth to speak and then stop yourself. I picture you beneath palm trees, drinking cold beer, your skin slick with sweat, supple shoulders bare in the close night, laughing in a language I can't understand. Guilt fills my mouth, dirty and acidic. I want you to go and be in your own life but you have done something to me I do not fully understand. I am used to being independent, swallowing my needs and getting on with things, but now I am itchy with want, on the soles of my feet and between my breasts. I am not the kind of person who falls in love easily. I am not the kind of person who lets myself curl up softly in the folds of someone else, but you took my mottled shell in your gentle fingers and I slid out, wanting.

'Let's leave it open for now.' You reach for me beneath the covers. 'We don't know what's going to happen.'

'No,' I say, truthfully. 'We don't.'

We wake at dawn, curled beneath the gold lip of morning, your heavy suitcase resting by the door.

'Do you think I've touched every single part of your body?' I ask with my arms wrapped around you, my belly curved into your back.

You laugh. 'I don't know. Probably not.'

'Don't you think so?' I want to press my fingers into every single part of you, to leave the marks of my finger-prints on your body like braille. I push my face into the pillow as your alarm rings, signalling an ending.

We stand on the platform as the train to the airport rushes into the station, tearing our hair away from our faces. You kiss me hard and say, 'You'll definitely visit?' I close my eyes. I want you to go and feel the sun split your skin, to move away from the yellowing bruise of your dad's death and to put down the heavy things you are carrying. I under-stand the importance of running away but I have opened myself up and I am afraid of sealing shut again. I am usually the person leaving and it feels strange to be on the other side. The knowledge twists like a fish in my stomach.

'Do you want me to?'

'Of course I do.'

I watch you wheel your suitcase onto the train in your black boots and dirty black jacket, dark curls falling into your eyes, like an alley cat. A stranger asks you a question and I watch through the window as you answer them, already out in the world and away from me. I imagine you walking through Barcelona in your colourful shirts, vines spilling from balconies and green parakeets in the trees, but I have never seen you in summer and don't know what it does to you. You press your nose to the window as your train pulls out of the station, waving your book like a handkerchief. I laugh and wave until the train pulls past me, then my face cracks open and my heart spills out.

26

When I was a child, my dad took me into Durham and hired a rowing boat for the afternoon. We pushed off from the shore and drifted beneath the old stone bridges, looking up at constellations of green moss and splinters of light reflected on the dirty bricks, reaching out to grab handfuls of weeping willow where it dripped into the muddy water. I relished his attention, watching his muscles bulge as he pushed the oars back and forth, the gold chain around his neck glinting in the sun. We reached a bend in the river and he put down the oars, letting us float for a while. I leaned over the side of the boat and put my hand in the cold water, watching as ripples moved in rings around us. I loved the feeling of being alone with my dad, away from the land, as though we were the only two people in the world.

The boat began to rock and I looked up to find my dad steering us to the river bank with his oar. He jumped onto land with a thud and sat on a tree stump, lighting a cigarette and laughing at my panicked face as I began to drift away from him.

'Dad?' I called, scrabbling at the heavy oars.

'You've just got to push.' He blew out smoke. 'Come on,' he laughed again. 'You can do it.' I reached for the oars, trying to push but they were wet and slippery and my arms were too small. I watched powerlessly as the boat was tugged away by the current, pulling me towards the bridge. I felt sick, imagining what would happen if I couldn't steer myself to safety, wondering if I would float all the way out to sea.

'Dad?' I shouted again and he put out his cigarette and strode along the river bank quickly with his long legs. He broke off a branch and held it out for me to grasp onto. I clasped my hands around it and he pulled me towards land, shaking his head.

'What was all that about?' He looked at my pale face and squeezed my arm, guiltily. 'There's no need to be so bloody soft.'

'I wasn't scared,' I lied, desperate to impress him. I had a hollow fear of not being good enough for my dad, afraid of disappointing him and giving him another reason to leave me behind. He pulled a fresh cigarette from his packet.

'That's my girl. Of course you weren't.'

27

The days grow a fungus, a fur around their edges. Winter settles into the cracks of the city and I go for walks on my own around Nunhead Cemetery, stepping through pearly frost. Rosa and I drink red wine on cold evenings and eat steamed dumplings afterwards. I go to the cinema alone on Sunday afternoons, wandering down the high street in the rain. I make chickpea stew in the evenings, applying for jobs I don't really want from the middle of my bed.

I soap my skin in the bath and find a small bruise on the inside of my thigh. I push my thumb into it until it is sore, imagining your fingers pressing into me. I notice it fade from black to purple, leaking into yellow like a polluted sky over a city at dawn, the last marker of a time when we almost belonged to each other. I imagine you working at the university, full of ideas, drinking beer in the dusk and making your colleagues laugh, your arms tanned beneath rolled-up shirtsleeves, a cigarette between your lips, asking a stranger for a light. I picture you inviting someone back to your apartment, your skin flecked with candlelight and a sharp pain catches in my chest. I wish I knew how to ask for the things I want instead of just swallowing them down, knotted with fear and shame. I do not want to own you but I want *something* and the thought burns my throat until my eyes begin to water, filling my mouth with a sour taste.

I cycle through the rain, tutoring students. The smell of onion and garlic browning in warm kitchens makes me feel lonely as I soak up their central heating. Children sulk their way through stories as I envy their organised pencil cases and handwritten timetables, the clockwork stability of their lives. Sometimes I wish their parents would invite me to stay for tea. I imagine them running me a hot bath, handing me a soft towel, making sure I have everything I need.

I pick up extra shifts at the café, watching people type on their laptops and burning my wrist on the milk frother. Customers with lingering eyes try to engage me in conversation and I entertain the thought of their hands on my waist for a moment, yet I can only think of you as I close up for the night, the streets haloed in electric light as people rush home to each other. I find a shopping list in your handwriting in my coat pocket and keep it there, rubbing it between my fingers as I ride the top deck of the bus into Soho, trying to remember what I once loved about the city. I press my face to the window, watching neon lights above kebab shops flicker and fade, their tubes cracked and broken, the mercury leaking out.

I walk through the wet, black streets, looking up at the lights on the ends of cranes, flashing red warning signs to low-flying planes. A thick fog settles over the river. I stand in the middle of London Bridge and I can't see anything. I squint into the white, thinking of you. I take out my phone and type,

'Where are you?' and then delete it.

28

One lunchtime at school, my best friend Tara tore a page out of her maths book and wrote our names across it in a purple swirl.

'Let's rate each other's features,' she said.

I looked at her, warily. 'What do you mean?'

She pressed her gel pen into the paper. 'Like, I would be the prettiest if I didn't have a big nose. So my nose gets a one. But my eyes can have an eight.'

I frowned at her. 'Why would we want to do that?'

'Oh, come on.' She rolled her eyes. 'It's just a game.' She drew a heart next to my name. 'Your hair gets a nine. But your legs are more of a six.' I felt queasy. I was so afraid of not being good enough, failing to meet the expectations that were set out for me. I crossed my thighs beneath my school skirt, trying to make my legs look neater. 'What?' she smirked. 'I'm just being honest. I hate my belly. So that's a zero for me.'

We queued in the cafeteria at lunchtime, antsy with hunger.

'You're gross,' a boy I didn't know sneered as he brushed past, hair slick with gel, shoulders straining through his school shirt. I rolled my eyes as his friends moved by in a wave of Lynx and coiled anger, chanting,

'Gross, gross, gross.'

I chose a ham and cheese panini, grease pooling in the paper wrapper. I slipped it into my blazer pocket and tore chunks from it, popping them into my mouth as I wandered around the school field, linking arms with Tara or sitting cross-legged in the grass.

'You know those have a lot of calories?' Tara wrinkled her nose.

'I'm hungry,' I shrugged. Tara pursed her lips and said nothing. I felt ashamed, pulling my skirt down over my thighs, vowing to make a better choice next time. I always gave in, choosing toasted bread and melted cheese over limp, wet salad, eating it in an awkward rush. I hadn't yet learned how to silence my desire and I gave into it guiltily, every single time.

Sometimes, I took a packed lunch. I sat in the common room with a group of girls, legs crossed and elbows tucked in, plastic lunchboxes on our knees. Some girls brought smelly food like tuna pasta or boiled eggs and we inched away from them, covering our mouths and noses with our hands as their faces burned. Some girls couldn't eat when other people were looking at them and they tore their sandwiches into tiny pieces, taking furtive bites when they thought no one was watching.

A couple of girls bit into hamburgers, sitting with their legs splayed, licking ketchup from the backs of their hands. They were funny and boyish, with loose ties and trainers, unconcerned with fitting into our anxious shapes. I watched their thick, clever fingers and the way they walked with their shoulders back and a slight bend to their knees, as if they owned the whole world.

29

I go out dancing with my housemates, dressed up in glitter and fur, passing a bottle of gin between us as we wait in the freezing queue.

'Are you alright?' asks Ada kindly, offering me a drag of her cigarette. 'You're a bit quiet.'

'She's lovesick,' trills Dan and I roll my eyes.

'That's not like you.' Ada finishes off the gin. 'You're usually so independent.'

'I'm fine.' I pull my coat around my body. 'Just tired. I'll be okay when we get inside.'

We offer our wrists to be stamped at the door, then we are hit by a wall of heat and sound. We hide our coats in a corner and I go to the bar, trying to shake away thoughts of you, but Ada's words are snagged on my skin. I am used to being independent, good at doing my own thing, but now all of my thoughts are caught up in you and I don't know how to let go of them. I feel angry at you for tearing the lid from my life and then leaving me here, dazzled by the sky. I order a drink and knock it back, relieved that you are not here drawing me towards you, remembering that I am my own person and can do as I please.

I find Ada and Dan in the crowd and we move together beneath the hot lights. Ada's gold crop top flashes in the strobes as Dan spins in circles, his tie-dye T-shirt soaked in sweat. I close my eyes and focus on my body, feeling stars rushing up inside me and filling my mouth. My blood is hot in my veins and my limbs are supple, buttery and light.

A stranger meets my gaze across the room and he moves towards me, rings on his fingers, a joint hanging from his lips. I dance closer, breathing in his beery musk, weed smoke curling in my hair. I don't want him but I want to be wanted, to feel shiny and powerful, less permeable, someone solid. He reaches for my waist, bare beneath my knotted shirt and I let him, sinking into the music, my arms making shapes in the air. He brings his face to mine and I think of Rosa trying to light her cigarette in the wind, telling me she wants to be loved. His tongue is fat and wet and I remember the taste of the word 'home' when it passed from your lips, glittering, safe and pure. The stranger presses his body closer and I put my hands on his shoulders and gently push him away.

'Just going outside for some air,' I say into his ear.

'I'll come with you.' He pats the tobacco in his shirt pocket.

'No, thanks. I'm okay.' I pass Ada and Dan on my way to the exit, swaying beneath the disco ball.

'Nice one, pal,' shouts Dan, giving me a thumbs up with spinning pupils, wiping his forehead with the back of his hand.

I relish the shock of the cold air, feeling the beads of sweat around my neck evaporate. I sit on an upturned beer keg and watch the people around me talking and swiping, the orange tips of their cigarettes splitting diamonds around the edges of my vision. Bass vibrates from the building but there is a flatness to it all. My phone flashes with a message from you.

'Fuck,' I mutter beneath my breath and then open it. You have sent me a picture of your hiking boots kicked off beneath a pine tree and the light looks so different, yellow and pure. There is a picture of a squat strung with paper garlands, people drinking beer outside on torn settees. There is a picture of a phrase you have underlined in a book but I can't take in the words because I am too distracted by the jagged line of your bitten thumb.

'I want you,' I type in reply and then delete it but the words flash neon behind my eyelids. I want you. I want the salt in your skin and the grey of your eyes and the way my name rolls wetly from your tongue. I am an expert in swallowing my needs and wants, pushing them down and getting on with things, but all my rules are broken and everything is spilling out. I send you a row of palm trees and you reply with a question mark.

30

Tara and I lay in the park drinking sticky sweet cider, walking arm in arm around housing estates, our cheap ballet flats soaked with rain. We watched *The Hills* and *The O.C.* on MTV, longing for honeyed limbs and pastel-pink sunsets, picturing boulevards lined with palm trees and jobs at *Teen Vogue*. We never dreamed of becoming doctors or lawyers or businesswomen, but we knew that beauty had the power to set us free. It was silky and spangled and a chance at something better. We smelled the glamour that seeped from the prettiest girls in sixth form, who got jobs dancing on podiums in their underwear in the swankiest club in Newcastle, where Kanye West was once spotted with a bottle of Grey Goose vodka. We knew a girl who spent her weekends standing in arrivals at the local airport with her sunglasses on, hoping to be scouted as a model and whisked off to a brighter place.

We watched Victoria Beckham shrink into her seat at the World Cup and traced the curve of Kate Moss's thighs in her gold lurex Glastonbury minidress. We swelled with longing as sequins dripped from the narrow shoulders of the Olsen twins and sighed with envy as the inky daisies tattooed around Peaches Geldof's stomach squeezed her into a smaller, more angular shape. We watched Alexa Chung form a long black line in her skinny jeans and ogled Cassie from *Skins*, angel-haired in a green-gold dress, spun out on pills in the dawn.

We learned the language of self-destruction, in hip bones and heroin chic. The women we admired could do anything if they were skinny and beautiful enough. They flaunted their appetites for sex and drugs, good-time girls who could take the whole rush of the world in their slender fingers, as long as they didn't eat too much. We drank it all in, understanding that we had to sacrifice flavour and fullness for beauty and the dazzle of club lights. We learned to suppress our needs so that we could touch pleasure, to reach out and grab it for ourselves.

All of the women we knew were on diets. There was the Atkins and the cabbage soup and the 2,4,6,8 and the fast, drastic one supposedly prescribed by the British Heart Foundation for patients about to undergo surgery. Celebrity magazines tore apart reality TV stars on the beach in their bikinis, circling their bellies in fluorescent rings of shame.

'Jade's kebab and pizza flab!' the covers screamed at us as we queued in the newsagent for packets of Space Raiders. *'Kerry's shocker belly bulge!'*

Beauty was transcendent, far away from the strip-lit lure of kebab shops and the 2-for-1 supermarket deals and the long, acrylic fingernails scrabbling with need. We pored over the Jack Wills catalogue, pressing our faces to posh girls with long legs languishing across hay bales, shining in the glow of an expensive-looking sun. Thinness seemed gorgeous, cultured and rich; women who were in control of their hunger because it could always be met. We gaped at the photos on pro-anorexia forums, inching towards danger, signing off our texts to each other with the words,

'Stay skinny <3'

We encouraged each other, skipping lunch together and drinking cans of Diet Coke to stave off our hunger, pooling our lunch money to spend on booze. I took a thermos of instant coffee to school and nursed watery cups of it all day, pressing my hands into my churning stomach, ignoring the thick, heavy feeling behind my eyes.

Sometimes we shared a box of salad or a packet of Quavers and watched each other shrink with envy, each of us wishing we were anybody other than ourselves.

One winter, Tara and I both caught glandular fever.

'I think you must get it from blow-jobs,' Tara said sagely, but it was more likely that we passed it between each other, sharing warm cans of Red Bull and sticky tubes of lip gloss. I spent a week in bed, slipping in and out of fevered dreams, my throat swollen and sore. Tara became so ill she was hospitalised and she had to stay off school for six weeks.

When she walked into the classroom on her first day back, the whole room went quiet. The girls crowded around her, jealously touching her wrists.

'You're so tiny,' they crowed, marvelling at her shrunken thighs and sharp cheekbones. I felt shaky when I saw her small face peering over at me, as though we were standing on a cliff edge and I had noticed the cavernous drop below us for the first time.

31

You send me long emails about your research, your new red bike, the artists and activists you are meeting, the libraries filled with light. You write about Catalan independence, the streets hung with gold ribbons, the tingle of rupture, the world tearing itself apart.

'*So many exits,*' you type, as the UK carves a scar into the skin of Europe. '*When will I find an entrance?*' You are full of ideas and observations, rushing forwards, leaving old things behind.

I print out your emails and keep them folded inside my notebook, so that I have something to hold on to. You write about our bodies pressing into each other, how you keep finding strands of my hair caught in your jumper. You say you think of me every time you swim naked in the cold, green sea. I trace my fingers over the letters you typed with your hands, imagining the texture of your skin, but all I can feel is your absence, aching and raw.

The chalky crusts of the days build up inside me. The tower blocks are sharp against the struggling sky. I apply to write articles for a hairdressing magazine, to babysit children, to sell theatre tickets and to intern at a gallery, but I hear nothing back. At the café, people send back their lattes, telling me, 'I want it extra hot,' and I make them a fresh one without bothering to explain that milk is delicate and it burns too quickly.

My students' parents stress about piano lessons, French classes and private school entrance exams.

'I don't know what we'll do if she doesn't get in,' an anxious mother whispers over the head of her eleven-year-old daughter. 'Our local school is a nightmare.'

'She'll get in,' I tell her, packing books away into my bag.

Her mother sighs, unloading her shopping bag on the kitchen island. 'Oh, crap.' She unzips her purse. 'I forgot to go to the cash machine. Can I pay you next week?'

'That's fine,' I smile brightly, even though I am already short on rent.

I check my phone as I unlock my bike and I have a new message from you.

'I'm sitting at the top of a hill overlooking the city. The streets feel as if they are on fire here. It has just rained and the sky is the colour of a cantaloupe melon. The clouds are bruised lemons and I'm sitting beneath an orange tree. I'm writing in my journal, wondering who collects the oranges when they fall from the trees and what happens to them afterwards. Which is the kind of question that you would ask, which made me realise that I'm actually writing to you. Why don't you come and stay with me for a month? We can live on olives and cheap beer. We can walk under palm trees and swim in the sea. You could teach some classes. We can make it work. What do you think?'

I cycle home through the failing light, flying past bus stops and corner shops, my hair streaming out behind me, braided with traffic fumes. I want to pack a bag and come straight to you, yet I am afraid of how quickly we have fallen into this and how little control I have over the way I feel.

You send photos of cypress trees, light on blue water, a sky the colour of possibility. I imagine us walking the old streets, eating oranges beneath a violet sky. I picture days spilling into wine-dark nights, mopeds backfiring, the sun trapped in our skin. I think about how easy everything seemed in the Highgate house and the memory is suffused with soft light. I know that I should try to forget you but the thought of you ignites the part of me that wants un-attainable things like beauty and thunder, hurtling towards a sense of something I cannot explain.

I remember how it feels to be leaving, watching people jogging or walking to work, everything washed in the knowledge that I am on my way out, light and untethered, the city growing smaller as I leave it behind, the whole sky pouring through the plane window.

Perhaps I could become a better version of myself in a new place with you, someone lighter and looser, less intense. Maybe I could smooth over all my sharp, jagged parts and you will never have to know them at all. I will always be shining, shimmery and bright, the kind of woman who knows the names of all the herbs and spices, who is unafraid of pleasure, who laughs long and loudly, showing all of her teeth.

Part Two

Part Two

32

The plane circles over the sea before landing. The sky is salmon pink and the air smells like hot butter. I wheel my suitcase between palm trees, untangling knots from my hair with hot fingers. The city is yours and there are no traces of me in it. I type you a fumbling message,

'*We are in the same time zone.*'

You reply quickly. '*Delicious.*'

I get off the train and wind through darkening streets towards your apartment, paid for by the university. Rubbery vines drip from balconies. There is washing strung through the heat like bunting, T-shirt armpits yellowed with old sweat. Men sit on tall stools in fluorescent bars, chewing octopus and watching football on big screens, flicking cigarette ash out of the windows. Women wear tight jeans and big blow-dries, drinking cold red wine at street-side tables, laughing and clattering their fingernails against their glasses. Punks sit in the park with shiny cans of Estrella, their dogs stretched out beside them, held by pieces of rope. I am self-conscious of my noisy wheelie suitcase, clammy beneath my thick black tights. My phone vibrates with a message from you.

'*Where are you? I can't bear it any longer.*' I turn the corner and find your apartment tucked into a crumbling corner of Poble-sec, bikes double-locked to the lampposts, graffiti scrawled across the walls. I press my finger to the bell and the intercom crackles.

'Come quick,' you breathe. 'Fourth floor. There's no lift. Do you need me to come and help with your stuff?' I linger for a moment, savouring the knowledge of you so close to me, nervous about how we might seem to each other, changed by the miles and the warm, yellow air. Your voice purrs from the metal box. 'Are you coming?'

'Don't worry. I can manage.'

The door to your apartment is ajar and I push it open. You are here, sun-bleached and rumpled in a cut-up vest, calves stained with bike oil beneath black denim shorts. We stare at each other for a moment, the months we have spent apart stretching between us like fog. I brush my hair from my eyes warily, wondering if I look different, wishing I had changed my clothes when I got off the plane.

'I can't believe you're here,' you say shyly, pulling me towards you, and my doubts dissipate in your hands. You smell of sweat and brine and my skin prickles. I bury my head in your shoulder, breathing you in.

'Bloody hell.' You notice my suitcase. 'Did you carry that up all them stairs? I would have helped you! Why didn't you say?' I press my finger to your lips and kiss you, hard.

'God,' you murmur. 'I missed you so much.' The walls flicker and I look around. The apartment is tall-ceilinged, crammed with dark furniture and purple shadows. You have arranged bunches of bright yellow mimosa flowers in old olive jars and their leaves make patterns on the ceiling. The surfaces are clustered with candles and steam curls above two bowls of stew.

'Are you hungry?' you ask.

I look at you softly. 'Did you do this for me?'

You bite the skin around your thumb. 'Yeah. Do you like it?' I imagine you walking home with your arms full of flowers, trimming the stems, rinsing salt from olive jars.

'Yes,' I say quietly, my face pink with pleasure.

I go to the balcony and look down onto the street. Mopeds sputter and skateboards clatter across the concrete. There is a row of orange trees beneath the window and there are people walking dogs along the pavement, barks echoing between the old buildings. I can see directly into the apartment opposite yours. An old man sits on a white bed beneath the open window, smoking a cigarette in the glow of a bedside lamp. I breathe in the texture of your new life, the pots and pans stacked in the small sink, a striped towel hung over the balcony to dry. I am worried that I might seem out of place to you here, my movements loud and ungainly, my pale skin almost translucent.

'Do you want to eat out here?' You bring over the bowls and a tall jug of water.

I nod. 'It smells so different here. I could smell it as soon as I got off the plane.'

'Do you think so?' You balance our food on a wooden stool, throwing me a cushion to sit on. 'What does it smell of?'

'Like burning. Or melting. As if everything is on fire.' I peel off my tights and drape them over the railings. The air is a balm on my hot legs.

'Oh.' You kneel on the floor and kiss my calves. 'I missed your legs.' I laugh and then tremble as you kiss my knees and the insides of my thighs, lifting up my skirt. You push your tongue inside of me and I close my eyes. I breathe in the singed air, exhaust fumes, hot candle wax. I have been afraid to see you in your new life, in a place that I do not know the shape of. I have been worried that all of the mercury between us might have dissipated through distance, but as heat rolls through my stomach I realise that we are beyond the point of choosing. We are moving deeper inside something wet and red and dangerous, a love so raw I can almost smell it. I dig my nails into your scalp as the city swelters below us. You are asking me a question with your tongue and I answer with my whole body.

You have a single bed and we sleep close together, stomach squashed against spine, knees tucked into each other. Daylight bleeds through the shutters. You stir and open your eyes, yawning like a cat, stretching your mouth wide.

'Hi,' I whisper and you run your fingers across my hips.

'You're actually here,' you murmur. 'I thought it was a dream.'

'Are you pleased it's real?' I ask, worried that I am intruding on your new life. You push your face close to mine, pulling my lip gently with your teeth.

'I'm very pleased,' you say into my mouth. I burrow my face into your neck and breathe in the bitter smell of your sleep. The hairs on your chest prick my tongue as I trace your outline. I don't know exactly what I am doing here but I am lost between the sour shock of your thighs. I know I am not supposed to put my need in you but it spills from my lips and bursts over your body, soaking you in want. You press your lips to the veins that purple my wrists and I want to unpeel you, to strip off the skin that covers your heart and find your glistering centre.

68

33

When I first moved to London, I felt clumsy and lumbering, as though I was different from the people I met in bars and at parties, whose skin shone with something I knew I could not afford. I thought that cultured, glamorous people would be in control of their appetites and I was surprised to find my new friends talked about food all of the time. They shared recipes from newspapers and glossy cookery books. They had favourite chefs and restaurants and they got sourdough pizza takeaways. I didn't understand their language. It was so different from the world I grew up in, where women shared Slimming World solidarity, talking in Magic Knickers and bathroom scales. My new friends competed with each other, each girl claiming she was hungrier than the rest. I couldn't tell if their hunger was genuine or if it was another kind of performance, one that I didn't understand. The women I knew from home were proud of how little they allowed themselves to take. They admired each other's discipline, their ability to wane.

At first, pushing away my hunger made more room inside me to feel everything else. I wanted colour, danger and beauty, things that felt removed from the daily grind of eating, sleeping and my new job at a pub. I shrank my needs for food, safety and comfort in pursuit of poetry and magic. I wanted to live like lightning, which seemed luxurious and out of my grasp.

I went out almost every night after work, linking arms with girls who smelled like Marlboros and patchouli, dancing on the pavement, kissing strangers in the dark. My days were compact and tightly controlled but at night I let it all unravel, surrendering to the tangle of sound, light and dreams. We went back to someone's flat, buying gin and lemons from the corner shop, dancing on the settee to Fleetwood Mac, grinding cigarette ash into the carpet. We lay in the wet grass in the park, catching stars on the ends of our eyelashes. My new friends said things like,

'This park has a bad heart,' or 'The sky is falling down,' and I knew what they meant, lacing my fingers through theirs and running through the lavender dawn, our long coats flying out behind us.

I met some art students who took me to a supermarket car park and I posed for their portfolios at midnight, naked beneath a fur coat, cigarette smoke swirling in car headlights. I met a group of women in a bar with tattoos on their faces and they bundled me into their taxi and poured me wine in their warehouse kitchen, disco balls scattering silver across the room. I drank Bloody Marys at lunchtime and then cycled to work, crashing into the wing mirror of a car and cutting my knees open, my dress getting caught in the sticky red wounds for the rest of my shift. I lived on black coffee, toast and vodka and I never got hangovers. I had bare legs in winter and I didn't feel the cold. I ran towards chaos and it felt good under certain conditions; if the chaos hung from my secret rules, a strong spine of control, a disorder with a logic inside of it.

I pinched a menthol cigarette from a man in a smoking area, his face flickering beneath a red light. I felt invincible, as though I needed less than other people. I didn't need to eat or sleep or spend my nights watching telly. I was flashing neon, my hair fibre-optic, static crackling between my teeth. None of my actions seemed to have any consequences.

'I feel like I'm at the end of a long tunnel,' I said to the man. 'And reality is at the other side. Do you know what I mean?'

He laughed, holding his lighter to my face. 'Not really, gorgeous. Sounds good, though. I want one of whatever you're on.'

34

You throw on a wrinkled shirt and run down the street to the bakery. I watch you from the balcony, your long legs sticking out of your denim shorts, hair tangled, nodding hello to the fruit seller standing outside his shop, brooding over crates of dark plums. I brew coffee on your little stove, looking around your apartment. I feel like a stranger as I touch the unfamiliar mugs and spoons, a giant girl in a doll's house. I look at your swimming trunks drying on the balcony and the unfamiliar pictures framed on the wall and feel uneasy, as though I barely know you at all. I am reassured by your old boots kicked off in the corner and your books stacked in piles on the kitchen table, their covers spelling titles I have seen before. My skin thrums with traces of you and I let it move through me, after feeling your absence for so long.

You pound up the stairs and burst through the door, clutching a paper bag, shiny with grease.

'I got pastries,' you smile, anticipation leaking out of you and my stomach contracts. I want to enjoy the small pleasure you are offering me without thinking about it, scattering pastry flakes into my lap, but I feel too raw beneath the acid sun and my throat tenses.

'Amazing,' I lie and carry a couple of plates to the balcony. We sit on the warm tiles with our bare feet pressed

71

against the railings. I close my eyes in the morning light and when I open them you have already finished your croissant, crumbs sticking to your lips.

'Aren't you eating yours?' you ask and my face is hot because you are giving me a simple joy and I can't take it.

'Not that hungry,' I mumble. 'Think it must be the flight.'

'Are you sure?' you frown. 'Do you want something else?'

'I'm fine.' I sip my coffee.

'Can I have it?' You reach out your hand. You look like a child for a moment and I smile and offer you my plate. I watch you chew and swallow, stretching out in the sun like a cat. My stomach rumbles and I press my hands into it to make it stop. You light a cigarette and I take a drag from between your fingers, filling the empty space inside me with smoke and tar.

35

As a teenager, I spent rainy weekends in the basement of a bookshop in Darlington, browsing the travel guides. I crossed my legs on the scratchy carpet and opened pages at random, tracing my fingers over terracotta rooftops and impossibly blue skies, reading words in different languages, testing them out on my tongue.

I found a book crammed with spiralling buildings encrusted with crowns and winged creatures, stone branches twisting around each other, windows wracked with light. The book said they were built by a Catalan architect called Antoni Gaudí and I read about him hungrily, holding his shapes and colours inside me as I stepped out onto the dank high street, past the shuttered Poundshop, the pavements grey with rain.

When I was living in London in my early twenties, I met Dylan. He was a graphic designer who liked clean, straight lines and plain black T-shirts. He rubbed a small vial of oil into his beard to make it soft and kept shoe trees inside his leather boots, so they would keep their shape. He was seven years older than me and his life seemed real and solid, whereas mine was a rough sketch, barely even formed.

One year into our relationship, he bought us plane tickets to Barcelona. We drank cold red wine outside small bars, watching parakeets and walking arm in arm through the hot, dense streets, taking pictures of each other on disposable cameras. I sat on the tiny balcony of our rented room, looking at the church lit up gold in the hills by Tibidabo, and it all seemed like a feverish dream.

We went to the Sagrada Família and Dylan refused to pay to go inside.

'It's a tourist trap.' He adjusted his sunglasses. 'Why don't we go and do something real?'

'But this *is* real.' I looked up at the half-built towers and curling spires, the angels stretching up into the sky.

'It's kind of ugly, anyway,' said Dylan and I was embarrassed for thinking it was beautiful, when he knew so much more about the world than me. 'And I've seen it before.' I lingered, watching light split the stained-glass windows, drinking in the palm trees in their deep and startling green.

'Come on.' He dragged me off to an art gallery. I watched him in his sharp black clothes against the stark gallery walls and I felt messy and ungainly, as though my dreams were tacky and heavy with angels; too much decoration, too many leaves and flowers. I listened to him talk about the smooth clay sculptures and I understood that I needed to refine my tastes, cut out the chaos, whittle myself down to the clean edge of a bone.

36

Gold bars flash across your face as the train pulls away from the city. I rest my head against the window and watch as sun-bleached tower blocks give way to a blaze of white stone. You read a book with your hand on my leg, the hairs on your arms prickling in the air-conditioning.

We get off the train at Vilanova i la Geltrú and walk past streetside cafés and fluorescent phone shops, tabacs selling cigarettes and scratch-cards, oranges and bananas piled outside fruit shops, their skins warm in the sun.

'Want to get a vermouth?' you ask, as we walk through a dappled square. Metal chairs scrape the pavement beneath a faded awning. We sit down, shielding our eyes from the light. You scan a menu.

'Look, they have honey aubergine. It's so good. Have you tried it before?' I shake my head. 'Shall we get some?' I clean my sunglasses on the hem of my dress. I find it difficult to try new foods and I am tentative here, uncertain of who I am beneath a brighter sky, afraid of getting it wrong and not being good enough.

'Yes.' I force a smile. 'Sounds good.'

You glance at me over the top of the menu. 'You're not sure.' Disappointment streaks your face for a second and I see it before you brush it away.

'I am,' I say, in a voice that isn't mine. 'Let's do it.'

The aubergine arrives, warm and lightly battered. You clink your glass with mine and dark grapes burst across my tongue.

'What do you think?' you ask, nervously. My throat is tense and my thighs stick to the chair. I spear the aubergine with a fork. It is soft and crunchy and I swallow the parts of myself that protest. I have already wasted so much time.

'Really good.' I ignore the oil on my lips and focus on sweetness, light batter, the soft, warm flesh inside. You tap salt into your hand from the shaker and sprinkle it with your fingers. I fish the olive from my drink and eat it, forcing myself to focus on your long arms, the white paper napkins, the wide-open sky.

'Life is so good here,' you say, leaning back in your chair, and I watch you uncertainly, envious of the way the city seems to have opened up for you and the seamless way in which you have stepped into it.

'What are you thinking?' you ask me, worry creasing around your eyes.

'Nothing.' I snap back into the present and smile.

'Shall we find the beach?' you ask, rooting through your pockets for change.

We reach a harbour and the sea crinkles below us like silver foil. Salt blows from the water, coating my hair and skin. I stop for a moment, breathing it in.

'I missed the sea,' I say softly.

You press your lips to my shoulder. 'I missed you.' We clamber over rocks and reach a winding coastal path. We walk alongside a train track and lean into wild rosemary bushes as trains rattle by in a blur of speed and light. The smell of lemon and eucalyptus rises from the baked earth. A plane passes overhead and I think of the heavy sky over

London and my mother in her small, bright kitchen in Bishop Auckland, all of the distance between us. I watch your boots kick up dust in front of me and wonder whether it is really possible to become someone different, who eats croissants and honeyed aubergine beneath an expanding sky, or whether I will always just be me.

We find a cove and scramble down a rocky path, throwing our backpacks onto the sand. The waves are enormous, crashing cream onto the shore. It is not yet spring but sweat still gathers in my creases and I pull off my clothes without thinking, longing to be in the cold water. There is no one else around and you look at my naked body and slither out of your shorts. We dive into the sea as foam fizzes around us. The icy surf is a relief on my skin. It takes our bodies, pulling us out in the surge. We are dragged beneath the waves and then come up laughing. Joy rises in me like a hard, bright jewel.

We bob on the surface for a moment and then swim back towards the beach. You take my hand and pull me up onto the rocks, your skin slippery against mine. Wanting tears through me and I give into it, letting go of my worry about the food and your unfamiliar apartment, the uncertainty of me in your new life. You taste of silt and brine and I open myself up to you. I feel as though my hunger could swallow the whole world.

Later, at home in your apartment, our hair crimped with seawater, we slice avocados with blunt kitchen knives, piling their hard skins on a wooden chopping board. I cut a mango into chunks and suck the orange pulp from my fingers. You whisk lemon and white wine vinegar in a mug and trickle it over rocket leaves. I toss in a handful of sunflower seeds and they hit the glass bowl like rain. I feel safe and I eat hungrily, sitting on your balcony as the peach dusk falls around us, ice melting quickly in our glasses.

You kiss my bare shoulder and say, 'Salty.' Planes leave burning trails in the sky above our heads.

'Do you think those planes are actually flying right over us?' I ask. 'Or are they somewhere else, further away?'

'I suppose they could be anywhere over the north of Spain,' you say. 'They just look like they're right above us. Think it's something to do with the light.' We sit quietly, our bodies wrung with salt and sugar. I bite into a square of dark chocolate and it leaves a bitter streak on my tongue.

We fall into your bed, leaving the shutters open so the moonlight will seep into us, sand caught in the sheets, my skin tingling with traces of sun.

'Did you have a nice day?' you murmur, your syllables thick with sleep.

'Yeah.' I curve my body into yours. 'Did you?' I close my eyes and the motion of the waves rolls through me. I think of the pink sky, the honeyed aubergine, the illusion of the planes moving over us, the way that things seem closer than they really are. I picture our naked bodies in the cold water, thrashing in the spray and something old and crusted over inside me begins to crack. It is a hairline fracture, a splinter of light, a glimmer of another way to be.

37

At the beginning of my sixteenth summer, I stood in an empty bath at the back of a beauty salon, shivering in a pair of paper knickers.

'Hands above your head,' the beautician smiled, wielding a nozzle spraying orange liquid. 'I've got to do your tits. Or it won't look natural.'

My mother's new boyfriend, Steve, took us on holiday to Greece. It was my first hot place and the sun warped the world into shapes I had never seen before. The bright light made the whitewashed houses and emerald water seem so pure, as if I had only ever seen a cheap imitation of the world until then.

Desire was taking root inside me, heavy and green. It unfurled in the yellow heat, pressing against the wall of my stomach, cramps curling around my spine. My mother slathered her legs in sun cream and I stretched out on my towel in my leopard-print bikini, counting my ribs with my fingers, nervous about my exposed stomach and the expanse of my thighs. I half closed my eyes behind my heart-shaped sunglasses, squinting into the boundless sky. I dozed off, and woke to a shadow looming over me.

'Big tits, no?' laughed a male voice and my body tensed in response.

'Alright, mate?' warned Steve, his characteristic soft syllables standing to attention. I opened my eyes to find a tall, tanned teenage boy standing above me, water glittering on his bare chest, dark curls silhouetted against the sky. His eyes shamelessly travelled the length of my body and I sucked in my stomach. 'Fuck off, mate,' Steve snarled and the boy shrugged and walked away.

My chest lurched with something dripping and dangerous that I couldn't name. I was afraid of the careless way the boy wore his wanting and I wanted that ease for myself. I knew that Steve had pushed the boy away in order to protect me but I didn't want to be protected.

I wanted to know about pleasure, to inhabit my skin easily beneath the sun. I was uncomfortable in my body but not in my sexuality; they felt like interconnected yet separate things. I wanted to be looked at and I wanted to look back.

The walls of our rented apartment were thin. I tossed and turned beneath a single sheet, sweat prickling me awake. My mother's bed squeaked through the darkness, gasps and grunts gathering in the corners of my room. I burrowed my face into the pillow, counting sheep and stars and bottles of beer, but the boy from the beach pushed his way into my dreams.

In the morning, I drank orange juice on a plastic patio chair and my fingers grazed a black insect bulging from my thigh. I tried to flick it away with my fingernail but it clung on.

'Oh, love.' My mother took off her sunglasses, sensing my panic. 'It's a tick. You must have picked it up in the long grass. Hang on a sec, I'll just get my tweezers.' Sickness rolled through me as I watched her clamp its swollen body, red and black and fat with my blood.

We went back to the beach and I winced across the hot pebbles in my bare feet, head pounding in the heat. My mother waded into the water and I noticed her hips spilling over her bikini bottoms and the wiry hairs coiled across Steve's back.

'Come in!' she laughed, splashing beneath the sky. 'We're in the Mediterranean Sea. Can you believe it?' I watched them swim out to a black rock in the water and I shielded my eyes from the glare, looking for the boy with the dark curls, hoping he would come back while they were far away. I wanted to cool off in the water but I was worried that it would wash off my spray tan and then people would know

I was pretending, that I was not at ease in my body, that I came from a cold place, that I had never watched the sun split a fig and that my desires never felt luxurious. They would know that I wanted too much and that I couldn't even name it, that I wanted to be looked at but I was too scared to look back.

38

The weekend is unexpectedly warm and we lie on a blanket on the sand, reading and drinking lemon beer. You pull out a tin of peaches in syrup, twisting the ring pull and peeling back the lid.

'I haven't had these since I was little,' I smile, fishing out a slippery segment, sweet juice running down my elbows.

'They're good for the beach.' You put your whole hand in the can. 'They don't rot in the sun.' I hold the soft peach slice on my tongue, trying to remember how it felt to be a child, when I ate whatever I hungered for, without thinking about it.

We watch the people around us, stretched out on the sand. A group of men play volleyball in black Speedos, their bellies soft around their waistbands, muscles straining as they reach for the ball. A woman wrings water from her hair and the droplets catch the light like glass beads. A small girl, aged five or six, runs across the beach in bikini bottoms, bare-chested.

'I feel so much more in my body here,' you say, sitting up with your knees bent and heels splayed.

'What do you mean?'

'I don't know. I suppose I'm at the beach a lot,' you smile. 'But people are more accepting of bodies here, I think. Less prudish.'

'Because of the hot weather?'

'Maybe. I just feel more present in my body. More comfortable with myself.' I look at your boyish chest and narrow hips, tattoo ink curled beneath your skin in leaves and petals.

'I like your body,' I say, from behind my sunglasses. You rest your hand on my back.

'I like yours, too.' I am aware of the elastic hem of my swimming costume digging into my thighs, the grains of sand sticking to my legs and the tight fabric stretched across my breasts. I feel conscious of the damp pucker of lycra as I step out of the sea, emphasising the curve of my hips and the bulge of my stomach, the eyes that linger on my chest for a moment too long as I make my way up the beach. I have always felt too much in my body, aware of the pull of my skin on my bones. I thought that freedom was the privilege of forgetting your body, but perhaps that is not true.

'Weren't you comfortable in your body before?' I ask, dropping a peach segment in the sand.

You think for a moment. 'Not really. I didn't feel *in* my body. It was like it just wasn't even there. Like I had gone missing from it.'

'That sounds kind of nice.'

'It wasn't.' You shield your eyes from the sun. 'It was like I only half-existed.'

'Why did you feel like that?'

'I don't know, really. I didn't hate it. Or love it. It was just nothing to me. Like a vessel.' I reach out and touch your arm. I wonder which is worse, being aware of your body with every small movement, or feeling that your body isn't there at all.

'I can't imagine it,' I say. I take a sip of my beer, feeling grit caught on the rim.

You push your fingers into the sand, awkwardly. 'Maybe it's different for women.'

I am quiet, thinking of all the too-small spaces my body has been forced into, the stray hands and lingering eyes that I did not ask for. I wonder what it means to accumulate these tiny shards of violence like beads on a necklace, commonplace and unremarkable, wound tightly around my throat.

The small girl races towards the water and trips in the sand. She bursts into tears and her mother rushes over and scoops her up, her own stomach soft and riven with stretch marks. I try to imagine how it would feel to carry another body inside my own and whether I would care for myself better then. I think of my own mother and the children she lost, wondering how it feels to lose a part of you that is part of someone else, too. I try to imagine how it would feel to go missing from my body in the way that you describe. I think that is what I was striving for with my drinking, starving, running, swimming, things that pulled me out of myself. And yet I could never escape; I was always dragged back to earth by the contours of my flesh, the inescapable fact of my skeleton beneath it all.

The mother dusts sand from her daughter's knees and kisses them. I remember my own mother doing the same for me, brushing my pain away, and my chest aches when I think of all the ways in which I have not looked after myself since then. I watch the girl's father opening a cool box filled with fizzy drinks and baguettes wrapped in tin foil. The girl takes a sandwich from him and he smiles at her. He unrolls a towel and wraps it tightly around her, keeping her safe and warm.

39

When I left school, we had a leavers' prom. Everyone fretted over it for years beforehand, poring over the photos of older girls who had been there before us, critiquing their hairstyles and admiring their dresses. We dreamed in spray tans and pastel colours, planning our hair, nails and after-parties, nervously wondering if anyone would ask us to be their date. People hired limousines to drive them to the venue, drinking Shloer from plastic champagne flutes and screaming out of the sunroof, the silty wind tangling their hair extensions.

My parents' divorce came through a few weeks before my prom and my mother took me dress shopping as a kind of apology. She looked tired as we fingered clouds of tulle and diamanté hair clips.

'They're like wedding dresses.' She shook her head, unconsciously twisting her empty ring finger. I ended up choosing something short and black from Topshop.

'Do you think it's alright?' I sucked in my stomach in the changing room.

'Do you like it?' She checked the price tag.

I frowned at my flushed reflection, fluffing up my hair. 'I think so.'

She smiled, approvingly. 'Well, that's the most important thing.'

*

The day of the prom, I felt sick with nerves. I shaved my legs carefully and lined my eyes in black. I strapped on my heels and tottered into the garden to have my photo taken. My body felt loud in my little black dress, my legs exposed and my breasts squashed together inside my new strapless bra.

'You look lovely.' My mother snapped away with her digital camera as I stood awkwardly beside a rose bush.

'Are you sure?' I fiddled with the hem of my dress. The phone began to ring and she went inside to answer it, leaving me sinking into the grass.

'It's your dad,' she said with a hurt expression, passing me the phone carefully, as if it was dangerous.

'Have a good time tonight.' His voice was hoarse. 'Get your mam to take lots of pictures. Look after yourself, alright?'

My mother was quiet as she drove me to Tara's house. The car seat made the backs of my legs itch and I felt jittery imagining the stares of everyone from school, the way they lodged in my skin like splinters.

My mother flashed a look at me as she changed gear. 'Be careful at the party afterwards. Call me if you want to come home.'

'I'll be fine,' I snapped. We drove in silence for a while and I chewed my lip.

'Do you think my dress is too short?' I worried, as we turned onto Tara's street.

My mother glanced at my legs. 'Well, it's a bit late, now.'

'So you do think it's too short?' I panicked.

My mother shook her head. 'That dress was expensive, love. You shouldn't have bought it if you weren't sure.'

My stomach felt hard. 'Does it look horrible?'

My mother's lips were thin. 'Stop it, you look lovely. What's the matter with you?'

We pulled up outside of Tara's house and the air in the car was charged. I felt queasy at the ripple of pink and yellow satin in the front garden and the ghostly flash of cameras in the daylight.

'Have a good time, then,' my mam said without looking at me. I swallowed hard and made for the door as Tara's mother breezed over to us in a long summer dress, holding a glass of prosecco.

'Sarah,' she trilled at my mother. 'Come in and have a drink.' My mother looked down at her jeans and old T-shirt.

'Oh.' She looked at me. 'No, I'd better get off. Look at the state of me.'

Tara's mother beamed down at us. 'Don't be daft. You're fine. Come on in. I'll get you a glass.'

My friends' parents stood in the front garden in short-sleeved shirts and floral dresses, smiling behind their sunglasses, clutching warm glasses of wine.

'You girls are all so beautiful,' winked a drunk dad wielding a camera. My friends did look beautiful in their slinky dresses, lips slick and shiny, eyes smoky and bright. I tugged at the hem of my own dress, pushing my shoulders back and breathing in. I looked around for Tara but I couldn't find her among the lip-glossed smiles and perfume flurry, a trail of plastic bunting fluttering in the breeze.

My mother stood at a table on her own, picking at a bowl of crisps. Someone asked her to take a picture and I watched as a dad in a checked shirt slipped his arm around his wife's waist, their daughter between them in a floor-length red dress, sparkling and proud. My mother's cheek twitched and I caught her eye.

'Are you embarrassed to be here with me?' she asked as I picked my way across the grass to her, my feet blistering in my heels.

'What?' I was taken aback. I wasn't embarrassed; I was too focused on feeling wrong in my body, wracked with nerves, already anticipating the Facebook pictures the next day.

My mother jangled her car keys. 'I'm going home.'

'What? Why?'

My mother's face was tight. 'You obviously don't want me here. You didn't even tell me it was happening.'

I looked around, worried that other people might be listening. 'I didn't know.' I wanted my mother to be there but I could see how much she was hurting, small against the drunk, smiling families in their radiant colours.

My mother put down her drink. 'I'm going. Have a nice night.'

I perched on the edge of a plastic chair, blinking back tears, watching my friends in their beautiful dresses. I couldn't understand what I had done wrong, only that my mother was hurting and the badness I felt clung to my body, dripping from the hem of my dress, exposing my thighs. I couldn't help but feel that my mother had left because I was not bright or pretty enough, that neither of us was good enough for my father and a sadness clung to us, giving our skin a sickly sheen. The promise of my classmates felt far away from me, as though they were moving somewhere filled with light, to a place I could not follow.

Afterwards, I looked at the photos on the internet and saw my failure written into my awkward pose and pained expression. I lived on toast and water for a whole week afterwards, punishing my body for letting me and my mother down.

40

You wake early, kissing my shoulder and slipping out of bed. I hear you clatter around the kitchen and then pound down the stairs on your way to work, slamming the door behind you. I lie alone in the darkness, watching yellow slats of light seep through the shutters, listening to voices I cannot understand echoing from the street below, the clang of the butano seller wheeling gas canisters between the tall buildings.

I make coffee on your stove and drink it on a wooden chair, noticing my suitcase shoved in the corner of the room. I look at your piles of books and paper, jackets hung on the back of the door, dishes stacked in the sink. I am comforted by your mess, evidence of living, yet I feel too aware that all of it belongs to you. I think of my scanty possessions in London, crammed into boxes and shoved beneath my bed while a stranger sublets my room. I want to spread out, untidy and expansive, yet I am afraid of having more than I can pack into a couple of cases, compact and easy to carry. A niggling part of me wonders if this is all just a distraction from building anything real in London, playing at living here with you.

I pull on a light dress and go out into the day, stopping at the fruit shop to fill a plastic bag with cherries, smiling at the fruit seller, hoping he will not ask me a question I cannot answer. I feel insubstantial, shy in my foreignness, unable to ask for what I need.

I walk through Sant Antoni and into El Raval, looking up at the vines curling from balconies, the narrow, crumbling buildings with washing strung high above the street. Some of the streets are so narrow that opposing apartments are only metres away from each other, leaning forwards, as though they might topple. It looks as if it would be so easy to jump between apartments, from balcony to balcony, but I think about how difficult it really is; to leave one life and slip into another.

The streets are chaotic and beautiful with patterned cobbles and mosaic tiles, grocery shops gilded with gold spices, shop windows glazed with pastries and squares drenched in light. I wonder if I could make my own life here, whether I might stay for longer, what it would mean to make a go of it properly and live with you, but then I remember we have only really just met and feel embarrassed, shaking my thoughts away.

The stink of piss and rotten fruit oozes from the gutters as I wind my way past red-lit bars and cluttered bazaars, strings of plastic lights and tangled plants hanging from doorways. I used to love the thrill of being in a new place, feeling my outer layers cracking, my skin unpeeling, learning the cadence of a different way to live, but as I peer into shop windows filled with fridge magnets and football shirts, watching people drinking beer in the midday sun, I feel detached from it all. I think of my mother at work at the call centre, answering phones all day, and the weight of it crushes me, making me feel ungrateful for being in a sun-wracked city, beneath a bright blue sky, unable to throw myself into it.

I walk past a group of men sitting in a square and they stare at me openly.

'*Hola, señorita*,' they call with smoky, teasing voices, their eyelids heavy, smiles loose on their faces. I ignore them and cross the square, feeling the sting of their eyes on my skin. I know they will forget me as soon as I turn the corner, which is a relief, yet there is an ache in me for something solid that is growing with every passing day. I am tired of living precariously and skirting the borders, a stranger caught on the periphery of a photograph, a passing, faceless woman without a name.

41

Dylan went away with work one weekend and left me the keys to his clean, white flat. I walked around barefoot, touching the empty counters. He liked plain walls and stark furniture, everything free of clutter. My suitcase vomited clothes into the hall, messy and chaotic. Dylan's life was sleek and curated and I felt ungainly inside it, as though I had no taste and too many cheap possessions, as if there was too much of me in his neat and tidy space.

I stood in front of his bedroom mirror, looking at the curve of my hips and my round breasts, my pale stomach, the stretch marks marbled across my thighs. My body looked so calm on the outside. There was no mark of any of the things I had done to it. No scars or cuts or bruises, no evidence of the hot, red discomfort that grew between my bones. I wondered how it was possible to exist like that; to look so ordinary and yet to be filled with such churning beneath the surface.

The window was open and there were builders working on the house across the street, standing on a scaffold, their bare chests burning in the sun. I heard a shout caught on the warm air and I ignored it, lifting my arms up above my head, watching my nipples rise. I breathed in, wondering how I would look if there was less of me, whether my body would fit me better if there was more empty space around it.

'Hey, gorgeous!' A voice thudded against the window. I peered into the glare, looking for the face that made the sound. 'Sexy!' The voice came again. 'Sexy lady!' I looked out of the window and saw a row of builders gathered on a wooden platform, staring through the window, right at me.

'Shit,' I breathed, dropping to my knees and crawling out of the bedroom. I almost laughed. I had to leave for work and I fretted as I pulled on a clean dress, anticipating the moment when I would have to walk out of flat and face the builders, without the protection of the outside wall, but there was no way around it. I took a deep breath and put on a pair of sunglasses, opened the door and stepped out into the light. I walked down the street quickly, without looking up, digging my nails into my palms, hoping they hadn't noticed me.

I was halfway down the street when I heard heavy footsteps pounding the pavement behind me. Someone was running towards me and I sped up, in a moment of panic. I felt hot and dizzy as the footsteps got closer. I heard the sound of jangling keys. A man reached out and grabbed my shoulder and I spun around to face him. It was one of the builders, covered in a layer of yellow dust, his T-shirt torn at the neck. I noted the bulge of muscle beneath his short sleeves, a black tattoo ringed around his bicep. He smelled like stale sweat and sunlight.

'I'm working on the house across from yours,' he smiled as I backed away from him, anger colouring my vision.

'Yeah,' I said. 'I noticed.'

He looked embarrassed for a moment and then smiled again. 'I just wanted to ask you for your number.'

'What?' I gaped at him.

'Your number? I want to take you on a date.'

'No.' I shook my head and turned away from him, fumbling for the right words. I felt like pure anger, a pulsing line of red. 'No,' I said again, my tongue fat and useless in my mouth. He watched me walk away down the street. My hands were shaking. I felt invaded, as though he had reached right through the window and touched my naked body with his strong, weathered hands. There was a horrible, niggling part of me that found approval in his actions, a suggestion that perhaps my body was not disgusting after all. I hated that thought because I didn't want my sense of self to be defined by men and yet, in lots of ways, it already was. I felt pathetic and ashamed as I got on the bus, as though I had let someone down.

Later, when I told Dylan, he said,

'It's weird, isn't it? How these kinds of things always happen to you.'

42

I go to the supermarket and buy everything we need for the week. I stack tins of chickpeas and lentils in the cupboards carefully, lining up jars of rice and pasta, rinsing vegetables and putting fruit in a bowl. I stand back and look at my work, feeling satisfied, but then a niggling fear creeps in and I begin to rearrange the shelves. I worry that I have bought too much and we will never be able to eat it all, that I have revealed something hungry and lacking in myself. I know I have to fight this feeling, that it is okay to buy what I need to survive and sometimes more but I still find myself shoving bulging bags of couscous and packets of salted crackers to the back of the cupboard, where I cannot see them.

I decide to visit Mercat de Sant Antoni before you get home from work. I take a little blue ticket from a plastic machine and wait patiently as a man in a white hat and gloves guts cod and drops handfuls of shrimp onto a pair of scales, their shells clattering on the metal. I pick out huge mussels with navy shells, crusted with algae and salt water. The man wraps them in plastic and I carry them to your apartment. I want to fill the space with something I have made and to prove that I am capable of choosing, that I am no longer captive to the fear that was coiled in me for so long.

I look up instructions on the internet, worried that I will cook the mussels wrong and poison us both. I fill a rusty pan with water and wait for it to bubble, then I add salt, garlic, parsley, lemon, a whole carton of cheap white wine. I play Billie Holiday, her crackly voice filling the echoey apartment, warm air blowing through the balcony doors. I plop a handful of mussels into the pan and hover nervously by the hob, watching as the steam prises their mouths open, briny and gasping for air. I scrape a thick dollop of butter onto a crusty baguette and warm it in the oven.

Your eyes are bleary when you get home. You kick off your boots and sniff the air cartoonishly, like a dog. The mussels slosh in their boozy broth as I carry them to the table.

'Jesus.' You take in my flushed cheeks and the pans in

the sink, the bottle of wine on the table. 'I'm not expecting you to cook for me.' You look apprehensive and I am embarrassed.

'I know.' I roll my eyes. 'I just wanted to try something.'

'Well, thank you.' You sit down at the table. 'I'm honoured.' I spoon broth into my bowl and bring it to my lips; hot, thick and bitter. You tear the shells apart hungrily, scattering them across the table.

'I was worried I might poison us,' I confess, dipping a crust of bread into my bowl.

'Nah.' You slurp broth from an empty shell. 'If they aren't cooked properly then they won't come apart easily. Don't eat the ones that are difficult to open.'

I pick at my mussels, unable to tell which shells I can prise apart easily and which ones are more difficult. I grow panicked and slurp the broth instead, ignoring the delicacies growing cold in my bowl. You reach over and crack them apart with ease.

'These ones are okay, look. They're easy to break.'

'I can't tell,' I say, hotly. 'What if I get it wrong and eat a bad one?'

You start to laugh and stop at my serious face. 'Just trust yourself. You're thinking about it too much.' I put down my spoon and rub my eyes. I am so tired of carrying this weight around, of letting its black shape come between me and other people, dark fingers caught in the back of my throat, scraping my gums.

'Are you alright?' You peer at me in the lamplight.

'Sorry.' I rub my eyes again. I glance at your concerned face and the words tumble out. 'I get weird about food sometimes.'

'What do you mean?'

'I don't know.' I fiddle with my glass. 'There was a time

when I didn't really eat much. And sometimes it creeps back in.'

'Yeah,' your voice is gentle. 'I kind of noticed.'

I feel exposed and fiddle with my cutlery, trying to find the right words. 'I'm sorry. I've been trying hard not to bring it here.'

'What do you mean?'

'I don't want it to come between us.'

'Why would it come between us?'

'It's happened before.'

'It's not a big deal.' You reach for your glass of water. It is a big deal but I don't know how to explain it. I want you to know how integral it has been to the way I have moved through the world, how I learned to push shame and anger deep into my body and yet speaking about it brings it into the present, when all I want is to leave it behind.

'Thanks,' I say, quietly. You light a candle and we watch it melt, leaking wax onto the table.

'The mussels are really okay, though,' you say, taking one from my plate. I pause for a moment, then lift the bowl to my lips and drink the broth until I am woozy. I prise the shells apart with my fingernails and tip the mussels into my mouth, until I am no longer thinking at all.

43

Dylan and I went to film screenings and art openings, clutching glasses of wine in stark white galleries, running for the last train home. We watched bands play in heaving pubs and spent Sundays in the park, slipping off our shoes and lying in the long grass, sipping lukewarm coffee from paper cups.

He invited friends over for Friday night dinners where he played obscure records and rolled cigarettes at the table, while I pushed food around my plate.

'Aren't you hungry?' asked one of Dylan's friends in a silver turtle-neck, eyes wide beneath her heavy fringe.

'She's never hungry,' Dylan laughed, getting up to change the record. His friend raised her eyebrows and I shrugged it off but my stomach clenched around his words.

Dylan's friends joked about artists I had not heard of, tossing back their heads in their shiny clothes. They were photographers and designers and they moved through the world in a way that seemed smooth to me, as though they were gliding on a lake of still water. My wanting came off me like a stink as I fumbled for the right words. They were calm and collected, their fingers tattooed with hearts and crescent moons, making plans for weekends in Italy or parties in dark basements that I could never go to because I was always at work. They didn't seem to need anything and I envied that as I pushed away my pasta and drank a pint of water to fill the hole inside me, drowning my animal self.

Dylan liked to link his thumb and little finger around my wrists. He did it absently, when we were sitting in the pub or lying in bed, as though he was checking that I still fitted. He bought his jeans from the women's section of expensive shops because he knew about shape and size, straight lines and smooth edges. He knew how to erase things and then put them back together and I believed in the way he viewed the world, because he was older and wiser than me, taller and flatter, an easier shape.

*

After a few months, he asked me to move in with him. I looked at his art books on the coffee table, his standing lamp, his tasteful prints hanging in wooden frames and said,

'That would be nice.'

Dylan fried sausages in the mornings, with garlic and herbs. I unpeeled a banana at the kitchen table, drinking black coffee, my skin pink and shiny from my run. We listened to records with the windows open, my feet bare on the wooden floorboards, bright light soaking our faces. While he was at work, I hung our washing to dry on his little balcony, my dresses and his T-shirts crinkling in the sun. I slipped into bed in the early hours when I got home from my shift at the pub, my arms aching and my legs streaked with beer. I climbed beneath the cool sheets, grateful for the still silence and Dylan's warm body breathing next to me.

He woke early, brewing coffee in the kitchen, listening to Philip Glass. I rubbed sleep from my eyes as he came into the bedroom clutching a steaming mug, looking for his laptop charger.

'Morning,' he said, stepping over my discarded underwear. He leaned over to kiss me and wrinkled his nose. 'Would you mind showering when you come home from work? The bed smells like a brewery.' I pulled the covers tightly around my body, smelling the stench of curdling hops, embarrassment coating my tongue.

'Oh,' I mumbled. 'Okay. Sorry.'

'Alright.' He shrugged on his jacket. 'See you later.' I watched his loping gait through the window as he walked down the street, joining the throng of early risers in their crisp, white shirts, on their way to air-conditioned offices.

44

We meet your friends at a small, dense bar packed with men with heavy sideburns and hoop earrings, the walls plastered with old punk flyers, candles stuck in wine bottles ridged with years of wax. There is a glass counter filled with olives and cockles, silver anchovies soaking in oil. Old men nurse small glasses of dark liqueur and smoke fat cigarettes on the pavement outside.

Your friends wave us over, calling your name above the noise. We wind our way through the crowd to join them, pulling rickety chairs up to their table.

'*Buenas*,' they smile, standing to kiss our cheeks.

'This is Nico.' You gesture to a pale man in a black turtle-neck, despite the heat. 'He teaches film at the university.' I kiss his cheeks. 'Laia is a writer. And Miguel works in my department.'

'This is my partner, Josep,' says Miguel and a man with short curls and tortoiseshell glasses raises his fingers in greeting.

'*Encantado*,' I mumble, ashamed about my lack of Catalan or Spanish. I studied Spanish for a couple of months at school and then dropped it. At the time, I couldn't imagine a life in which I might need it, but now I am here.

'I'll get the drinks,' I say to you, then I go to the bar and order two cold beers.

When I return, you are deep in conversation, laughing and shouting in accented Spanish. You say something I can't make out and Miguel claps you on the back with wide eyes, speaking in a hushed tone, then the table erupts in laughter. I smile along, picking up on social cues, trying not to reveal how little I understand. I notice Nico staring at me and snap back into the conversation.

'Sorry. What did you say?'

Nico smiles. 'I asked how long you are staying here.'

'Oh.' I glance at you and you sip your beer without looking at me. 'For a couple more weeks, I think.'

'And then what?'

'What do you mean?'

Laia shakes her head. 'Just ignore him.' Her voice is rich and rasping. 'He can be very blunt.'

'That's okay,' I smile at her. Nico looks at you and you get up to go to the bathroom. I try to catch your eye but you move too quickly. We haven't really talked about what will happen next. We are just inside things as they are unfolding. I have a ticket for a flight back to London at the end of the month but I have been trying not to think about it.

Josep speaks quickly in Catalan and Laia translates for me.

'He is talking about a book he has written,' she says, kindly. 'It is about the rise of the far-right in Europe, linked to the history of Catalan anarchism.'

'Sounds interesting.'

'Yes,' she nods. 'You should read it. Although I don't think it is translated yet.'

'They will not translate me into English.' Josep clicks his tongue. 'You have to be very successful for that.' I nod awkwardly, embarrassed by the dominance of my native tongue, while Josep is moving fluidly between three languages and I am blindly trapped within one.

You come back from the bathroom and the conversation drifts between Spanish and Catalan, as everyone discusses the Catalan independence movement and the treatment of political prisoners. I try to pick out individual words but the conversation becomes heated and everyone speaks too quickly, so I sit back and let the cadence wash over me. You are louder in another language, your movements bigger and your gestures wider, curling your tongue around the words. I watch your full lips and your wiry, girlish beauty, the long, dark lashes around your eyes. The table bursts into laughter again and I squeeze your elbow.

'What did you say?' I ask, but you brush me off and start speaking to Miguel. Laia notices and tries to engage me in conversation but I feel untethered, as though I am floating somewhere outside.

I feel small and self-conscious around your university colleagues. When I finished school, I worked in a café in town for a couple of years, reading novels on my lunch break and trying to work out what I wanted to do. When I moved to London, I took an evening course in English Literature, with the thought of maybe doing a degree one day, but I got too nervous in seminars and couldn't bring myself to speak. My ideas were founded on emotion and connected to my own experiences, without roots in critical theory or stylistic movements, simply raging through me in bolts of love and anger that I couldn't always articulate; unfounded, chaotic and wild.

'Would you like another beer?' Laia jolts me out of my thoughts.

'Okay,' I smile. 'Thanks.' She goes to the bar and I try to reach you but you are ignoring me. I realise we have not spent much time around other people together and it makes me feel lonely, as though I barely know you at all.

We are both drunk as we walk home together through the old, dark streets. The alleyways smell of piss and hot concrete. You take my hand and I pull away.

99

'What's the matter?' You frown at me.

'Nothing.' We walk for a while in silence.

'Are you sure?' We reach Parallel and you light a cigarette. I resent the ease with which you lean against the traffic lights, tall and unafraid.

'Why were you being like that?' I ask you. 'In the bar.'

'Like what?'

'Ignoring me.' The green light flashes and we cross the road.

'I wasn't ignoring you.'

'What were you doing, then?'

You clench your jaw and a muscle in your neck twitches. 'I was just hanging out with my friends. Is that not okay?' You gesture between us. 'We're together every day.' I look at you in disbelief. I have no problem with you being with your friends or doing things without me. You are twisting the night, making me feel as though I am an intruder, a clinging, needy person whom you must look after.

We turn onto your street and I am suddenly exhausted. I am used to being alone in unfamiliar places but it is different here because it feels like yours. I was caught up in the rush of you but now I realise that I don't have a plan or any sense of the future. I don't know what I will do when I go back to London or what kind of life I want to build. I am supposed to be living in a way that feels more concrete, but instead I am floating in a grey space, faltering between your new life and my old one. I am frustrated that I could not articulate my ideas in the bar in either language, insecure that I exposed my vulnerabilities. We climb the stairs to your apartment in silence. You pour yourself a glass of water, swaying slightly and rubbing your eyes.

'I'm going to bed.' You throw your jacket onto the settee.

'Okay.' I open the balcony doors. 'I'm going to sit out here for a while.' You pull off your shirt without looking at me and go into the bedroom.

I make a cup of tea and sit on the balcony with steam curling between my fingers, listening to your bed springs rattle. I look up at the purple sky but it is thick with smog and I cannot see a single star. I think of you in the bar, avoiding my eyes, speaking in a different voice, and I wonder if I have made a mistake. You came here because you wanted to choose your life and I wonder whether I am merely following you along dark alleyways. I want to live in a deeper way than I have in the past, to put down roots and stop just scratching the surface. I wonder if I could do that here, or whether it is better to construct my own life on my own terms. I notice the man across the street at his window. He looks straight at me and I raise my arm in greeting but he just closes the shutters without a response, as though I am barely here at all.

45

I had a summer job in London, working front of house at an immersive theatre production. The show was set over five floors of a warehouse and the design team erected an indoor forest with real trees and a desert, with tonnes of sand sculpted into dunes for the audience to clamber over. A live band played in the velvet jazz bar and the audience mingled with the actors, sipping champagne from vintage coupes. The audience wore masks, to differentiate them from the performers, and my job was to stand in the basement dressed in black, wearing my own mask, hidden in the shadows.

'You should be invisible,' the stage manager said to me. 'Don't speak to anyone unless it's an emergency, even if someone asks you a question.'

'What kind of emergency?'

'A fire. Or a medical emergency. Quite a few people have panic attacks.'

'Really?'

'Yes. You need to show them to the nearest exit and we'll get them first aid.'

'Got it.'

The building was a maze and I walked up and down, learning the floor plan, weaving around tree trunks and the fake operating room, the glittering ice palace and the fluorescent pool.

'Watch out for people having sex,' winked one of my colleagues, on his way out for a cigarette. 'It happens more often than you'd think.'

'Right,' I laughed uncertainly.

'Wearing masks does strange things to people. They think no one else can see them.'

'Thanks for the heads up.'

I stood in the basement for six hours a day, sweating into my mask. Sometimes people found me and asked me directions but I just stood there impassively, ignoring their confused whispers and frantic hands waving in front of my face. Now and again an actor whisked past with a trail of dazed onlookers, hissing the name of a missing prop into my ear and I ran backstage to find it.

For the most part, I was invisible. I watched the dancers as they leaped and spun in circles, carving proudly through the darkness with their shoulders pushed back. I noted their toned calves and the tattoos slipping from the hems of their costumes, the angles of their collarbones, the sinews arched around their necks.

I watched the audience move around the room uncertainly. Some people held on to each other tightly, shuffling slowly, jumping at sudden sounds. Others walked alone with their heads held high, standing too close to the actors, touching the set and picking up props. The masks made everyone anonymous and yet they all moved differently. They brought all of their experiences to that dark, charged space and they could not be separated from them. Some people became bolder when their faces were covered and others grew afraid, stripped of the markers that usually gave them a smooth passage through the world.

I had often dreamed of being invisible; moving through the streets without being reminded of the shape of my body by the flash of a stranger's eyes or a call from a car window. I had often wondered whether my passage through the world would be different if I wasn't a young woman, whether I would be taken more seriously or if I would have more power. I had tried to imagine how it might feel to inhabit a body that I was less aware of, that I rarely really thought about, that was just a part of me. I brought it up with my mother once and she said,

'I wish that people would look at me. You'll miss it when you're older. I feel invisible, now.'

At the time, I thought that sounded like freedom, but in the basement, where I was invisible, I did not feel free at all. When I cycled home at night after the last show, I sometimes drifted into the path of a speeding car, forcing the driver to swerve to avoid me, honking the horn and swearing through the window. I spent so long pretending I was not there, I forgot that I was made of muscle, tooth and bone, something solid that could be broken.

46

I walk up to Montjuïc while you are at work and go swimming in the outdoor pool. It was built for the Olympics in the nineties and the changing room is cavernous, breeze-blocks furry with mould and metal pipework exposed. I stand beneath the cold shower and imagine the athletes warming up, flexing their broad shoulders and solid biceps, walking across the cool tiles with their heads held high, safe in the knowledge of their strength and power.

The swimming pool is an aqua rectangle jutting above the sprawl of terracotta rooftops and the hazy hills in the distance, the Sagrada Família rising up like a dragon from the heat and smog. There is an abandoned diving pool to my left filled with leaves and dead insects, the water dark and cold. It makes me feel strange and I turn my back on it, diving into the bright pool and kicking my legs urgently, pushing out the tension coiled in my muscles, the fear of not being good enough for you beneath this sun-split sky, the worry that we might lose this dark, strange red between us, as though it might bleed away.

The water is freezing but the sun warms my face, pulling freckles from my cheeks, and I swim length after length until my arms grow heavy. I have always stored my fear of not being good enough in my body; pushed my failures and anxieties deep into my tissues and cells where they cramp and burn until I pound them all out. I swim until my body grows too weak to push through the water and then I climb out and sit on the damp concrete by the glass barrier that separates the pool from the sky, imagining how it might feel to fall. I look out across the city and wonder if I could make a life here. I look at the palm trees and the crumbling yellow buildings, the colourful graffiti, the green flash of the sea. It is all so beautiful; sun-drenched and dazzling and I feel like something darker, hard-edged and silver, struggling towards the light.

I walk back to your apartment beneath a fading sky, my blood thick and heavy like syrup. I look at the people drinking beers outside cafés, eating hot bravas, seemingly unafraid. I wish that I was like them, that I didn't have to swim and starve and purge things out of myself. I wish I could just enjoy all of the beauty, instead of jangling with nervous energy, all caught up inside.

You arrive home soon after me, carrying a baguette. We haven't spoken about the night in the bar with your friends and there is a hard feeling between us, like something stretched too tightly.

'What did you do today?' You open the fridge without looking at me.

'Mostly reading,' I lie. 'And I went for a walk.' I don't tell you that I went swimming beneath the hot sun in a bid to erase myself, that your nonchalance in the bar filled my lungs like water, making it difficult to breathe.

'What shall we have for dinner?' you ask and I shrug as if it is nothing. 'Do you like tapenade?' You pull out a small jar and hand it to me. I break a small crust from the end of the bread and scoop dark paste from the jar. 'I can never decide if I really like it,' you say. 'The flavour is so strong.'

'I like it,' I say, defiantly. I like biting straight into limes and swallowing mouthfuls of seawater. I like dark wine, aniseed, wasabi, fennel. My body craves density; honey from the jar and teaspoons of salt. Once, I ate a spoonful of dried coffee granules just to hold bitterness on my tongue. 'I like things that are on the verge of disgusting. Like fish.'

You raise your eyebrows. 'Fish isn't disgusting.'

'It almost is. All slimy and salty. It tastes right on the edge and that's what makes it good.'

'Is that why you like me?' You avoid my eyes. 'Because I'm on the verge of disgusting?'

'Must be.' I want to puncture the distance between us but I don't know how to begin. I am so afraid of not being good enough. I don't want to talk about what will happen when I go back to London because I can already sense you pulling away.

'Have you ever eaten octopus?' you ask.

'No, I haven't.'

'Do you want to try it now?'

'Right now?' My stomach makes a fist.

'Yeah. There's a place at the end of the street I pass every day. It looks cheap. Dark wood. Plastic tablecloths.'

'Okay,' I swallow. I don't want to eat octopus but I want to be the kind of person who does. 'Let's go.'

We sit in the empty restaurant, cheap glasses of cava fizzing between us. Your eyes are lined in black, oil-slicked in the candlelight. I want to ask you what is wrong but I am afraid of the answer. The octopus arrives on a plate, curled like a flower. You look worried.

'It's boiled.'

'Is that bad?'

'No. I've just never had it boiled. I think it was fried

when I tried it before.' I look at the coiled purple tentacles, suckers oozing stock.

'They're supposed to be very clever, aren't they?' I ask, biting my lip. Your face is pale.

'I think so,' you say. 'But we can't think about it now.' We leave the octopus on the table in front of us and rub garlic cloves onto thin slices of toasted bread. There is a silence and you take your phone out of your pocket and frown at it, then put it face-down on the table. You seem tired and distracted, fiddling with a stray cigarette filter, avoiding my eyes.

'Is everything okay?' I ask you.

'Yeah. Why?'

'You seem a bit distant.'

'I'm fine.'

'Are you sure?'

'Yes,' you snap. 'Stop asking me that. It makes me feel paranoid.' Your phone vibrates and you pick it up and start typing. I poke the octopus with my fork.

'My mam told me that when she first saw me, she thought she had given birth to an octopus.'

You put your phone down. 'What? Why?'

'My umbilical cord was wrapped around my neck and I was all blue and tangled, with long arms and legs.'

'What an image.'

'I was alright, though.' I cut off a piece of tentacle and spear it with my fork. 'I think it's quite common.' I put the octopus in my mouth. It is chewy and rubbery and I'm not sure if I like it but I want to prove something to you and to myself; that I can be present and powerful, that I can take the world in my mouth and hold it on my tongue.

'How is it?'

'It's good.' I gesture towards your empty plate. 'Aren't

you going to try some?' You cut off a small piece and chew with a grimace. 'I thought you liked octopus.'

'I like it fried.' You take a sip of your drink. 'This is a bit much.' I shrug and pull the plate towards me. Your eyes widen as I lift another tentacle to my lips, feeling power rush through me at the sight of your dazed face.

'So, what will we do when I go back to London?' I ask, feeling emboldened and looking straight at you. Your eyes widen for a moment and you rub them with the heels of your hands.

'I don't know.'

'What do you want to do?'

You run your hand through your hair. 'What do *you* want to do?' I bring my glass to my lips, holding silver bubbles on my tongue. I want to be with you and to be wanted by you, but I am afraid to say it because I have only just begun to name the things I want, to speak my desires instead of swallowing them down. I am afraid of having but I am also afraid of not-having, of asking for something and then being denied it, of never having enough.

'I don't know,' I tell you.

You look at the tablecloth. 'I don't know, either.'

'Right.' My eyes feel hot. A waiter brings over a plate of bravas and you take one with your fingers.

'Do we have to talk about it now?' you say. 'Can we not just have a nice time?' I don't know how to have a nice time when it feels as though everything is crumbling.

'Okay. Fine.'

We walk back to your apartment in silence. We climb the stairs and unlock the door and then you pull me inside and push me up against the wall. You look me straight in the eyes.

'This is stupid.' You bring your face close to mine.

'Is it?' I ask and you kiss me in reply. I reach for you breathlessly as you pull my dress over my head and I unfasten your belt. My body is strung with want and anger, wrapped around each other like vines. Your hair smells of cooking oil and your mouth tastes of sour wine. You bite my lip hard and I press myself into you, drenched in a craving I cannot contain.

'I want you,' you say into my mouth and I grasp you tighter. I think of the huge expanse of sky between here and London. You push yourself inside me and I remember your tall, easy beauty beneath the traffic lights, a language I do not yet understand curling around your tongue. Your face is slick with sweat and suddenly I want to hurt you, not out of cruelty but to prove I have agency, to assert my presence. I press my nails into your back and think about the way you dug your fingers into my life and tore everything wide open. You gasp in pleasure and I grip harder. I want you to feel the sting of it, to know how it is when you can never satisfy your hunger, when the weight of your inadequacy eats into your bones.

'Fuck,' you breathe as my fingernails break your skin, drawing blood. I picture my tiny blue body bursting into the world, strangled and choking for air.

47

Shaun was my first boyfriend. We learned the shapes of our outlines together, drinking Red Diesel in dirty pubs, spending school nights pressed between sweaty strangers at heaving gigs. We spent whole weekends buried beneath his musty sheets, exploring each other with abandon.

When Shaun turned eighteen, we went to stay with his Uncle Joey in Liverpool. Joey was a builder in his late twenties. He wore polo shirts over tracksuit bottoms, whisking us off in a taxi to his favourite pub and showing us off to the landlady, pulling pints in her shimmery blouse.

'This is me nephew.' Joey ruffled Shaun's hair, an unlit cigarette dangling from his lips. 'And this is his bird,' he winked at me. 'Tell her what yer want,' he told me, gesturing towards the bar.

'A glass of white wine, please.'

The landlady looked at me. 'You got ID?'

Joey waved her away. 'Come on, Liz. She's with me.'

We felt famous when we went out with Joey. He dragged us from bar to bar, flashing his big smile at all the regulars, ordering rounds of tequila shots. He pulled wads of notes from his pockets, waving our protests away.

'I'm your Uncle Joey, alright?' he said. 'Tonight's on me.' We stopped off at the bookies to put money on the dogs. I chose the ones with the best names like *Curling Chaos* and *Butterfly John*. I won fifty quid and Joey lifted me up on his shoulders, parading me along the street as I shrieked and tried to pull my little dress down to cover my knickers.

He took us to a drag bar to sing karaoke. The queens on the door smiled at us in their glittery stilettos. They knew Joey and waved us in for free as he slipped them a couple of cigarettes from a fresh packet. The walls were covered in pink tinsel and we slipped into a booth at the back, beneath a heart-shaped disco ball. The lights made my head swim as Shaun grew drunker and louder, his hand on my thigh beneath the table.

Joey bounded onto the stage to sing a Verve song and Shaun's hand inched up my skirt. He kissed my neck, pressing his body into mine. Acid burned the back of my throat and I felt jittery as Joey crooned into the microphone.

'Don't,' I said, inching away from Shaun.

'What's the matter?' His words ran into each other. 'Don't be frigid.' The disco lights streaked my body in red, like a warning. Laughter rippled across tables and Joey's rasping voice filled the small room. Shaun shoved his hand between my legs and I let him. His breath was heavy with vodka and I closed my eyes.

'Do you like that?' Shaun breathed into my ear as his fingernails dug into me. I nodded, pretending that I did. I didn't want to be frigid or boring, the kind of girl who always said no. I wanted to say yes to the world like Uncle Joey, to be a man about town, loose and up for anything, to let pleasure and sensation linger beneath my skin.

'This one's for the lovebirds in the corner,' crooned Joey, beaming at us from the stage and I smiled back at him, raising my glass in a silent toast.

48

Restlessness coils inside both of us, feverish and wild. It is the weekend before I am due to leave and there is still a sharpness between us, catching on my hair and skin. You move faster than usual, making too many plans and rushing out of the door on your way to work, avoiding silence and stillness, leaving no space for us to think. I am vibrating with frustration; angry that a part of you is unreachable, after you asked me to come and stay.

'I know what we should do.' You pour red vermouth into a glass, making the ice crackle like static.

'What?'

'We should go dancing.' A shard of danger glints in your eye and I am drawn to it.

'Do you think so?'

'Yeah. We'll feel better.' I pull on a glittery dress, painting my eyes in black and pulling a dark lipstick across my mouth.

'A beauty,' you say, as I fasten a choker around my neck. Your words are magnetic but I pull away from them, letting the friction between us linger. You wear black jeans and a New York Dolls T-shirt, silver hoops fastened in both of your ears. I lean forward to kiss you and bite your lip, hard.

'Oh.' You press your hand to your mouth and check for blood. 'That hurt.'

'Sorry,' I say, but I'm not.

We take the metro to Gràcia, sharing a plastic bottle filled with gin and tonic on the train. I pull strands of lemon from between my teeth as we ring a bell outside of a shuttered warehouse, constellations spilling across the metal in silver paint.

'*Buenas.*' A tall man with heavy sideburns glances up and down the empty street, then ushers us inside. The room is small and dark, jittering projections of shapes and colours rippling across the back wall. It is early and you tell me that people don't usually arrive until two or three in the morning, when the neighbouring bars begin to close.

A group of thin men in long coats smoke sullenly in the corner. A woman in red vinyl trousers dances alone with her eyes closed. The music is heavy and brooding, scratching and rattling, drowning out my thoughts. You order a couple of rums at the bar and we drink them straight, with a twist of lime.

'Do you feel better yet?' I ask you.

'No,' you say into my ear and I can feel your hot breath on my neck.

I pull you into the middle of the room and begin to move my hips. You spin in circles, your face sharp and serious, eyes like onyx beneath the lights. I push white noise out of my stomach and into my limbs. We move faster and the air changes shape around us, viscous and malleable, as though we could take it in our hands and mould it into something new. You move towards me and we linger for a moment before I pull away. The music is grinding, filling my skull, like metal between my teeth. You are a fizzing, silver danger in the heat and smoke, red light striking your face. I realise I do not want to leave you, then you grab my shoulders and say something I cannot hear.

'What?' I shout above the music.

'I'm sorry!'

'What for?'

You spin across the floor without replying. I close my eyes and let the night swallow me. I stamp my feet and feel the impact in my elbows. We are bone-popping punk dancing, throwing ourselves at the sound.

We buy cans of cold beer at the bar and go outside for a cigarette. There is a church at the end of the street and we climb the stone steps, resting our backs against the old wooden door. I feel drunk and the air flickers around me. You smell of sweat and old leather and it makes me dizzy.

You crack open your can and drink thirstily. You swallow and I watch your throat contract.

'This was a good decision.' You wipe your forehead with the back of your hand. The moon has an orange glow, like an electric streetlight. I suddenly feel tired, thinking of the vast distance that is about to open up between us, wondering what it would mean if I stayed.

'Why did you say sorry?' I ask. 'When we were dancing?' You bite the skin around your fingers. They look ragged and sore. I take your hand and put them in my mouth, sucking away the blood. Something falls in your face and you pull away. 'What's wrong?' You pull out a pouch of tobacco and begin to roll a cigarette.

'I don't know.' Your lips are tight and your movements are jerky.

'You don't know?'

'No.' We sit in silence and my anger clots like tar. You have pulled me out of my life and now that I am here, I feel as though I am not good enough for you, as though you are sealing up and pulling away, waiting for me to go. You light your cigarette and lean back against the door with your eyes closed. You look so dark and handsome with your black curls and bitten lips, a shadow of stubble across your jaw and I hate you for it. You blow smoke into the night and open your eyes.

'I get scared sometimes,' you say quietly. 'That this won't last.' My stomach contracts. I am so afraid that all of this is too good, that you will peel off my skin and find my twisted heart and then everything will be broken.

'What do you mean?'

'It goes back to my dad dying, I suppose. I have this feeling that everything is always slipping away. I feel like I've been losing love my whole life.' I am quiet, watching smoke curl from your lips. 'Sometimes it's like I can feel time falling through my fingers. And even though we're here together and it all feels so fucking good, I'm just waiting for it to fall apart.' I move closer to you, until our arms are touching.

'But I'm right here.'

'What about when you go back? It makes me feel so lonely. Like, we have this connection but you'll go back to your life or whatever.' You stub out your cigarette. 'We're all alone, really. At the end of the day.'

'That's depressing.'

'Yeah.' The hairs on my arms prickle with sadness but I am relieved that this fear is what you have been holding and you're not just tired of me. Perhaps we should stop resisting the strange pull between us and simply submit to it, to draw our lives tightly together, even if it is not practical, so that it doesn't all slip away.

'But you do have control over things,' I say. 'Not over your dad dying. But over other stuff. Like this.'

'Do we really, though? Do we really have control over what happens to us? Or are we just pulled around by things?' I want, so badly, to believe we have control over what is happening, but my whole life has been a battle with control, an attempt to assert agency in a world that does not want me to have it. 'It's like there's never enough time.' You look young in the pale streetlight. 'Don't you ever feel like that?'

I am quiet. I don't know what to say. You are the first person I have ever wanted to hold on to. I usually just leave and give everything away.

'We can find a way to make it work,' I say, softly. 'If you want to.'

You take my hand and kiss the inside of my wrist. 'I'm tired. Shall we go home?'

I look at the dark street, the orange moon, the trees making shadows on the walls. I want to be in your apartment beneath your cool sheets, our bodies pressed together in the dark. 'Okay.'

You link your fingers through mine. 'Shall we run?'

'What?'

'Come on.'

You pull me down the steps and through the stifling streets, dodging groups of people smoking outside bars, neon lights blurring into streaks. We run past revving scooters and the green glow of late-night pharmacies, closed kiosks on street corners, restaurants swollen with light. We run until our lungs burn and our legs ache, your boots pounding the pavement, my dress iridescent in car headlights. We are running away from a dark thing, slipping down alleyways as it snaps at our heels, or perhaps we are running towards something new, a vast and shimmering future, an uncertain expanse of sky. I wonder if you are just another way for me to outrun myself, but this feels different, like I want to be present, rooted in time and place. We reach your apartment and you fumble for your keys, panting. I am tired and my muscles are sore. I wonder if I could let myself stay in one place, if I might learn to be here.

49

Someone Dylan knew worked at a fashion magazine and they offered me an internship. I didn't particularly want to work in fashion but I wanted to do something, to move through the city in a way that felt purposeful, instead of just scrabbling around. It was unpaid and I cycled through rush-hour traffic to the Soho office each morning, the bottom of my long, charity shop coat furred with silt and rain.

I sat nervously behind my desk on my first day as a woman my own age in a Chanel skirt-suit and a pair of Gucci loafers smiled down at me.

'Did you bring your laptop, babe?'

'Oh.' I crossed and uncrossed my legs. 'I don't have one.' The woman frowned. 'My boyfriend does, though. Maybe I can borrow his.'

She beamed. 'That would be perfect. Don't worry about today. We're going to a press day. You can take some photos of the products and upload them to Instagram. I'll give you our login now.'

'Ah.' I tensed my toes inside of my boots. 'I don't have Instagram.'

'Well, you can download it.'

'I mean, I don't have a smartphone.' I pulled out my cheap plastic phone and the woman laughed.

'Are you joking?'

'No.' I smiled, uncertainly. 'It's ancient, I know. But it has a fake call function.'

'A what?'

'You can press a button when you're in an awkward conversation and it'll ring, so you can make an excuse and leave.'

The woman stared at me. 'Right. Weird.'

For several months, I worked in the office all day, sourcing images of shoes and handbags that cost more money than I had ever had in my bank account, proofreading website content and picking up dry-cleaning. Afterwards, I cycled straight to the pub for my evening shift, pulling pints and scrubbing the toilets at the end of the night, riding home beneath the moon around two in the morning. Once, I got knocked off my bike by a passing van as I gazed blearily at the traffic lights, not noticing that they had slipped from red to green. I spent my nights off in the bath, soaking the days away, trying to sink into the silence but hearing drunk voices calling out to me.

I made friends with some freelancers who worked for the magazine. They dyed their hair in pastel colours and wore thin gold hoops in their ears, black ink etched beneath the skin of their wrists. They dropped into the office clutching takeaway coffee cups and stacks of magazines, eyeballing my ratty coat and the shadows purpling beneath my eyes.

'Coming for a drink?' they asked, one sunlit afternoon and I left my desk and went to the pub with them, ordering an Aperol spritz and laughing in the gold light dripping through the window, pretending I was one of them and everything was that easy.

I met up with them in pink-walled cafés bulging with cheese plants, their MacBooks open beside cooling flat whites in lipstick-rimmed mugs, packets of American Spirit and stray filters strewn across the table.

'Freelancing is a nightmare.' They shook their heads as they ordered doorstep slices of coffee and walnut cake. 'No one ever pays you on time.' I tipped a handful of almonds onto my saucer and nibbled them slowly. One of the girls opened her lilac backpack and showed me a tangle of rubies and sapphires glinting inside.

'They're for a shoot on Saturday,' she laughed, zipping

up her bag tightly. 'The designer gave them to me this morning. I've been freaking out all day.' The tiny pendant around her neck glimmered in the warm light.

'Shall we get some food?' asked one of the others, snapping her laptop shut. 'I'm starving. There's a good burger place around here.' Everyone nodded in agreement and I made an excuse to leave.

My new friends' lives seemed gilded, filled with films and plays and trips to faraway places, wine-soaked dinners and bitter cocktails, their tasteful apartments crammed with kitsch cushions and salvaged furniture, art posters fixed in pastel frames.

'Did you read that *New Yorker* article?' they asked me. 'Are you going to the film festival? Have you tried that new sushi place? Shall we have dinner at mine?'

They seemed like adult women, paying the bill on their credit cards, brewing fresh coffee and nibbling pastries in the morning, burning scented candles, buying tasteful clothes without thinking twice, hanging them on wooden hangers, safe behind wardrobe doors. I envied their lack of self-consciousness, the way they wanted so openly, without trying to hide it. Their needs were thoughtless because they had the means to meet them, so they didn't have to push them down.

I wanted to be like them, to wear the city loose around my shoulders and to take all of the good things in my hands, yet there was a hard thing inside me that resented them, too. Their lives had a shiny, plastic veneer, removed from the blood and gristle of things. I told myself the scrabbling way in which I lived was more real and yet I didn't feel solid at all. I got snagged on everything, my knees black with bruises, twigs and leaves caught in my hair.

I couldn't fulfil my basic needs, like having enough

119

money to pay my rent, for my tube journeys and my groceries or to replace whatever was broken. The things I wanted were bigger than the place I came from and more than I felt I deserved. I spent the money I saved by skipping meals on glasses of wine in dark, sticky bars with electric people or bus journeys through the city at night, travelling nowhere in particular, sitting on the top deck and watching the buildings crackle and fizz, as though the whole dazzling blaze of it was mine. At first, the trade-off was worth it but it began to seem unfair as I watched my new friends enjoy their wants, rolling their hunger around their mouths and then satiating it, whereas I just wanted, all of the time.

The barbed space at the edges became my comfort zone and it validated the beliefs I held about myself; that I did not deserve as much as other people and I should take as little as I could. I didn't know how to make it to the other side, to always have enough of everything, to be safe, warm and full.

50

The evening before I go back to London, we sit on the beach as the night sets in, pushing our bare feet into the cold sand. The last light washes everything in violet, like spilled ink. I rub a smooth pebble between my fingers anxiously. You light a cigarette and your face flares in the dark.

'I've been thinking about our chat the other night,' I start, hesitantly. I look at you but I can't read your expression.

'Me too.' A silver plume escapes your lips.

'Do you want to try?' I ask. 'To make things work?'

You trace your fingers in the sand. 'I'd like to. Would you?'

'I think so.'

'Will you come back here?'

'Do you mean for good?'

You squint up at the sky, avoiding my gaze. 'Maybe.' I want to be with you but I am afraid, too. Everything is rushing so fast that I can't keep up with it. You look at me and smile. 'What have you got to go back to in London, anyway?'

'I've got stuff to go back to,' I snap. I know that my work seems less important than yours and it makes me feel small and stupid. You reach for me but I clench my jaw and pull away. My life is small and shabby in London but it belongs to me.

'I know,' you frown. 'I didn't mean it like that.'

'What did you mean, then?'

'Nothing,' you sigh.

I am quiet, looking at the water as it rolls towards us like black fog. You get to your feet, brushing sand from your legs.

'Shall we get a beer or something? It's your last night. Let's not be like this.'

I stand up and we walk across the sand to a nearby bar but the night has lost its sheen for me, a sharp sting I cannot quite articulate caught in the salt air.

My flight is the next evening and the sky is the colour of watermelon flesh. The plane turns around over the black water, passing above ships in the harbour licked with gold. I press my face to the window and imagine you smoking on your little balcony, heat caught in the tiles.

I find the smooth pebble from the beach in my pocket

and run my fingers over it, thinking of our conversation in the dark. Now that I am further away from you and the magnetic pull you exert on my body feels weaker, our plan seems impossibly vague. We didn't talk about when I might come back, or whether you might visit me in London. We didn't discuss the parameters of our relationship; whether things are still open and it feels loose and undefined. You are asking me to take a big leap for you and anger grinds in me, as though my life is less important and as if my choices carry less weight than your own.

The plane judders in the wind and my hands grow clammy. I open a book to try and distract myself. I inhale deeply and the man next to me notices my clenched fists and smiles.

'Don't you like flying?' he asks.

'Not really.' I close my book. 'I never used to mind. I don't know what changed.'

The man adjusts his glasses. 'I'm the same. Didn't used to think twice, until I had children. And now I hate it. I've got too many people to come home to.' He raises a plastic cup of red wine. 'This helps, though. I recommend it.'

I smile at him and try to settle into my book but I can't focus on the words because I'm wondering where home is and who I'm going back to, whether I have become afraid of flying because I have too much to lose. I think that I always had a lot to lose but I just couldn't see it before. My younger self threw her body into dangerous places, chasing the night and the whirling stars, never caring about whether she came back alive. Sometimes I wonder if she could have done it all differently, made other decisions and grown into someone better. I wish I had held on to her dreams like balloons, tied their strings around her wrists so that I could look up now and remember them.

I am lost in thought when London appears in the darkness, lit up like a broken necklace, beads of light scattered across the ground. Your body feels so far away from mine, nestled in the mountains of a different world, and I wonder whether all of this is good for me, if it would be better to focus on my own life, to build something here instead of chasing you across the sky.

'We made it,' my neighbour says as we hit the tarmac.

'We did.' I check to see if the clock on my phone has updated, giving me an extra hour of time.

51

When I was a child, I always tucked my vest tightly into my knickers. I zipped my coat right up to my neck and begged my mother to lace my trainers as tight as they would go.

'I can't get them any tighter, love.' She kneeled at my feet, exasperated, and then bundled me into the car where I sulked in the back seat, pulling my seat belt until it cut into my stomach.

'You'll hurt yourself.' My mother reached over to adjust my belt and I pushed her away, wanting to be tucked in, safe and secure.

In my early twenties, I chased sensation. I went to parties with people I barely knew, dancing all night strung up in sequins and reaching for disco balls with outstretched fingers, grasping at splinters of light until I woke up in my bed with cavities in my memory and blood dried across my knees.

One morning, I was walking home from a party when

my phone alarm went off to get up for work. I fumbled in my bag to turn it off and leaned against a wall for a moment, closing my eyes and willing the world to stop spinning. When I opened them again, I noticed a launderette across the road, filled with warm light. It looked inviting so I went inside.

There was a man sitting on a bench, watching his clothes spin in the machine. He took in my glazed expression the glitter crusted on my cheeks.

'You alright?' he asked me.

'I'm alright.' I blinked at him. We sat quietly, listening to the swoosh of water and the thump of the metal drum. The smell of soap made me think of my mother with her boxes of washing powder and starched cotton; white and pure. I looked at the man's laundry bag and his bright trainers, the newspaper folded by his side.

'Why are you here?' I asked him.

'You what?'

'Why are you doing your washing at half six on a Saturday morning?'

The man shifted on the bench and then laughed slowly. 'I could ask the same of you.'

'I'm not doing any washing.'

He raised his eyebrows. 'I noticed.'

I looked at him properly. His clothes were neat and sharp but his eyes were puffy with black shadows carved beneath them.

'I don't sleep,' he admitted. 'The noise of the machines makes me feel calm.' I rubbed my eyes and he stared at me. 'What about you, then?'

'I'm just having a rest. I start work in forty minutes.'

The man laughed another long, slow laugh. 'Are you joking?'

'No.' My head began to pound. I wanted to stay in the launderette, held by the rhythm of the dryers and the promise of redemption, entering dirty and leaving clean.

'Will you be okay?' the man asked me as I stood up to leave and I smiled and waved him away.

I was half an hour late to work and I got through my shift on black coffee and digestive biscuits, thinking about the man in the launderette and laughing to myself about the night's antics. The line between self-control and self-destruction was so thin. I couldn't see that obliteration was just another way to restrain myself, a desperate attempt to be held.

52

I throw myself back into London with a kind of fury. Rosa comes into the café and sits at the bar while I'm at work. I ply her with free coffees and huge chunks of carrot cake, tall gin and tonics, mixing Negronis without measures. We go out after my shift, spritzing deodorant over my work clothes, sharing lipstick in the toilets, drinking tequila in the pool hall down the road. We slurp steaming bowls of pho and blag our way into clubs on weeknights, pressing our bodies up to the front of the DJ booth, our necks damp with other people's sweat. On my afternoons off, I watch films that make me cry in the dark and visit free exhibitions, scribbling in my notebook in the gallery café, watching people drinking wine in colourful clothes. I cycle along the canal on bright, sunny mornings feeling strong and untethered, my dress tied in a knot above my thighs, hair tangled in the wind.

You text me sporadically; pictures of the sun setting purple from your balcony, a pink full moon, palm trees jagged with light. I don't want to think about who you are with or what you are doing and I try to detach myself, to become strong and impenetrable, less vulnerable to hurt.

You write, *'What are you up to?'*

I reply, *'Not much,'* feeling hollow and meaningless, as though our words are bricks obstructing our feelings, crushing all of the things we really want to say. I am trying to be happy here, to remember how my life felt before you burned a hole in it, to understand what it means to feel rooted and learn how to be full on my own.

'Maybe you could come back again next month?' you type and I chew my lip. I want to be close to you but I don't know if it is right for you to keep pulling me out of my life like this.

'I'll think about it,' I send, but you do not reply.

Rosa has a birthday party and we fill her house with tulips and daffodils, stringing coloured lights through the trees in her scrubby garden. We light candles and buy cheap fizzy wine, pressing glitter onto our eyelids in her poky bedroom. We are drunk before anyone arrives, dancing to the Supremes in the kitchen with her girlfriend Emily, as her housemates clear away dinner.

Guests begin to arrive and Rosa dances on the table in her pink platform boots. Men in black hoodies light spliffs in the garden and we drink shots of vodka from candle-holders. A stranger trips over a plant pot and cuts his hand on broken glass. The house throbs with people and Rosa throws her arms around me, a lit cigarette between her fingers and a red lipstick kiss on her cheek.

'I'm so glad you're here.' Her breath is smoke and sweet wine. 'And not in fucking Spain.'

'Me too,' I tell her, breathing her in, but I feel a pang in my stomach at the mention of Spain, thinking of you with your friends in some hot, dark bar, wishing that you were here. Someone has baked Rosa a birthday cake and I eat a big slice of it, licking the cream from my fingers.

'You must be hungry,' says someone's boyfriend, gesturing at my paper plate.

'I am,' I tell him defiantly, chewing with my mouth open and he laughs nervously and turns away.

Rosa's housemate puts on records in his bedroom and we all pile in there, drinking wine from the bottle, dancing on the unmade bed. I am wearing a silver jumpsuit and I feel fast and slippery, wiggling my hips and spinning in circles, trying to bury your name.

'Shall we play spin the bottle?' asks Emily, winking at Rosa, and we gather around her in a circle, all lips and tongues and laughter, the alcohol making us bold. I kiss Max, who works at the gallery with Rosa. He wraps his arms around my waist and pulls me close and I like it, letting his hands rub you away. Rosa's eyes widen as Max and I leave the circle and get up to dance, locking eyes then hands and mouths, the room falling away.

'I've always liked you,' Max whispers in my ear and I tell him I have always liked him too, which isn't true, but I like him now in this moment, masking the pull of you.

We end up pressed together in the bathroom, Max unpeeling my jumpsuit, his shirt in a ball on the floor. His hands seem big and rough compared to yours, his chest broad, his hair thick and coarse. He pushes himself into me clumsily and I press my fingers over his lips.

'They'll hear us,' I murmur, one foot on the toilet seat.

'So what?' says Max and I laugh. I close my eyes and your face flashes behind them, your body swimming through green water, salt caught in your hair. I bury my face into Max, trying to obscure you but an ache blooms in my belly, twisted in the shape of you. Max pulls out of me and steadies himself on the bath.

'Christ,' he says and we dress hurriedly, laughing and whispering, then go to find our friends.

I go downstairs and pour the dregs of a bottle of whiskey into a mug. I slip out of the back door and into the garden, shivering in the grass in my jumpsuit, sticky between my legs. I pinch a cigarette from one of Rosa's friends and sit on the doorstep, listening to techno pulsing upstairs. The garden swims and you are there behind my eyelids, frying mushrooms in your tiny kitchen, smiling at me through the dark. I pull out my phone and check my messages but there are none from you. The symbol next to your name that means you are online lights up. I stare at your picture for a moment, trying to imagine how I would feel if you were here next to me, but it is all too impossible and I turn my phone off.

53

Things became strained between Dylan and me. He grew impatient with my clothes strewn around his tidy flat, my beer-stained boots cluttering his floor. I spilled everywhere, unkempt and uncontainable, unable to squeeze myself into his compact, organised space. I understood that I could only learn how to develop taste if I eradicated my own. I put so much energy into suppressing my appetite that it began to disappear altogether. At night I turned away from him in bed, afraid that his yearning hands might pull me back into my body and into the smallness he made me feel.

'Is everything okay?' he asked as I rolled away from him in bed, pressing my knees against the wall.

'Just tired.' I ignored his sighs in the darkness and I slipped into thick, unsettling dreams.

One weekend, we went to a festival. People dressed in feathered capes and gold hotpants, disco lights sparking the gems glued to their faces, scattering prisms into the grass. When it got dark, I saw the glimmer of glow-worms in the bushes.

'You're imagining things,' Dylan laughed when I tried to point them out, but I wasn't.

We got drunk outside our tent, passing a bottle of bubbly wine between us and holding the fizz in our mouths.

'I know you're disgusted by me,' Dylan said unexpectedly, his words tumbling into each other.

'What?' I twisted the bottle into my empty boot to keep it upright. 'What do you mean?'

'You don't want to touch me. It makes me feel horrible.'

I didn't know what to say. I felt hurt for Dylan, that I had made him feel unwanted. I knew he worked hard to maintain a façade, that he was insecure beneath his smart clothes and nice glasses but it wasn't really about him; I was disgusted by myself. My body didn't fit into the right spaces; the gap between his thumb and forefinger or between his clean, white walls.

'I'm sorry,' I said, quietly.

'What is this about?'

'I don't know.' I pulled the sleeves of my jumper down

over my hands. Dylan took a swig from the bottle of wine. He tried to pull me close and I wriggled away.

'Shall we go and dance?' I asked him.

He looked at me hotly, stung with rejection. 'Yeah.' He polished off the wine. 'Okay.'

We danced for hours in a red circus tent. I threw back my head and flailed my arms wildly, trying to pretend that everything was fine. Dylan's hands caught my waist and he leaned in to kiss me but I wriggled away from him, feigning drunkenness. He walked away to get another beer, emanating bitterness, making me feel on edge.

We stumbled back to our tent in the early hours, streaked with mud and beer. Dylan reached for me and I kept very still, my body unresponsive. He kissed my neck and my bare shoulder and I rolled over and opened myself up for him, even though I didn't want to. I felt as though I owed him something because I had made him feel unwanted, even though the root of it was in me. I felt drunk and the tent swayed around us. Bass wobbled across the fields and people laughed in the distance. I made my body limp and waited for it to be over. Tears pricked my eyelids and stung my cheeks.

'Are you okay?' he asked me afterwards. I closed my eyes and said nothing, my head spinning in the dark. 'I don't know what you do to me,' he whispered, as he settled into his sleeping bag. I felt responsible for the shape of my body and the way it made him feel, as though it was my fault.

We woke with the sunrise, hot and sticky. Dylan climbed out of the tent and pissed in the cool air, silhouetted in the grapefruit dawn. The screech of laughing gas canisters tore through the morning. I pulled the sleeping bag around my body, feeling it snug and secure around my limbs. The delicate skin between my legs was tender and swollen.

'I'm going for a shower,' Dylan called.

'What, now?' I squinted in the bright light.

'It's the best time. There won't be a queue.' He poked his head inside of the tent. 'Are you coming?' I wanted to wash his smell from my clammy skin, sour with sweat and muck but I didn't want to undress in front of him, my body tired and sore. I didn't want him to see what he had done to me, although I wasn't exactly sure if he had done anything at all.

'No, thanks.'

Dylan shrugged and walked off into the distance. I lay in the tent and watched him go through the flap, silhouetted against the sky, growing smaller and smaller until he seemed insignificant, eclipsed by the endless blue.

54

I am late for my class the day after Rosa's party. I am too bleary to cycle so I jump on the tube, rushing through the barrier and up into Balham, half running past quaint cafés and pastel-coloured florists, stopping to catch my breath on a street corner. My eyes sting and my skin feels hot to the touch. Sick swells in the back of my throat and I swallow it, smoothing down my dress and hoisting up my tights where they have wrinkled around my ankles.

My student's mother answers the door distractedly.

'Come in.' She ushers me into her warm kitchen. 'I hope you don't mind me hanging around. We have some friends coming over later and I'm just getting everything ready.'

'That's fine.' I tense inwardly. My student is ten and he can sense that I am hungover. He looks at me sulkily, rolling his eyes whenever I ask him a question, replying in monosyllabic tones.

'Come on, Isaac,' his mother says, over her shoulder. 'Make an effort for your teacher. You can say more than that.' Isaac sticks out his tongue as his mother turns away and I pretend not to notice. I set him a writing exercise so that he doesn't have to speak to me and my brain feels like cardboard as I watch him press the nib of his pen into the page.

I look around the stylish kitchen at the teal-green tiles and wooden worktops, the shiny appliances, a bouquet of lilies in a tall glass vase. I am self-conscious of my body tucked beneath the expensive dining table, feeling cheap and dirty, my unwashed hair full of smoke, my scruffy backpack dirtying the wooden floor. The fridge is covered in children's drawings and there are wicker baskets filled with toys. There is a calendar scribbled with work meetings and school trips, dates written down and then crossed out. I can see a shoe rack crammed with wellies and trainers in a range of sizes, a wooden sign spelling 'HOME' hanging on the back of the door. I wonder if this is what a home looks like; steamy windows and honey-glazed carrots roasting in the oven, everything polished and clean.

I am envious of Isaac in his neat uniform from his expensive school, his family around him, London on his doorstep, the fridge filled with food. I try to imagine living here, making coffee with the espresso machine, drinking wine from large glasses, but it makes me feel claustrophobic, as though my life is fixed and decided, the parameters of it stifling, rigid and walled.

And yet I feel heavy thinking of my own ragged world, the mould on the walls of my sublet bedroom, the smell of cat piss in the hall. I wonder what exactly it is that I'm chasing, throwing myself into the whirl of the night. The people I grew up with are buying houses and getting married, carrying seeds in their bellies, watching things grow and yet there is something in me that cannot settle, that can see the goodness in these things but cannot imagine that goodness as my own. I picture you smoking in a doorway, your coat collar turned up against the cold, and my stomach twists in longing. I wonder if I can imagine a future with you, when a future with another person is something I have never dared to visualise before.

'I'm finished,' says Isaac and I pull his exercise book towards me. I asked him to describe his favourite hobby and he has written about eating pizza.

'I love pizza because it is cheesy and tomatoey,' he reads. 'It is chewy and stringy and soft.'

'Can you write a simile?' I ask him. 'If you had to compare pizza to something, what would you compare it to?'

He thinks for a while, chewing the end of his pen. 'Pizza is like a soft, warm bed,' he writes, and I smile.

'Do you like pizza?' he asks me.

'I love pizza,' I lie. Isaac smiles happily, drawing an orange circle on the paper, and I wonder how I could possibly build a home when I am incapable of nourishing myself properly.

Isaac looks up at me. 'Why are you sad, miss?'

'I'm not sad.' I brighten my face. 'I'm just hungry. All this talk of pizza.'

'Can my teacher stay for dinner, Mum?' asks Isaac.

His mother laughs. 'Your teacher has her own home to go to, darling.' She winks at me and I force a smile.

55

Dylan and I broke up and I found a mezzanine room in a warehouse unit built into an old toffee factory by the canal. It was illegal and we weren't allowed to hang our washing outside in case the council noticed it and began an investigation. The rent cost more than half of my pub wages. The landlord erected cheap plywood walls and wooden staircases, cramming as many people into each space as possible. He kept the original factory windows, rotting at the edges, so the wind blew through the cracks and forced them open in the night. There was no heating and he didn't wire the ceilings, so the spaces were dark, lit by table lamps and fairy lights. There were communal showers on every floor, silverfish flickering beneath fluorescent bars of light. Old machinery rusted in the corridors, skeletal and sharp.

At first, the factory seemed romantic, filled with incense and music, closer to the kind of life I was reaching for, precarious yet haloed in glamour. Whoever lived on the mezzanine before me had painted the walls pink and pasted glow-in-the-dark constellations across the ceiling. There was a piano and one of my flatmates played classical music in the mornings, his billowing shirtsleeves falling over his thin wrists, coffee bubbling in a silver pot on the stove. We found all our furniture on the street and nailed our pans to a wooden beam above the sink. Someone had drawn a mermaid on the toilet wall, dripping scales and sea foam. Laundry flopped from the beams and dried baby's breath hung from the ceiling on pieces of string. After Dylan's neat flat it felt wild and expansive. Sometimes bands played an impromptu set in someone's kitchen and we climbed through the fire escape and up onto the roof afterwards, watching the dawn stain the clouds yellow, skyscrapers shimmering in the first light.

The sheen began to wear off when my broken bed slats collapsed repeatedly in the middle of the night. The lock on the front door was faulty and I often wondered whether my scanty possessions would still be there when I got home from work. I woke up in the morning with frost clinging to my duvet in a silver sheen. We bought electric radiators to heat our rooms, which made our windows glow amber and the electricity bills rocket. The landlord pounded on the door, tanned from a month in Bali, where he was building a yoga retreat.

'You've got to stop with these heaters,' he said. 'I'm going to have to raise your rent to afford the bills.'

'The shower isn't working again,' I told him.

'I'll have someone over to fix it today, princess,' he replied, but nobody ever came.

My flatmate had a puppy and it barked all night. The fuzz of weed and wet dog wound its way into my hair and the fibres of my clothes. I became conscious of it seeping out of me as I sat in cafés or on the bus with other people, as though they could smell my strangeness, the grasping, dirty facts of my life. I walked around the city at night, looking at the golden rectangles of other people's lives, drinking in their fat bookshelves and standing lamps, their shiny kitchens with wine glasses laid out on the tables. The windows were like small television screens, flickering and luminescent. I imagined stepping into them, taking off my shoes and padding across the plush carpet, locking the door from the inside, claiming the space as mine. Sometimes I fantasised about checking into a hotel for a night, stretching out into the silent darkness, feeling the clean, starched sheets, staying in the bath until my skin turned raw, sweating all of my bad parts out.

56

'Are you okay?' you text me late at night, while I am lying in bed.

'I'm okay,' I reply, squinting in the glare of my phone. 'Why?'

'You feel far away.'

'I am far away.'

'Emotionally, I mean.'

I scrunch my eyes tightly shut and then open them again. 'You feel far away too.'

'I miss you.'

'I miss you too.'

'I wish you were here.'

'Do you?'

'Yes. I miss your body next to me.'

'I miss your body too,' I type and then delete it. It feels too exposing to say I miss your body, too needy and raw, but I do miss the bitter smell of your sweat and the curls on the back of your neck. I miss our bodies when they are together, the ache and shine of them, your hands moving across my stomach, the dark thrum of your blood.

'Please come back,' you write. 'And stay this time?' I turn my phone screen off and press my face into the pillow. I am trying to seal myself up again, to be safe and whole on my own. I am afraid of needing you after years of trying to need nothing at all, but your name is filling my lungs and throat, the sharp lines of your consonants slicing my gums. I sit up and look through the open curtains at the dark street outside, the damp, grey rooftops and the flickering streetlight. I remember the sun and salt water, the way the light split the sky wide open, your hand on my bare shoulder, tinned peaches in sweet syrup. My phone flashes and I pick it up.

'Will you come? Soon?'

I send Rosa a screenshot of our conversation. 'What shall I do?' I ask her.

'Omg. Just go.'

'Really?'

'You never let yourself have the things you want.'

'What do I want?'

'For fuck's sake.'

'What?'

'Go and find out.'

'Ok.'

'Ok?'

'I'll go.'

Part Three

57

I book a one-way flight to Barcelona and find someone to fill my room. I am tired of moving and I am dreaming of being rooted in one place, somewhere I can unpack and spread out properly. I spend my first few days back in Spain feeling tentative, layers of myself stripped away but there is a spark in you as you share a can of beer between two glasses, slipping your arm through mine as we walk along the beach at night. You press your body close in bed and I bury my face in you, splintered by the sun and your tobacco-tipped fingers, trying to hold on to myself as your tongue splits me open like fruit.

'Are you okay?' you ask, sticking bread under the grill as I drink coffee at the kitchen table, rubbing sleep from my eyes.

'Yeah.' I wrap my fingers around my mug. 'Just acclimatising.' Your toast begins to smoke and you crack open a window.

'Shall we go away somewhere this weekend?' you ask.

'That would be nice.' I take a sip of coffee. 'Maybe we could go to the mountains?'

'Good idea.' You throw a blackened slice of toast into the bin and kiss me lightly on the shoulder. 'It'll be good to get out of the city.'

*

We borrow Miguel's car and drive towards the Pre-Pyrenees. There are cypress trees scribbled across the blue and we wind down the windows, singing along to a scratched Paul Simon CD, eating cinnamon rolls from a brown paper bag. I lick grains of sugar from my fingers, kicking off my sandals and pressing my bare feet against the dashboard. We pass boarded-up towns peppered with parched buildings, shutters pulled tightly closed. I give directions from a road map we bought from a tabac. I frown at the tangle of coloured lines.

'You need to take a right here.'

'Where?' You glance in your wing mirror.

'Here. Oh wait, no. Back there.'

'Really?' you sigh.

'Sorry.'

You pull into an empty car park outside a closed restaurant. You take the map and study it while I open the door and drink in the clean air.

'It's not very clear, is it?' you frown.

'No.' I roll my eyes. 'It isn't.'

'Don't worry.' You lean over and twist your hand through my hair. 'You're an excellent co-pilot. I wouldn't want to be lost in the mountains with anyone else.' I wrinkle my nose. 'Look.' You point across the road. 'Is that a supermarket? Let's go and stock up.'

We buy glass jars of chickpeas and tins of chopped tomatoes, a loaf of crusty bread, dark chocolate wrapped in silver foil. We find a deep green bunch of spinach and a handful of oranges with emerald leaves, two dark bottles of Catalan wine.

'Do we need stock, or spices, or anything like that?' I ask you.

'I brought some from home. Have a look in my bag.'

I put my hand in your backpack and pull out a selection of zip-lock bags with paprika, sage, cumin and turmeric neatly labelled, clumps of bay leaves and rosemary held together with elastic bands.

'Oh,' I say. 'Very impressive.'

You flush and look at a display of orange mushrooms. 'My mum always does it. So we don't waste anything. There's no point buying things we already have.' I spend the rest of the drive thinking about abundance; your tiny, careful handwriting, the spices on the ends of your fingers in flakes of gold and rust.

The valley is known as the Valley of the Vultures, on account of the birds of prey swooping over imposing red rocks. The old stone walls have shrines built into them, painted figurines cooling in the shadows. The sky is orange and the trees are the colour of saffron. Miguel told us there used to be a small village here that fell into disrepair when the older generations died and their children moved to the cities to make a living. The yellow buildings fell into ruin, lizards and weeds settling into the cracks until a group of goat farmers moved in and began to sell milk and cheese, which brought new people to the area. Now, a handful of people from across Europe live and work nearby. He told us people grow their own vegetables and fit their own plumbing, living in caravans while they repair the old houses. At night they sit around bonfires beneath the stars, goat bells ringing across the fields.

We drive along a dirt track and stop outside a wooden cabin clustered with olive trees.

'Is this the place?' I ask you.

'Think so.' A vine drips purple grapes over the wooden porch. There are life-sized human sculptures carved from wood in the garden, covered in moss and dirt. A string of coloured lights glows softly in the dusk.

'*Hola.*' A woman in denim dungarees walks across the grass towards us, a packet of rolling tobacco in her hand. '*Soy Maria*. Welcome.'

'*Hola.*' I hold out my hand. '*Gracias por acogernos.*'

'*Claro,*' she smiles. 'Any friend of Miguel's is welcome here.'

'It's beautiful.' I look up at the mountains, fading to purple in the creeping dark.

'*Sí.*' Maria sits on the porch and rolls a cigarette. '*Lo es.*'

'Have you lived here a long time?'

She runs her tongue along the paper. 'Fifteen years, *más o menos*. I built this house.' She gestures across the fields. 'And now I am fixing a place over there. I raised my sons here. They are teenagers now. Soon they will want to leave and go to the city. Go to nightclubs or something.' She blows out a cloud of brown smoke and I breathe it in.

'Are these your sculptures?' I ask her, gesturing at the figures in the grass.

'*Sí.*' She stands up. 'This is my army. They keep me safe.' I meet her eyes, to show her that I understand. 'So,' she rattles a bunch of keys. 'You should have everything you need. I put the wood burner on for you because it gets cold at night. Make sure you leave the grille open when you sleep, or there is poisonous gas.'

'Right.' You wink at me.

'I forgot to get firelighters. You have enough for tonight. I will go into town one of these days and buy some more.'

'We'll manage,' I smile. '*Gracias.*'

'Anything you need, I'm just over there.'

You say something in Spanish that I don't catch and Maria laughs.

'What did you say?' I ask you as she walks away. You shake your head and go inside without answering. My muscles tense, remembering how small I feel here sometimes, when I cannot interpret everything or express all of the things I want to say. I think about all of the years I have struggled to articulate myself in my own language, pushing my words into my body instead.

'I hate it when you do that,' I mutter, following you inside.

'Do what?' You stand at the sink, looking out of the window at the darkening mountains, your eyes lit with excitement.

'Never mind.'

We sit on the wooden deck, listening to the trees throb with cicadas, an orange glow settling over the hills. I open a bottle of wine and pour it into a couple of dusty tumblers. I clink my glass with yours and you look at me shyly.

'I'm glad you came back,' you say, a twinge of guilt passing across your face. I look at the scorched grass and the yellow freesia, jasmine spilling over the washing-line. I am glad to be here in this moment, but I am uncertain about what my life means in Spain. I want to be with you but I also want to be my own person, to live in a way that I have chosen.

'Are you glad you came back?' you ask, tentatively. I breathe in the night and the wild rosemary, wondering if I should tell you about Max in London, then I look at your worried face and change my mind.

'I'm happy to be here,' I say, carefully. In the past, I thought nothing of uprooting my life and moving to

145

another city, but something is shifting and I can't quite let go of the versions of myself I was once so desperate to leave behind.

'What are you thinking about?' you ask me.

'Nothing, really.'

'Nothing?'

'Well.' I pause. 'I'm just wondering what I'm going to do here. In Spain.'

You sigh and gesture at the blazing hills and the tangerine sky. 'Do we have to go into it now? Can we not just enjoy being here?' I want you to acknowledge that I am taking a risk for you, making myself vulnerable in a place that belongs mostly to you.

'Okay,' I say, quietly. A tension settles between us and I try to brush it away. My wooden chair is warm to the touch and it is difficult to imagine the clamour of London while I am here, so close to your body and the bitter thrill of your skin. I think of my damp room in Peckham and the wet streets, the rubbery smell of the trains. I remember how you belittled my life in London, the last time I was here and I wonder for a moment whether London is mine simply because I chose it, in the same way that you have chosen Spain.

'Are you hungry?' you ask me. 'Shall we get dinner on?'

'Yeah, alright,' I say, standing up and going inside.

You glance at my closed face. 'We can talk about it another day.'

'Okay,' I say curtly, then head inside.

I rinse the long drive from my skin in the tiny shower as spices simmer in a pan. The temperature drops outside and I pull on a woollen shirt and a thick pair of socks, my blood feeling close to the surface. Candles spit shadows onto the walls as you stand at the hob, turmeric bubbling gold. You are playing Etta James from a small speaker, a stained tea towel slung over your shoulder, the starless night heaped against the window. I pull a wooden chair from beneath the table and you pass me a glass thick with black wine, your skin slick with pepper and sweat, rimmed in the blue glow of the gas cooker. You press your lips to my shoulder and I lean towards you, falling into danger, twisting the rind of you around my tongue. You slip your fingers past the hem of my shirt, press your hands into my hips. The floor is cold and I give into the night, brushing off the questions caught in my skin like teeth, trying so hard to be present. My hips spill around you, hair streaming across the tiles. The air is creamed with coconut milk and I pull you closer, tasting the gold of you, choking on endless yellow.

We leave our bowls slopped with stew on the table, candle wax melting into stalactites. The wood burner is sweet with resin.

'Listen,' you whisper.

'What?'

'The silence. I haven't heard silence in such a long time.' I pull back the heavy curtain and a sheet of silver falls across the table.

'The moon,' I gasp, looking through the steamy glass. You open the door and go out in your bare feet, wincing at the cold.

'Come.' Your voice is hushed. 'Quick.' I follow you outside and look up at the sky. The moon is full and enormous, like an electric light. You cross the porch and lie down in the damp grass.

'What are you doing?' I laugh.

'Moonbathing. Come and join me.' I press my body into the earth, feeling held by solid ground. The light turns our limbs to bone.

'That's the brightest moon I've ever seen,' I say.

'It's an omen,' you reply, in a sinister voice.

'What kind of omen?'

'We'll have to wait and see.'

58

When I was a teenager, my mother noticed me eating less and tried to talk to me about it.

'You need to think about your body,' she said. 'You'll make yourself ill.' She looked at the posters of Kate Moss and Alexa Chung I had pasted around my room and sat me down with a panicked look.

'Why do you want to look like that? You're perfect as you are.' I sealed up and pushed her away, closing my eyes and refusing to discuss it because I didn't have the words to explain. I felt like I was growing stronger in my tough, closed body, rising above my needs and wants. I couldn't really tell if I was bigger or smaller. I couldn't really see the shape of my body at all. I felt like I was doing something right by practising denial, growing into a woman; empty and hard.

We started arguing about the food I left on my plate and the lies I told her about where Tara and I went after school, her concern twisting to anger at my refusal to let her in. We seethed alone in separate rooms of the house and then I crept into the kitchen, heavy with regret.

'I'm sorry for being horrible,' I said and my mother softened at my red eyes.

'You haven't got a horrible bone in your body.' She wrapped her arms around me. I wanted to cry because she was wrong. I knew there was a horrible bone inside me. I could feel it, black and rotting, digging into my belly, giving off a putrid smell. I knew I had to conceal it, to cover it up and bury it deep inside where no one else could see.

My mother opened the fridge. 'What shall we have for tea?'

'I don't know.' I turned away from her. The horrible bone swelled inside me, taking up all of the space, tricking me into forgetting my hunger, filling me up with fear and shame.

59

We wake to clean air pricking our skin through the blankets. I watch you making coffee in your boxer shorts, studying a crumpled map. I look at our clothes tangled on the floor and the day seeping through the window. It all seems too good, despite my uncertainty, and I am afraid for a moment, waiting for something bad to come and catch us out. You carry a steaming cup into the bedroom, your feet bare on the cool tiles and I pull back the curtains, pushing my thoughts away, drenching the room in light.

I slice figs on a slab of sanded wood and we eat yoghurt and honey outside in the garden, coffee poured into small white cups. The grass flickers with insects, and flamenco from the direction of Maria's house rolls across the fields towards us. I watch you run your finger around the rim of your bowl and lick it. I pick at my figs nervously, leaving their sticky hearts untouched.

'What do you think Maria's story is?' you ask, lounging back in your chair. 'How do you think she ended up here?'

'I don't know.' I play with my spoon. 'I think she probably has a nice life.'

You look around. 'Do you not think she feels isolated? She's so far away from everything.'

'Maybe she likes it.'

You wrinkle your nose. 'But she's so cut off from the world.'

'I kind of like it.'

'You would.' You roll your eyes.

'What's that supposed to mean?'

You stand up and begin to clear the table. 'Nothing. Never mind.'

After breakfast, we walk up into the hills, scrambling over dirt, our clothes streaked with yellow dust. We gaze up at the red rocks, listening to the call of goat bells. It is warm along the ridges of the hills and we peel off our layers, letting the sun raze our bare skin. We stop for lunch on an old stone wall outside a ruined church. You hand me a clementine and I split it in half with my thumb.

'I wasn't sure if you wanted me to come back,' I say, as citrus bursts across my tongue.

'What do you mean? We said we were going to try and make it work.'

'Yeah. But we didn't really talk about what that looks like.'

You are quiet for a moment, rolling a small stone between your fingers. 'I didn't know if you would come back.'

'Why not?'

'I don't know. I just had this feeling we'd lost something. After you left.'

My throat tightens. 'Do you still feel like that?'

You pull at the weeds in the cracks of the wall. 'No. Not now you're here.' You look at me, nervously. 'Are you glad you came back?' I look at your dirty trainers and bitten fingernails, your eyes creased with worry.

'I'm glad to be with you,' I say tentatively and my words hang in the air between us.

'You need to give it a chance,' you say, breaking away from me, and anger flares in my gut. I do need to give it a chance but it is not your decision to make. 'Come on,' you say before I can answer, picking up your rucksack. 'Let's go.'

I swallow my words and we press our fingers into yellow flowers, trying to identify plants and birds that we don't know the names of. We walk through a field of copper rocks, like remnants from a distant planet as the sun bleeds through the trees. The ground crunches below us and I look at my feet and find it is littered with bones. I pick up a tiny pelvis.

'What is it?' I ask you.

'Sheep.' You inspect it. 'Or probably goats.'

'What do you think happened to them? Did they get eaten?'

You run your finger along the dirty hip joint. 'I don't know. Maybe. Probably just old.'

'Shall we take some back with us?' I say, raking in the dirt.

You scrunch your face. 'They might have diseases.'

'Really?'

'Why are you so interested?' you laugh. 'Have you never seen bones before?'

'Not really. Not like this. Have you?'

'I think so, yeah.'

'Where?'

'I used to go camping a lot with my dad.' I try to imagine my own father putting up a tent and building a fire, cooking dinner on a camping stove, fastening my waterproofs, teaching me the names of plants and bones, but the impossibility of it is crushing and I push the image away.

We reach a dried-up river bed, the rocks smooth from centuries of water rushing over them. I stand in the middle of the valley and I can almost feel it, the trace of an enormous energy, cutting through the earth. I close my eyes for a moment and think of currents pulling silt towards the sea.

'Do rocks have memories?' I ask you. 'Do you think they know they were underwater once?' You kneel in the riverbed and press your ear to a rock.

'He says he remembers,' you say with wide eyes and I laugh.

Back at the cabin, we pick wild rosemary from the garden and roast it with tomatoes, peppers and thinly sliced potatoes, lighting long dinner candles in metal holders. I roll twists of newspaper and douse them in petrol, to try and coax a fire into life. I look at the ripples of light on the walls, your face stippled gold in the dark. I notice our dusty shoes and our pile of jumpers and the longing for a home rolls through me like a cramp. I forget to be scared of everything breaking and wish that we could stay still in this moment, to preserve our lives in amber and forget about being anywhere else.

'Are you alright?' You frown at me.

'Yeah.' I pull cutlery from the drawer and start setting the table. 'Just hungry.'

'Dinner's almost ready.'

'Great.'

We sit on the porch until the cold makes us bristle and we head inside, pulling the curtains closed against the night. Twigs rake the windows like fingers as we climb into bed, pressing our bodies close together for warmth. I run my fingers over your skin and think of the memories trapped in the rocks, the broken bones littered across the forest floor, the spices labelled in your careful handwriting, everything we do not know the names of. I think of your lost dad and my own missing one, the twisted knot of that difficult love, and I grab your hips, right here where I can touch you, and I feel sick with want. I sense a hot, wet presence in the centre of your chest and I move towards the beating of your heart.

We drive back to Barcelona the following evening. I am quiet in the passenger seat, watching the roads wind below us. Light flashes through the trees as the moon rises pale in the fading sky. The smell of petrol swells through the open window. I remember your words about giving it a chance here and I wonder if taking chances is something I have begun to fear.

'I am giving it a chance, you know,' I mumble. I glance at you but you keep your eyes on the road.

'That's good.' You switch lanes carefully, looking over your shoulder. 'You're always thinking about being somewhere else. You just need to give yourself some time.' I swallow and dig my nails into my palms. You don't seem to recognise that I am taking a risk and moving my whole life for you, whereas you are doing what you already wanted to. I fall silent as we drive towards the burning sky.

'What's the matter?' You frown.

'Nothing.'

'What is it?'

I turn away from you and look out of the window. 'I can't explain.'

'Maybe it's the moon,' you joke, trying to make light of things, and I roll my eyes to mask my unease. I imagine the omen seeping into my skin, confirming my fear that all of this is too easy, too good for someone like me. I am waiting to pay the price for all this joy, all of the good things shimmering around me like plankton, waiting for the danger to catch us up.

60

One summer evening, when I was seventeen, I waited at the bus stop on my way to a party. A floral breeze grazed my bare legs as I stood on tiptoe in my black Converse, a plastic bag clinking gently as it swung from my wrist. There was a glitter in my belly at the promise of a party and the glimmer of trouble. I was always looking to come undone.

A white Honda Civic pulled up next to me and the driver wound down the window. The buzz of a lawnmower cut through the dusk as a youngish man's face smiled up at me. I moved closer, waiting for him to ask directions. I peered into the car and he unzipped his jeans and pulled out his hard, pink penis. I tried to back away in disbelief but my feet were frozen. He looked me in the eyes and moved his hand up and down. I fumbled for the words that would make him stop but my tongue was too thick in my mouth. His hand moved faster. A gasp escaped my lips and the man laughed.

'Fuck you,' I spat but the words broke against my teeth and my voice sounded small and muffled. My bus arrived and the man drove off with a wink.

When I got to the party, I told Shaun what had happened.

'Dirty bastard.' He squeezed my arm. 'Are you okay? Did you get his registration?' I poured myself a vodka shot.

'I'm okay.' I brushed him off. 'No, I didn't get his registration. I'm fine. Don't worry.'

I was fine as I danced in the garden, the grass damp beneath my bare feet. I twisted my hips through a blur of hands and faces, laughing and shrieking until the dawn split the conservatory and my eyes burned with cigarette smoke. I twirled in circles, drinking wine from a chipped mug, laughing in my short skirt and my brand-new body that already felt unruly and out of control; an animal that deserved to be punished.

61

I am walking through El Gòtic alone one afternoon. You are at work and the heat presses down on me like a heavy blanket. I stop in a shady square beneath mimosa trees, their green fronds casting shadows across my skin. I sit down at a table outside a bar and order an Aperol spritz. The waiter brings it over with a bowl of dark olives and I spit the pits into my palm. Drinking alone in the daytime feels luxurious. The city is getting warmer and the sun warps the hours, elongated and strange. I try to think about how to make things work in Barcelona but the alcohol thickens my thoughts and my eyes begin to ache. I don't even know what I would do if I went back to London, where I would work or how I might live, but I have given up so much so I can choose my own life and I can't relinquish that for you.

My phone lights up with a message from Rosa. She sends me pictures of her weekend; a can of beer and a glittering skyline, a group of our friends smoking on a picnic bench, a fresh tattoo of a lemon on her ankle, a mug with dark lipstick smudged across the rim. The images pull at me, tugging the ends of my hair until I am sore. I send Rosa some of my own pictures in return; you silhouetted against the blue mountains, the silver moon, my shadow caught on red rock.

'It looks so beautiful,' writes Rosa. 'I'm jealous.'

'Yeah,' I reply uncertainly. 'I suppose it is.'

'You suppose?'

'I dunno. I feel weird.'

Rosa sends an eye roll. 'You're supposed to be trying it.'

I take a picture of my Aperol, glowing in the sun. 'I am.'

She sends a photo of her knees on the bus, squashed against the back of a dirty seat and I laugh and then put my phone away. I look up at the bright sky and count the petals heaped on the ornate paving stones. I try to notice the good things around me, instead of wishing I was elsewhere.

*

'I'm going to apply for some jobs,' I tell you that night, eating roasted aubergine at your kitchen table.

'I think that's a great idea,' you say quickly, your face bright with promise.

I spoon rice onto my plate carefully, ignoring the drone in the back of my head, warning me that something bad is lurking in the future. 'I'm trying to be present.'

'Present is good.' You smile tentatively. I catch your eye for a moment and then look away.

62

After my parents split up, I saw my dad less frequently. We met up occasionally in cafés, our conversation stilted, too much coffee making my palms sweat. On my eighteenth birthday, I decided to book us a table at an Italian restaurant.

'He'll want to see you.' My mother squeezed my arm. 'It's the right thing to do.'

I dressed up for the meal in a short, sparkly dress and a pair of high heels. I wanted my dad to be proud of me and to look at me and understand that I was an adult with my own life, capable of taking control over the distance between us. I arrived early and sat at the table with a glass of rosé, watching the families and couples around me, tacky with hairspray and perfume, mounds of steaming pasta on their plates.

Fifteen minutes passed and I checked my phone.

'He isn't here yet,' I texted my mother.

'Don't worry,' she replied. *'He's always late.'* I went to the toilet and reapplied my eyeliner, fluffing my hair in the

mirror, trying to brighten my worried face. When I got back to the table he still hadn't arrived.

'Would you like to order?' asked the waiter. I considered ordering something to eat but the thought of pizza or pasta felt heavy and suffocating.

'Not yet,' I smiled up at him. 'I'm waiting for someone.'

The waiter looked at me sympathetically and I hated him. 'No problem. Just let me know when you're ready.'

Half an hour passed and I tried to call my dad but his phone went to voicemail. The waiter brought over a basket of bread and I pushed it away. The wine was too sweet and it made me feel queasy. I fiddled with my earrings and anxiously checked the entrance, searching for my dad's tall frame tucked into blue jeans, Harrington jacket flung over his shoulder.

After forty-five minutes, the waiter returned to the table. 'I'm very sorry but you need to order now. We have another booking later. Perhaps your friend is not coming?' He looked pointedly at the empty seat opposite me.

'Just give me five more minutes,' I said to him. 'Please?' I rang my dad's phone again and there was still no answer. The smell of oil and cheese clung to me, making my skin itch. The couple at the next table kept looking at me and I felt hot and panicked. I stood up too quickly, knocking into the table and making the cutlery rattle. I left some money for my wine and went out into the night, too embarrassed to offer the waiter an explanation.

I sat at the bus stop with goosepimpled legs, shivering in my fake leather jacket. Bitterness burrowed inside me as I watched cars glitter on the road, carrying people with purpose, on their way elsewhere. I didn't think that I needed my dad but I knew that I wanted him there. I felt like I wasn't good enough for him, as if he would rather be anywhere else than with me.

Later, I discovered that he had been drinking and his phone was dead and he lost all perception of time.

'I'm sorry, love.' My mother pulled me into a hug. 'It's not your fault. He'll always find an excuse.' I understood that I wasn't enough and that he would always choose his own problems over me.

Addiction runs through the men in my family like an old rope, binding them through the years. My grandfathers on both sides were alcoholics, and their fathers before them. I also know the pull of addiction; the safety of rules, chasing a feeling, the flash of hunger behind my eyes. The men in my family cried, pissed and vomited, stumbling in the street and tearing holes in the centres of other people's lives, whereas I tucked my compulsions neatly inside me, showing up for other people but creating an absence inside myself. I stayed tightly in control. I felt the pull of addiction but different things were expected of me, so I buried myself in denial instead.

63

After a few weeks of fruitless searching, I embellish my qualifications and I am offered a job teaching English at a language school in Collblanc. Each morning, I cycle along the wide roads, dodging the traffic at Plaça d'Espanya, weaving through the sugary smell of fresh pastries mingled with exhaust fumes. The roads are damp from the street cleaners and droplets cling to my legs as I speed over the warm concrete, my hair fat with humidity. I pass fruit shops shiny with apples, dazzling sprays of mimosa flowers in plastic buckets, old men drinking beer outside cafés, the Mercat d'Hostafrancs hung with nightgowns in pastel colours, rows of sunglasses flashing in the light.

In the evenings, I frantically make notes from a grammar textbook, so that I can list nouns, adjectives and verbs on the board the next morning at school, colour-coding tenses, prefixes and suffixes, explaining clauses and prepositions. My students learn quickly, twisting their tongues around unfamiliar vowel sounds and pushing them out. I read novels with my advanced pupils, arranging the chairs in a circle and encouraging them to discuss the texts, surprising myself with the ease at which I hold this unfamiliar space. Most of my students are bilingual in Spanish and Catalan and some of them speak other languages, too. I ask them how it feels to hold so many different names for things inside them and they wrinkle their noses, trying to find the words in English for what they want to say.

'Different languages have different flavours,' says a teenage girl in my Friday morning class. 'Catalan tastes like family, because that is how it feels to me. It is difficult to explain. Like I can taste the history behind the words.'

'That's interesting. What does English taste like?'

She looks embarrassed. 'Really? It tastes hard. Like rock. Or the black thing they put on the roads.'

'Tar?'

'Yes, like tar. Or something solid. Spanish is more like a liquid to me but English is definitely hard.'

*

My classes give the days shape and purpose, which smooths my knotted thoughts. I meet you for vermouth after work and we sit at high stools around bodega barrels, sharing bitter olives and roasted corn. Something loosens in me as we meet friends in plazas as the night draws in, sitting cross-legged on the tarmac, sharing joints and buying cans of Estrella from street sellers, our bikes leaning against the wall. Our lives fold into a shape and I let myself be held by it, thinking only of the heat caught in your skin and your hand on my back in the dark.

We go to cheap bars together and eat lemony anchovies in pools of sunflower oil, plates of bravas in spicy salsa. We try burrata with peppery rocket, thin slices of coca bread brushed with garlic, drinking cheap cava and fizzy water, bubbles glittering in our mouths. Sometimes we go to a Syrian restaurant in Sants and sit outside in the petrol fumes, watching the traffic, dipping warm flatbread into thick hummus, eating stuffed vine leaves with our fingers, then stringy baklava and mint tea with lots of sugar in tiny glasses. We get Japanese takeaways, sticky with soy, swallowing pink slivers of sashimi and sucking edamame from their pods.

You ask me what I want and I dare myself to reach out and take it, possibility caught in my skin like salt. I am buoyed on the gleam of us together beneath the sun and I gorge myself on the colour of you and this quicksilver city, where want prickles our tongues like sour cherries and we satiate each other, the air thick with heat and smoke, clouds clotted with dirty rain.

We walk past old warehouses in El Poblenou as the light drips neon down the skyscrapers. We abandon our clothes on the sand at Playa de Bogatell and dive into the metallic water, our bodies grateful for the cool waves, swimming out past soggy cigarette ends and washed-up plastic bags like wrinkled jellyfish. You swim right out to the open water, where the sea meets the ocean and it turns deep and cold.

'I like to feel the pull of it,' you tell me, floating on your back like a starfish, looking up at the fading sky. 'To stretch out into the blue.' I swim out past the buoys with you, trusting my body to carry me. I feel afraid when we turn back and look at the tiny beach in the distance, as though I have gone too far and I will never be strong enough to swim back to land.

64

When I lived in the factory, I had a job at a busy pub. City boys flocked to us after work, spilling onto the pavement outside and talking in loud voices. I slipped between them collecting glasses as they flicked their cigarette butts onto the ground and watched me sweep them up. My manager was always in trouble. He did lines of coke alone in the cellar to get him through double shifts. He kept getting into fights and often rang me up last minute, asking me to cover for him.

'I've fractured my jaw,' he said, thickly. 'Had an accident on my bike. Come on, baby, do it for me.'

When we worked together, he watched me with greasy eyes, mixing different concoctions and decanting them into shot glasses, opening a bottle of red wine whenever we did an evening shift.

'Why do you never eat, baby?' he asked me one day,

watching me push my staff meal around on my plate. 'Do you have some kind of problem?' He gestured to my colleague, pulling pints in an oversized Nirvana T-shirt and a pair of tights. 'I would get it, if you were skinny, like Kate. But you're not.'

He was married and secretly sleeping with a lawyer who propped up the bar on weeknights, her glossy hair shining beneath the warm lights, her expensive handbag propped in the service area. She drank bottles of cold Picpoul wine and she looked through me, waving a ten-pound note in my general direction, telling me to keep the change.

It was a sweltering summer and sweat beaded on my face during my shifts, catching in my creases, my lips tasting of salt. I pulled on a pair of denim shorts and a cropped T-shirt, feeling self-conscious of my exposed thighs. My jaw clenched as I approached the pub and saw the heaving crowd packed onto the pavement, sunlight falling through pints of beer, women twisting their hair away from hot necks. I fought through dank bodies to reach the bar, avoiding mirrors and reflective surfaces, feeling raw in my skin. I cringed as rows of bloodshot eyes traced my calf muscles when I stood on my tiptoes to reach the gin. I pulled pint after pint, serving glass bottles straight from the cardboard box, without any time to restock the fridges. I felt aware of the soft expanse of my skin beneath my crop top, damp beneath the waistband of my shorts.

I rested against the till for a moment, drinking a glass of cold water, wiping sweat from beneath my eyes. My manager appeared behind the bar in a floral shirt, a pair of Ray-Bans clipped onto his breast pocket.

'Baby?' he said, quietly. The lawyer was sitting at the bar in a smart linen dress and she met my eyes and then looked away quickly. 'I'm sorry,' he spoke softly. 'But you need to wear more clothes at work.' My pale legs jerked beneath my shorts.

'Are you joking? It's the hottest day of the year.'

He laughed, awkwardly. 'Yeah. But people are looking at you.' He gestured to the lawyer. 'She doesn't think it's right.' He leaned over me to mix himself a gin and tonic. 'You can handle it, baby. Alright?' I turned away and went to serve the line of customers, my body like a flare, desperate for my shift to end so I could stretch out in the dark of my room, away from the heat and the stares that pierced my skin like shards of glass.

65

Carla, a colleague from the language school, invites me to a party in her barrio. There are long tables laid out in the street and coloured streamers strung between lampposts, a man playing guitar on a makeshift stage. Carla's friends are huddled around one end of a table, sharing bottles of wine in plastic cups, slipping between languages and laughing loudly, their syllables softened by the alcohol. They welcome me warmly, standing to kiss my cheeks.

'Have you ever had calçots?' Carla's friend Elena asks me, her ears ringed in silver, vines tattooed around her wrists. I shake my head. 'You are lucky,' she says, solemnly. 'It is the end of the season.' She smiles at me. 'I wish that I was eating calçots for the first time.'

The calçots are long green onions, blackened on a huge barbecue. We gather around it with paper plates and someone adds sardines to the flames, grilled in their skins, smelling of charcoal and the sea. One of Carla's friends carries armfuls of calçots wrapped in newspaper to our table and the group descend on them, tipping back their heads and dropping them into their mouths, smearing thick, orange sauce across their lips. Elena takes me by the arm and guides me to the calçots.

'You have to eat quickly. Or they will be gone.' I unwrap the pile of newspaper and drop a handful of calçots onto my plate. They are thick with coal and it covers my hands and gets beneath my fingernails.

'Dip it in the romesco.' Elena gestures to the orange sauce. 'That's the best part.' Carla fills a porrón with wine and passes it around. Everyone takes turns drinking from it, trying not to spill the liquid as it arcs from the long spout in a scarlet ribbon. The Catalans are well practised and laugh as the others spill wine down their chins, soaking their clothes.

I am nervous but I tip my head back like the others and eat my calçot gingerly. It is delicious, tangy and sweet, crispy then soft inside. The others eat frenziedly, chewing with their mouths open, oil and dirt smeared across their faces. I hesitate for a moment and then I throw myself into it, grabbing the long onions and drinking too quickly, my fingers streaked with charcoal and grease. Someone puts a plate of sardines down on the table and I take one, biting straight into it. No one knows my secret here and I am free to eat rapaciously, to pretend I am the kind of person who takes things easily, who eats when she is hungry and sometimes even when she is not.

'You're a natural,' laughs Carla, nodding at my blackened teeth, the fish bones between my fingers.

'No,' I tell her honestly, shaking my head. 'I'm not.'

66

I was walking home from a day shift at the pub when my throat began to tighten. My lungs felt crushed, as though there were sharp fingers scrabbling in my chest. My hands began to shake and my legs moved slowly, as if I was wading through water. It happened quickly and I was afraid. Reality suddenly seemed separate, something glimmering far away in the distance. I passed a bus stop and sat down on a plastic seat, trying to catch my breath. The flats and the grocery shops warped around me and the air began to shimmer, like heat rising from tarmac. I felt removed from myself, as though I was watching from a distance, inside and outside my body at the same time. There weren't many people around and I pressed my sweating palms into the seat, pushing my feet into the pavement, trying to ground myself. Fear rolled through me in a black wave and my heart jolted against my ribs. I tried to pull out my phone to call someone, but the screen blurred in front of my eyes and I pushed it away.

I closed my eyes and tried to breathe deeply and the feeling began to subside. The buildings around me resumed their usual shape and I felt shaky, my limbs weightless, a dull pain in the base of my skull. I walked slowly to a newsagent across the road, focusing on putting one foot in front of the other. The passing cars made me shudder with their noise and metal, sunlight hitting their bonnets. I chose a bar of Dairy Milk chocolate and pushed some change over the counter, worried that my blood sugar was low because I had not eaten enough. I sat on a stranger's door-step trying to make sense of it, light-headed with shock.

*

A few days later, I was sitting in a pub garden with Rosa and the same thing began to happen again. A thick, heavy fear swept over me and I moved from the picnic bench and sat down on the concrete, sticking my head between my legs.

'What's wrong?' asked Rosa, kneeling beside me and putting her hand on my back, her mouth puckered with concern.

'I don't know. This happened the other day.' I screwed my eyes tightly shut. 'Just give me a minute.' I tried to breathe evenly as the sky shattered into pieces above my head. I felt as though Rosa was very far away from me, a light I couldn't reach. She got me a glass of water and a packet of crisps and I ate them quickly, feeling afraid. I thought perhaps I deserved whatever was happening to me, that my body was repaying me for all of the ways I had punished it, all those months and years of neglect.

When I felt better, I tried to explain to Rosa what had happened, but talking about it brought the sensation on again. I could feel it at the edges of my vision, pressing up against the backs of my eyes, pulling me away from Rosa's soft hands and the rough wooden table, the bright garden clinking with glasses.

'I don't know what's happening to me,' I said with my eyes closed. Rosa pressed her cool hand to my back. I pulled my hair away from my face and my forehead was damp with cold sweat.

'I think you might be having panic attacks,' Rosa said, softly.

'Really? Have you ever had one before?'

'Once.' She rubbed my back. 'It was horrible. You just have to remember to breathe.'

'But what am I panicked about?'

She looked at me softly. 'It's adrenaline. If you store lots of anxiety in your body and it doesn't have an outlet, then it hits you all at once like that.' I sat in the grass trying to breathe evenly, thinking about all the years I had spent burrowing my feelings in the darkness of my body. I wondered if I could learn how to braid them into the rope of a sentence, so I could reach down my throat and pull it out.

67

Mimosa trees burst into fireworks. Hot-pink bougainvillea grows over buildings like a rash. Cacti flower in orange and yellow as people shed their layers like falling petals, the city thick with pollen and salt. I stuff my blouses and denim into your old rucksack and we board the coach to Cadaqués, a few hours north of the city. The air on the bus is stale and the lurching hills make us queasy until we see the sea, spangling in bottle green below us. We carry our bags through cobbled streets, looking up at white walls and painted plant pots, red hibiscus tumbling over doorways, cobbles stained purple with crushed figs. We follow the map on my phone to a ground-floor apartment, clean towels and bedsheets strung out in the sun.

The house is small and smells like the sea, a surfboard propped against the wall. You find a couple of snorkels under the bed and we fill a straw basket with our books and towels, black grapes in a brown paper bag. We wind our way through narrow streets to a square filled with people wearing white linen and Ray-Bans, drinking sparkling wine in the sun. We follow a curving road along the water and the bars and restaurants give way to silver cliffs. The bay is stippled with sailing boats and we clamber along the rocks until we find a patch of sand sheltered by boulders. We climb down and slip out of our clothes, stretching out on our towels like big cats, our bodies pale in the soft glare. I half close my eyes and watch the sun tessellate the waves from behind my lashes. You rest your hand on my stomach.

'Shall we swim?' I ask, feeling my scalp burning through my hair.

'Do we have to?' you groan.

'Come on.' I climb to my feet, scattering sand across our towels. 'Let's go.'

The water is cold and I dive down into it, feeling the long, strong pull of my muscles, my body eagerly expanding to fill the space around it. I turn and see you bobbing on the shoreline like a seal, your hair slicked back, skin slippery with salt. The sun strikes gems from my eyelashes as you splash towards me, waving the snorkels above your head.

'Shall we?' You hand me a pair of goggles.

'What do I have to do? I've never done it before.'

'It's easy. You just have to remember to breathe through your mouth.' You put your snorkel between your lips and blow through it like a whale, then you disappear beneath the blue, the plastic tube making ripples on the surface. I pull my goggles over my head. They cling to my face and strands of my hair get caught in the rubber. I put my head beneath the water and swallow mouthfuls of brine.

'Wait.' I come up coughing, readjusting my snorkel. You are already far away and I stall. I don't trust the flimsy piece of plastic. I am afraid of not being able to breathe

the only way I know how. Nerves rake my skin but I take a deep breath and push myself beneath the waves.

Time moves differently beneath the water. Rays of sunlight are caught in the swell, dappling the grains of sand caught in the drift like phosphorescence. Bits of seaweed and algae float, untethered. A school of tiny silver fish dart beneath me, oblivious to the dark shape of my body. I breathe through my mouth and think about the way that time passes differently when we are together, like being underwater, the minutes and hours stretched out. I feel inside time, not dragged along or just skimming the surface. I want to wrap you up in our time, safe from your fear of loss, but I know it is slipping away as we live it. I wonder if it is really possible to hold on to anything at all.

I try to float with the current, feeling the swell of it in my skull, but my goggles steam up and the world becomes a blur of green light. My breath rattles in my ears. Your legs appear in front of me, moving in slow motion, as though you are dancing. The light silvers your body and turns you opalescent, kicking up cubic zirconia. I reach for your pearly feet but my goggles fill up with water and I breathe through my nose in panic, inhaling huge gulps. I thrash my arms and legs, propelling myself upwards. I pull off my mask, spluttering in the bright daylight. You bob up beside me, laughing.

'Are you okay?' you ask and I shake my head. 'It just takes practice.' You laugh at my red face and I turn away from you, swimming back towards the shore. 'Where are you going?' you call after me and I ignore you, desperate to feel solid ground beneath my feet.

I sink onto my towel, damp and shivering, pulling my jumper over my wet swimming costume, seawater soaking into the wool. I remember the beauty of your body beneath the water, your hair like seaweed and your legs rippling like long pieces of ribbon. You have an ease in your body that I will never experience, a fluidity of movement that is not charged with hurt. I want, more than anything, to exist like that, easy and pearlescent, to forget the shape of my body as I drag it through the days.

You climb out of the water and walk towards me, wincing at the hot sand.

'What happened?' you ask, your skin glittering with droplets. You are so beautiful that you are almost painful to look at, your body tanned beneath the blinding sky, tattoos curled beneath your skin like question marks.

'I don't know.' I shield my eyes from the sun. 'I just panicked.'

You reach out to touch me but I pull away. 'What's wrong?' you frown and I shake my head. You reach into the basket and pull out a beer and I watch you drinking thirstily, without thinking about it.

68

One morning in the warehouse, I woke up on my mezzanine with a squeezing feeling in my chest, spasms of pain fluttering around my heart. I made a cup of coffee and tried to eat some breakfast but the sensation was crushing, rolling in waves. I anxiously looked up my symptoms on my phone and it told me to go to the hospital. I grew scared and called in sick to my shift at the pub. My manager sighed down the phone.

'Fine,' he said. 'But I can't guarantee you enough hours next week.'

'Okay,' I replied distractedly, making anxious circles on my chest with my fist.

I decided to go to the walk-in centre and I sat in the waiting room for hours as people rushed in and out, red-faced and crying with swollen ankles, cradling their stomachs, faces cracked with pain. My chest ached and I flicked through a magazine as though I was at the hair-dresser, trying to focus on anything else. The waiting room was part of the hospital and I watched the little screen above reception that warned the doctors when an ambulance was on its way, short words describing the severity of the conditions of the people inside. My stomach clenched when I heard someone wailing, the whisk of a curtain drawn quickly around a bed. I didn't have a word, or an ambulance, or even a prescription. I didn't know if I was supposed to be there at all. I didn't want to go back to the mezzanine to sit in my room with my heart rushing through me, worrying that something bad was going to happen.

I lay on the bed in the consultation room, the paper sheet sticking to the backs of my thighs beneath my thin summer dress. A nurse wiped away a sheen of sweat and pressed electrodes to my chest.

'Good news,' the doctor said briskly, peering at the screen. 'The reading is absolutely fine.'

I sat up, peeling the small white stickers from my skin. 'Then what is it? The squeezing feeling?' The nurse left the room and the doctor glanced at his watch and then looked at me, kindly.

'Would you say you've been feeling anxious lately? Are you going through something stressful, at home or at work?'

I shook my head. 'Not really. Nothing specific.' The

doctor peeled off his gloves and rubbed alcohol gel between his palms. 'I go running a lot.' I slid off the bed and picked up my jacket. 'Do you think I should stop?'

The doctor smiled. 'No, no. Running is good. It keeps your heart healthy.' My cheeks burned as I left the room.

'I'm sorry,' I told him. 'For wasting your time.'

I walked home through the darkening streets, watching car headlights flicker like dirty rubies. The smell of fried chicken and hot concrete coated my skin. I felt stupid for going to see the doctor but I didn't know what else to do. I needed an explanation for the way that I felt; a diagnosis, a record, some kind of proof. I needed a word that described what I was, a name that I could hold on to.

69

We go back to the little white house to rinse the salt from our hair. I hang our swimming things on the washing line and they drip into the plants. The hot shower calms me, slowing my thoughts and thickening my blood. You watch me in the mirror as I dress. Your eyes are like sea glass, freckles breaking across your nose. You press your lips to the back of my neck and a rich heat rises in my stomach. My body feels warm beneath my cotton dress, tingling with traces of light.

We go out into the warm night. The streets smell of hot stone and cigarettes. The houses in the hills are lit up like candles and brine blows over the water. Laughter leaks from restaurants and is stifled in the heavy air, the threat of a storm rattling the fishing boats anchored in the bay.

Waves hit the harbour wall and rise up over the pavement like clouds of smoke. Teenage boys push each other into the spray, hair gel running down their faces.

We sit outside a small restaurant, tucked into a quiet square. The street is cobbled and lilac wisteria clings to the awning, a red Vespa parked on the kerb.

'I glance at the menu. 'What are you going to get?'

'Langoustines,' you read, excitedly. 'And razor clams.' The waiter comes to our table with glasses of cava. I look at the menu again and order salmon in one breath.

'I've never done that before,' I tell you, as the waiter carries our order inside.

'What?'

'Ordered salmon.'

'Well.' You raise your glass. 'Cheers to that.' The bubbles are bitter and fizz in my stomach. The people next to us are eating sticky black rice, pink prawns cracked from their shells. The men have dark beards and oily hair and the women drip silver bangles over leathery wrists. Someone lights a cigar and the animal smell clots the air.

Our food arrives and my stomach flips. The razor clams bleed butter and garlic. My salmon is burnished in butter on a bed of asparagus tips. I squeeze lemon over my plate.

'Have a clam.' You push them towards me.

'How do I eat it?'

'You just pull it apart and suck.'

I raise my eyebrows. The flesh is tender, garlic tart on my tongue.

'What do you think?'

'Really good.'

The salmon is like creamed velvet and hot, wet drops fall from the sky and burst on the table. The boats clink in the distance as the storm moves closer and I feel deep in my body in the best sort of way, my skin sore with sun, the damp smell of the pavements, the bitter wine and cigar smoke, the thrill of your legs beneath the table.

You watch me eating and it makes me self-conscious.

'What?' I put down my knife and fork.

'Nothing.' You look away.

'What is it?' My stomach clenches. You are quiet for a moment, cutlery scraping your plate. You look up again with a strange smile on your face. 'Why are you looking at me like that?' I ask you.

You reach for my hand across the table. 'I think you're brave.'

'What?'

'I think you're brave,' you repeat, gesturing towards the food on the table. 'I know this is difficult for you.'

I pull my hand away from yours. I remember the ease of your body beneath the water and heat flares in my gut.

'No.' My throat tightens. 'You don't know.' I know you are trying to be kind but it feels patronising. I don't want to be brave; I just want to be normal, to move through the world without getting snagged on jagged edges. 'You don't know what it's like.'

'What do you mean?' I am silent and you put down your fork in exasperation. 'Don't be like that.'

'Like what?' I draw away from you.

'Like that.'

My body tenses. 'But you don't know what it's like. I'm not brave.' My voice is too loud and the bearded men look over at us. Thunder breaks above us and your face falls. You push your plate away and sit back in your chair with your arms folded.

'I was just trying to be nice.'

I feel as though you have punctured something I cannot

name, slippery with rainwater, sliding out of my grasp. I pull some crumpled notes from my purse and throw them on the table, where they get soaked in the rain. You cover them with an empty glass as I stand up.

'Where are you going?' Your mouth twists in confusion.

'Sorry.' The rain plasters my dress to my body. 'I just need a bit of space.'

I walk out onto the slick, black cobbles. Fat rain bounces on the old stone.

'¿Necesitas un paraguas?' the waiter calls after me and I shake my head and walk towards the water as a shard of light splits the sky. Restaurants pull up their awnings and people scatter. Everything smells metallic as I stand on the edge of the water, the boats rattling wildly in the waves. The rain falls through the streetlights in glittering sheets. People stare at me but I ignore them, feeling the air crackle. I am upset with myself for being angry at you, afraid that I have broken something, but your words stuck their teeth in me in a way I cannot define; something to do with the calm of your body beneath the water and the scrabbling, choking feeling that is always in me. I know you were trying to be kind but you will never understand. It is a distance between us that will never be crossed. There is no bridge, no tunnel, no way to reach the other side.

You appear in the darkness, running towards me and holding your jacket uselessly over your head, your shoes leaking water, dark curls plastered to your forehead. You reach out and grab me by the wrist.

'What are you doing?' you ask me. The sky flashes white and anger boils inside me. I pull my arm out of your grip.

'What the fuck?' you say and I look at your worried face

beneath the black clouds, your shirt soaked right through, and my anger spirals into guilt.

'I'm sorry.' I look at the churning water. Thunder echoes around us and you squint at me through the downpour.

'Shall we go home?' you ask and I nod. We splash through the puddles, the empty streets eerie in the streetlight, the sky rippling above our heads.

We light candles back in our small, dry room, shivering beneath the duvet. You boil a pan of water on the stove for cups of mint tea.

'I'm sorry.' I untangle the knots in my hair with my fingers, feeling embarrassed. 'For ruining the meal.'

'What happened?' Your voice is sharp, then you soften. 'I don't really understand. I've never seen you like that before.' You pass me a mug and the hot ceramic burns my palms and makes me feel grounded. The windows rattle beneath the force of the rain and the candles spit shadows on the walls.

'I don't know.' I lie back on the pillows and you put down your tea and lie next to me, tracing your fingers slowly across my arm. I close my eyes, dizzy with the cava, the clams and the salmon, thunder caught beneath my skin.

'Can I show you?' I ask you.

'Show me what?'

I sit up and press my hands into your stomach, one on top of the other, palms facing down.

'What are you doing?' you gasp and I press harder. I don't want to hurt you but I need you to know what it's like when you cannot find the name for what you are feeling, when you have buried language in your body for so long that it begins to speak for you instead.

'Stop,' you say, with fear in your eyes and I pull my hands away and sit back.

'It's like that. A kind of pressure that you can't get away from. Some days it's harder and other days it's softer but it's always there.' You pull me close and wrap your arms around me.

'That's fucked up,' you whisper.

'Yeah.'

The storm passes and we lie quietly, listening as the rain slows and water trickles down the drainpipe, the rise and fall of our breath. You blow out the candles and we slip into dreams and in the morning the sky is bright and clear again.

70

I wanted to leave London; my broken bed in the toffee factory and my stifling job at the pub. I wanted to live in a place where I could be anyone, far away from the bus stops and pawn shops of my childhood, to move through a city wracked with light. I thought I had chosen London as the place where I would make my own life, but its edges were sharp and cruel and I got caught on them, bloodying my ankles and wrists.

I decided to go to Paris, smoky and sepia, far away from the trundling buses and terraced houses, fat with the possibility of becoming someone else. I pictured pink cherry blossoms, red lipstick, cheap cigarettes in the dawn. The woman I wanted to be seemed far away from me but I felt certain she was in Paris, waiting in the future in her glossy fur coat, drinking wine at a red-lit café in the rain, laughing with all of her teeth.

The only room I could afford was an attic in the old servant's quarters at the top of a grand art nouveau building in the 14th arrondissement. I emailed the landlord three times before I left, to check that it was still available. I always felt as though everything would be taken by someone else.

'Don't worry,' he wrote. 'The room will be waiting for you.'

There was a polished mahogany door leading to a marble staircase and a gold cage lift with numbered brass buttons. My room was small and dark with a slanted ceiling and a thin, rectangular window above the bed. I had a little hotplate and a cold-water sink, a broken bookshelf and a cracked mirror.

I stuck candles in old wine bottles and tacked postcards and photographs to the peeling walls. I found a fruit crate on the street outside and kept my jar of coffee and my tea bags in it with a packet of lentils and crumbling stock cubes. I tacked a map of the city above my bed and went to sleep at night memorising the curves of the street names and the colours of the metro line, new words building beneath my gums. In the morning I looked at the rooftops through my tiny window and felt dizzy with the glitz of it all, the allure of a threshold, the lustre of choosing something else.

I shared a rickety toilet at the end of the corridor with an older woman, who shouted at me for walking past her room too noisily, but there wasn't anywhere to shower.

'Previous tenants used the facilities at the local swimming pool,' the landlord assured me. 'And there is a launderette just down the street.'

The pool was only open between seven and eight in the morning. I woke early to glittering frost and jogged around the periphery of the city when it was still dark, my shampoo bottle bouncing around in my backpack. The showers were communal and I faced the wall in my little blue swimming costume, rinsing suds from my hair as old men in speedos rubbed soap into their willies, the skin on their bare chests wrinkled and sagging with age.

Occasionally, kindly women with muscled arms tried to engage me in conversation and I stumbled to answer them in halting French. I fantasised that one day, when I was better at the language, I could explain my predicament to them and they would invite me to their houses to use their marbled bathrooms, where I would smear my legs in their expensive creams and wrap myself in a big, fluffy towel, warm from the radiator. Until then, I showered quickly, avoiding the stares of the old men. I went back out onto the cold street in my dank running clothes, my hair wet on the back of my neck.

71

Summer stretches before us and our lives settle into a rhythm. We wake early in the heat and drink coffee on the balcony, before getting on our bikes and cycling to our jobs in different parts of the city. You meet friends after work while I walk on the beach or drink cold red wine with Carla, the sky glazed purple above our heads. Our lives are abundant, tropical and streaked with light. My teaching job does not pay a lot but it pays enough and for the first time in my life, I have enough of everything.

I know I should be content but as I choose fresh vegetables in the supermarket, or swim in green water, or drink cold beer in a dappled square, there is something twisted inside me that doesn't feel right and I am frustrated with myself for being difficult, unable to settle.

I spend a Saturday alone while you are in the library working on your research and I don't know what to do with myself. The feeling swells behind my eyes, clouding my vision and making me listless. I don't want to drink a cup of coffee, or read a book, or see a film, or look at the whitewashed walls of a gallery. I don't want to meet a friend or run my fingers along racks of flea-market dresses. I don't want to sit down and eat something, even though I can do that now. I don't know what is wrong with me and I walk the streets for hours, turning my thoughts over and over, trying to work it out.

I climb up to the old civil war bunkers at the top of El Guinardó and look out over the city, skirting groups of teenagers smoking joints and playing reggaeton from crackling speakers, watching the horizon blaze orange then fade into pink. I sit on a concrete slab as electric light prickles the streets and I realise that I don't know what to do now that I can pay my rent and I always have enough to eat and I come home to a person who loves me. I am afraid of this feeling. It is soft and swaddling, wraps me up warm. I am used to night-time, danger, the purple shock of adrenaline around my heart. I have spent so long being empty that I don't know how to be full. I am constantly waiting for the danger to come, for reality to creep up and catch me out.

*

We eat steaming ravioli in your apartment at night and I try to explain it to you but I can't find the right words.

'I never felt like this in London,' I say. 'I always felt alive there, like I was close to something real.'

You look tired in the lamplight. 'What do you mean?'

I don't know how to describe what I am feeling, only that the way I live now feels cushioned and comfortable, and because I am not used to it, it makes me feel less real. I think back to the scrabbling feeling I used to have, pushed up against the edges of the city, and in a strange way I miss it, even though I didn't have much power then, less than I have now.

'I can't explain it.'

You run your hand through your hair in exasperation. 'Sometimes I worry this thing will follow us everywhere.'

'What thing?'

'Are you just going to keep running forever?'

I bite my lip until I taste copper. I know you will never understand. You had heavy things of your own to bury in London but you were never trying to outrun yourself, to leave your own body behind. I stand up and begin to clear the table.

'Stop.' You reach for me but I pull back. We lock eyes for a moment and I wish I was different, someone easier and less intense, able to take what I need.

'Sorry,' I say, moving away. Something small and fragile catches in your face. You blink it away like a shutter coming down between us. I know that I am bad because I cannot settle, that I am trapped within the bounds of the things that have shaped me and the kinds of things I think I deserve. I wonder if love is a need or a want and whether that means I can have it. I wonder if you would be better off without me, with someone who knows how to stay.

72

I found a job as a nanny in Paris, looking after a family of small children. Every afternoon, I collected Alec from his childminder, Léa from nursery and Emilie from school. We walked to the local park together, Alec in the pushchair and the girls running beside us like unicorns, their pink schoolbags dangling from the handles. I pushed Alec on the swings as his sisters hung from the monkey bars in their matching blue dresses, until it was time to go home.

The children lived by the Eiffel Tower and I sometimes sat on the balcony until Alec's mother came home, watching it spangle with gold light. There were wine glasses with silty pits stacked in the sink and I imagined her curled up on the settee with her husband, a bottle of velvety red between them, entertaining friends, their hands on each other's knees, picking at hard cheese and salty olives while their children dreamed. I thought of my own parents, my mother making lists of bills to be paid in her small, round handwriting, and my dad out chasing the night somewhere, hungry to forget himself. A shard of loss bit into me but I couldn't work out if it was for them or for myself.

On Wednesdays, Emilie finished school early and I took her for lunch on the way to her music lesson. We walked through her neighbourhood holding hands, looking up at the tall buildings with red flowers spilling from balconies, the fruit shops piled with mangoes and pineapples, coral-coloured lobsters with their claws tied together, reclining on beds of ice. The 15th arrondissement was like a painting of Paris; old women drinking espressos in fur coats and gold jewellery, fluffy dogs perched on their knees. There were toy shops selling wooden trains and ragdolls, waiters in crisp white aprons serving people at round tables on the street. The light punctured glasses of white wine, picking out red lipstick bitten on the rim, the bulb smeared with greasy fingertips.

Emilie liked to go to a glass-walled sushi restaurant and her mother gave me a voucher to pay for her meal. I listened to her flit between languages, ordering dishes I had never heard of in either of them.

'Why aren't you getting anything?' she asked me.

'I don't have enough money,' I told her, which was true, but it was also only half of the story.

'Why don't you ask your *maman* for some money?' Her eyes were wide, lips stained with soy sauce.

'Yeah.' I took a sip of water. 'Maybe.'

Sometimes their mother came home late from work and I helped the children with their homework and put them to bed. Alec cried and I turned on his moon-shaped night light and stroked his hair.

'*Maman* will be home soon,' I murmured. 'Try to get some sleep.'

'But what about you?' he sniffed into his pillow.

'What do you mean?'

'What about your *maman*?'

'Mine?'

'You're only small and you need a *maman*, too.' I tucked the blankets tightly around his small body. 'Where does your *maman* live? Is it far away?'

'Yes,' I said, softly. 'But yours will be home soon.'

184

73

I sit on a bench in a square in Poble-sec and call my mother. She is doing housework and she answers slightly out of breath, her familiar voice falling across the world and into my ear.

'Is it hot there?' she asks.

'Boiling.' I touch my hand to my damp forehead.

'Lucky you. It's bloody freezing here. Been raining all week.'

'Yeah?'

'It's miserable. How are you, then?'

'I'm okay.'

'Are you sure?'

'Yeah.' I don't know how to put my feelings into words; that I am homesick but I don't know where home is, that I can't work out what I need. I want her to tell me what to do but I know that she can't, or that I wouldn't really listen if she did. 'Just feel a bit. I dunno.'

'What have you been up to?'

'Just working. Going to the beach and stuff.'

'Hold on a sec,' my mother says. The line goes muffled and I watch parakeets fluttering in the orange trees above me, children sticking their heads beneath the silver rush of the water fountain. A man pulls out a painted guitar and starts playing flamenco.

'Sorry about that,' my mother says in my ear. 'It was work on the house phone. I'm trying to get some extra hours.'

'Really? Is everything okay?'

'Oh, you know. Just the usual. What were you saying? Are you feeling unwell?'

'No, not unwell. It's more like—' I hear the kettle boiling

in the background and picture my mother in her small kitchen wearing her paint-stained house jeans, piles of washing on the table, a week of long shifts at the call centre looming in front of her.

'I can't hear you very well. It's very noisy, wherever you are. I can hear people talking in Spanish.'

'Don't worry.' I swallow. 'I miss you.'

'Miss you too. Maybe I can come and visit, if I can get some time off?'

'That would be nice.'

'It would, wouldn't it? I could do with a bit of sun.'

We say goodbye and I look up at the bright blue sky, the heat of the day trapped in the metal bench, warming the backs of my legs. I feel sickened by myself, unable to appreciate the good things, to reach out and take what is mine. I am guilty for choosing a different life, as if my mother's world wasn't good enough for me, with her broken heart and her lost children, and yet here, where my life is about more than simply survival and I do not have to work as hard as she does, I am still not satisfied. I picture her pouring hot water into her favourite mug, fishing out the tea bag, tipping a couple of chocolate digestives onto a plate. I feel homesick but my home is not there with her and not quite here with you.

74

I took a cheap flight from Paris to Newcastle, to visit my mother at Christmas. I felt dirty in her spotless house, as though the dust from the crumbling Parisian buildings and cobbled streets was caught in my hair and skin. My mother's widescreen telly and bright pink toaster felt like the future, whereas my attic in Paris seemed as though it existed in the past.

I met Tara for a drink in Durham on Boxing Day. The pubs were packed with people in sparkly dresses and fruity after-shave, brand-new high heels blistering fake-tanned feet. Tara booked us a table at the champagne bar and she looked beautiful in a cream satin blouse, her false nails coated in glitter. I felt like a child in my scuffed boots and big denim jacket. I went to the bar and ordered a beer.

'It's a champagne bar, love,' said the barman, a crisp tea towel slung over his shoulder. 'We do prosecco or cham-pagne.' My stomach tensed as I ordered two glasses of prosecco and passed over my bank card, praying that it wouldn't get declined.

'You look smaller,' Tara frowned when I sat down at the table. I felt pleased and wondered which form of myself she liked best. She had recently gotten breast implants and she pulled down her blouse to show me her new cleavage, deep and proud.

'You look great.' I sipped my drink. 'What do they feel like?'

She pushed her shoulders back. 'You can touch them if you want.'

'Oh, no. It's okay.'

'Why not?' She pursed her lips.

'I don't know. It seems weird for me to touch your body like that.'

Tara rolled her eyes. 'Suit yourself. Liam loves them.'

'I bet he does.' A group of men at the bar peered over at our table and Tara smiled and tossed her hair. I felt conflicted, caught between two different versions of myself; the teenage girl who wore her sexuality like an armour and the uncertain, child-like woman I worried I had become.

I told Tara about my nanny job and my attic in Paris, embellishing details to make it seem romantic.

'Sounds lush.' She sipped her drink. 'Do you eat croissants on the Champs-Élysées and that?'

'Not exactly,' I laughed.

I tried to imagine how my life might look through her eyes but it seemed small and grimy; my furtive showers in the swimming pool, cycling home through the freezing dark. I told myself that I was pursuing something different, a way of living that felt meaningful to me, but I looked at Tara's shiny iPhone and her patent-leather handbag and felt unconvinced.

She was saving up for a deposit on a brand-new house with her boyfriend and she flashed through photos of the show home on her phone.

'It's lovely,' I said as she scrolled through stainless-steel appliances and laminate flooring, but I thought it looked bland and cold.

Our conversation grew stilted. She told me about friends from school having babies or affairs and I laughed along and asked the right questions but it all seemed far away. I thought I was reaching for freedom in my quest to become a different kind of person, but I looked at Tara with her job as a mortgage advisor and her musky perfume and she seemed like an adult, with glamour and power, and I wondered which of us was more free.

'Will you take a picture of me?' Tara asked after another drink, re-applying her lip gloss and handing me her phone. I watched as she filled the screen, glossy and gorgeous with her perfect new breasts, and I felt the weight of the distance between us, all the ways in which I was shrinking, even though I thought I was broadening the parameters of my world.

We stopped exchanging messages when I went back to Paris. I didn't know how to reconcile our jagged teenage years with the person I was becoming. I felt afraid of that world, the things it made me confront about myself, the danger of being pulled back in, unable to climb out again. I didn't stop to wonder how Tara felt around me. I just knew we were moving in different directions. She sent me a photo of her new house keys and I left the message unread.

75

We take the train to the science museum, in the hills of Vallcarca, close to the gold-lit church hanging in Tibidabo like a star. We walk through streets filled with mansions faded to pastel colours by the sun, empty swimming pools and cacti cracked with heat. We pay our entrance fee and follow a line of comets and meteors to the planetarium.

'*Lo siento,*' says the attendant when we show her our tickets. '*Llegas muy tarde. Es nuestro último espectáculo del dia.*'

'We're too late to see the stars,' you say, as we walk towards the aquarium. 'Can you believe it?'

I shrug and head towards the aquarium. The air between us is swollen, filled with things we can't say. I look at the angelfish hiding behind seagrass with sad eyes. Seahorses move their brittle bodies beneath electric lights. An octopus flails in bright blue water and I press my hand against the glass.

'I can't believe you ate one of those,' you say.

'Don't make me feel bad about it.'

'I was joking.' Your words are hard.

'No, you weren't.'

We pause in front of the hermit crabs, scuttling among rocks and making homes in the shells of other creatures. There is a piece of text on the wall and I read it aloud.

'Living in empty snail shells forces hermit crabs to contort their bodies to unimaginable extremes. This affects the size of their pincers.' I look pointedly at you and a muscle in your cheek twitches. 'The hermit crab changes its shell, or moults, once a year, forced to leave its home by its increase in size. Just when it is most vulnerable, it has to leave its refuge and expose its clumsy body to predators. This is the hermit crab's moment of greatest uncertainty.' The crab waves its pincers at us.

'He looks angry,' you say.

'Of course he's angry,' I frown.

You shake your head and move into the next room without replying. I bite my tongue and follow you to a row of glass cases filled with brains preserved in liquid, arranged in size order. The smallest is a mouse, followed by a cat, a dog, a sheep and then a monkey.

'The last one's human,' you grimace. 'I don't think I can deal with that today.' I kneel down to get a better look. It makes me queasy to think that a whole world can be squashed into something so small. I wonder who the person was who donated their brain to the museum.

It looks so fragile and I am uneasy thinking of all of the ways in which I have not looked after my own brain, deprived it of food and nutrients, experimented with pain. I feel exposed, as though the skin has been peeled off the world.

We move past taxidermy birds and butterflies, into the final room. There is a living mangrove swamp behind glass, water snakes lurking in the murky roots and insects skittering through rot. Orange light glazes the water, casting ripples across our faces and I momentarily forget that I am upset. We walk around the forest entranced, feeling the artificial humidity pumped into the air. A capybara looks at us mournfully.

'It's kind of sad, isn't it?' you say. 'All of these creatures living in a fake swamp in the city, not knowing that it's all just created by humans.'

'It is sad. Maybe they do know, though.'

'How would they know?'

'Hormones. Intuition. A feeling in their bones.'

You laugh. 'Do insects have bones?'

'A feeling in their blood, then.'

I think about the mangrove forest for a long time afterwards, growing in the city beneath closed stars. I think of the flailing octopus, the skeletal seahorses, the world with its skin peeled off. I think of the problem of finding the right home. I think of the brains in glass cases, separated from their bodies. I wonder if they remember pain. I wonder if the creatures know they are living in the wrong places, whether they dream of seawater, if they feel it in their blood.

76

In Paris, I spent weekends wandering the streets, avoiding my reflection in the dark river and the sludgy canal, looking at the grey slate rooftops and the musicians on street corners, searching for a place where I might fit. The things I needed and wanted were small and ordinary; a safe place to live, a warm winter coat, a hot cup of coffee, a glass of wine in the rain, but they felt huge and dazzling because it was a world I was not supposed to have, one that was outside the bounds of the life that was set out for me and I didn't have the means to attain it. They were gilded dreams and teetering risks and the thrill of it all tore through me.

I went out dancing alone and met an actor called Louis who bought me gin and tonics, which oiled the new words I had been collecting and they began to slide out of me with pursed lips and long vowels. He had soft, dark hair that fell past his shoulders and he wore tight jeans with big boots. His arms were strong and riven with brown scars. He held a beer between his lips and looked at me with intensity. I felt the pull of him, the tingle of standing on a threshold, the prospect of erasure, of becoming someone new.

'Do you want to go for a walk?' he asked, when the lights came on. I pictured my slanting attic room and the old woman who shared my hallway screaming at me to be quiet. I thought of Tara drinking champagne with manicured fingernails, a gold locket dangling between her new breasts.

'Okay,' I said, finishing my drink in a single gulp.

Louis wore skull-shaped rings, smoked Pueblo tobacco and had a special spray for his boots to keep them shiny. He picked me up on his moped and took me for rides around the city, his long hair streaming into my face. I learned how to wrap my legs around him so the engine didn't burn my bare skin. Once, he turned up outside my apartment with a white rose tucked inside his helmet and it made me feel embarrassed. The first time we had sex, he said,

'You have a sadness deep inside you and that is what makes you beautiful.'

I turned away and frowned at the wall. My sadness was not beautiful; it was scalding, destructive and heavy. It was not alluring or mysterious. It did not give me hidden depths. It was something the world outside me had pushed into my body and forced me to carry. Louis was mistaken when he glimpsed the glimmer and shine of it. He could not feel the jagged edges; the broken shards of glass.

'You don't eat much,' he said, when I turned down another offer of dinner.

'No,' I stalled, looking for an explanation. 'I don't get very hungry.'

He raised his eyebrows. 'In Paris, the women are always hungry.'

My face grew hot. I wanted to be like the women I saw at the restaurants that lined the canal, eating long, luxurious lunches, slipping their feet out of their sandals beneath the table, letting pleasure pool in their skin like sunlight on water. I wanted to be someone who ordered wine for the table and paid for it, who slept in a sunlit apartment beneath cool, clean sheets. I did not want to be tired and bone-heavy, always scratching at the limits, living on scraps.

'All of the women in Paris are hungry?' I asked him, sarcastically.

He leaned over and bit my shoulder. 'And all of the men, too.'

77

We drink bottles of beer on your balcony with a bowl of crisps between us. You are restless and distracted, biting your nails and playing with your lighter, glancing at me and then looking away.

'What's wrong?' I ask.

You take a swig of your beer. 'I got that grant I applied for.' You wrap your arms around your knees. The hairs on your legs are bleached white from cycling in the sun.

'What? That's amazing. Why didn't you say?'

You pick at the label on your bottle. 'I dunno.' We sit in uncomfortable silence for a moment. 'Sometimes I think I might break things if I say them out loud.'

'What do you mean?'

'Like saying something curses it. Makes it not real.' I look at you. I don't think I can afford to live like that; keeping things inside me in fear of breaking them. I am trying to get better at verbalising things so they don't weigh me down.

'I don't think it works like that,' I say, quietly.

'Well, anyway. It means I can stay here for another year at least.' You look at me sideways.

'That's great.' I try to seem bright.

You watch me carefully. 'Is it?'

'Is it not what you want?'

'Yeah. I think so. But what about you?' I look through the railings at the opposite apartments. I want to be where you are but I want to make my own decisions, too. I am not used to having my wants met and it makes me feel stifled, afraid of needing you.

'I don't know.' Sometimes I worry that I am not making

the right choices and the years will go by and I will end up in the wrong future, unable to go backwards, to stop the churning cogs of the life that I have already put into motion.

You look down at the street, avoiding my gaze. 'Do you want to stay here?'

'For now. But a year's a long time.'

'Maybe we could move into a different apartment.' You look around at the furniture. 'Choose somewhere together.'

'Maybe.' I finish my beer too quickly and the bubbles get trapped in my chest. My throat feels tight but I don't know why. I stand up too fast and my glass bottle smashes.

'Shit. Sorry.' I step over the broken glass and you climb to your feet.

'Don't worry.' You head into the kitchen. 'I'll get it.' You come back with a dustpan and I sit on the peeling settee, picking at a tiny sliver of glass wedged in my toe. 'Are you okay?' you ask, tossing the shards into the bin.

'I'm fine.'

'Are you sure?'

'Yes.'

You look at me as if you are about to speak and then change your mind, sitting down at the kitchen table and opening your laptop. 'I just have to send a couple of emails.'

'Okay.'

'Then shall we have dinner?'

'Sure.'

You look at me over the edge of your laptop and I turn away.

I pick up my phone and scroll through social media while you are working. My eyes skim the lives of people I have not seen for years; bright white smiles and plates piled with pasta, a flaming sunset, a field of sunflowers, a misshapen loaf of bread. I get snagged on the image of a thin wrist against a green hospital gown, a plastic wristband with *Tara* spelled across it. There is a long, sprawling caption sparkling with pink hearts and shooting stars. I read it quickly with a strange, floating feeling, as though I am not quite in the room.

'Had my first round of chemo today. Feeling wobbly but okay. Very grateful for all my friends and family. Especially Liam who is my rock. Thank you for all the well wishes. Might not be on here for a little while.'

I put down my phone with a ringing in my ears. I look at you typing on your laptop and you seem far away. I pick up my phone again and press my finger into Tara's photo. We have not spoken for a couple of years. I watch her online, from a distance, as though we never shared those sticky, fractious nights, as though we barely know each other at all. I saw pictures of her wedding; her big white dress, a diamanté tiara woven into her hair, pink rose petals on her cake. I know that she lives in a brand-new house with a kitchen island, that her bedroom mirror is edged in light bulbs, that she drinks prosecco on a Friday night in her silky dressing gown from a tall, thin glass emblazoned with her name.

I scroll through her profile but I can't find out any more information, only that she is having chemotherapy and that Liam bought her a set of pyjamas with bears printed on them to take to the hospital. She looks so thin. I feel sick thinking of all of the ways in which we hurt and starved our bodies, how little we valued them and how much we wished them away. I go back to the picture of the hospital band and zoom in on her small wrist. Her hands are exactly as I remember them, her neat knuckles and stubby fingers with perfect half-moons, bare without her false nails. My arms prickle with cold, despite the hot, heavy air in your apartment. I feel staticky, a metallic shock closing around my throat, my finger stuck on her name. You keep typing and the noise cuts through me.

'I'm just going for a walk,' I say, slipping on my sandals.

'Okay.' You barely look up. 'See you in a bit.'

I walk up the hill to Montjuïc, past pomegranate trees heavy with fruit, the night vibrating with motorbikes and cicadas, the city razed below me in orange light. There is a band practising in a square; a man playing a double bass, a long-haired violinist, a woman leaning into a trombone. The music is thick with joy and it presses into me like wet sand.

The steps of the Museu Nacional d'Art de Catalunya at the top of the hill are full of people speaking in different languages, sharing joints and drinking beer. The Font Màgica de Montjuïc is lit up gold below us and the *manteros* throw blue lights into the air, then they fall to the ground like broken stars. I sit on the steps and think of Tara. It seems wrong that I am here in the world while she is alone in a hospital bed, the curtains drawn around her, too sick to look at her phone. I feel horrible for not replying to her messages, for not holding on to her tightly enough.

My restlessness feels gaudy and trivial. I think of all of the ways I have not looked after my own body, all of the ways in which I have hated it and all of the unsafe places I have dragged it through. I always thought that she made better choices; that I was bad for disappearing, for wanting too much, more than I deserve. Tara stayed within the bounds of her world and I struck out into danger, taking too many careless risks. It doesn't seem fair that her life is in crisis and I am here in the cloying heat, my life shot through with love and abundance and still it is not enough for me, still there is something in me that does not know how to have.

I wish that I could reach back through the years, find us smoking in some doorway in our tiny dresses, drunk, hungry and cold. I would step out of the shadows and stub out our cigarettes, grab us by the wrists and tell us that our bodies are valuable in ways we do not know. A teenage boy darts past and knocks into me, interrupting my thoughts. I reach out to steady myself and he laughs and darts away, without looking back.

78

When we were teenagers, Tara's parents were strict and she got into piercings to spite them, smuggling silver secrets beneath her clothes. She ringed her ears in stainless steel and put a metal bar through her tongue. One Saturday afternoon, before a night out, we went to a piercing shop in the centre of town and I held her hand as a man with stars tattooed across his knuckles put a ring through her nipple. I helped her bathe the puckered skin in salt water as we got ready in a rush, squeezing ourselves into bodycon dresses and drinking sickly glasses of rosé, rubbing instant tan across each other's shoulders and backcombing our hair with toothbrushes.

'God, I'm so bloated,' said Tara, looking at her stomach in the mirror.

'Don't be daft. You look gorgeous.'

Tara wrinkled her nose. 'I'll just get mortal. And then it won't matter.'

We smiled at the bouncer and tottered into the pub in

our platform heels, enjoying the power shimmering in our limbs as heads turned to watch us pass, youth dripping from our bodies like expensive jewellery. We knocked back our drinks quickly, aiming to get as drunk as possible. We liked to push our bodies to their limits, to feel the slap and sting of the night, to dangle over a brink and come back alive and dazzling. When we were drunk, we didn't care about anything. We let our wanting spill out of us, drowning everything in its path.

We did tequila shots until the walls rippled and we swayed on packed dancefloors, taking pictures with strangers, spilling beer down our dresses. Disco balls spun above our heads like planets and we felt as if we could dance forever, as though our bodies were boundless, the gold ends of our cigarettes like comets in the dark.

When the club closed, we skittered into the chip shop. We hadn't eaten all day and we were desperate for polystyrene cartons of ketchup and grease. Tara was standing in the queue beside me when her legs suddenly gave way beneath her. She buckled like a fawn and I caught her weight.

'Tara?' I gasped, steering her to a table. The man behind the counter passed us a bottle of water.

'She alright?'

Tara propped herself up on her elbow. 'I'm fine,' she slurred, peeling off a false eyelash. 'I just need to go home.'

I went outside and flagged a taxi. 'My friend's not very well,' I said to the driver. 'Can you help me get her in?'

The driver sighed and climbed out of his cab. 'She'd better not be sick in me car, mind. It's a fifty-quid fine.' He scooped Tara in his arms like a child and laid her across the back seat. I scrambled in after her, stroking her hair as the streetlamps scattered her face with light.

'I'm okay,' she smiled weakly, raising the bottle of water to her lips. 'Honestly.' She waved my worrying hands away. 'I'm fine.'

We woke up the next day squashed together in her single bed, our shoes and dresses strewn around the room.

'Have you seen my phone?' Tara clutched her head, mascara smudged across her face. I looked around half-heartedly, squinting through a haze of vodka and sweat. 'Shit,' she said. 'I think I must have lost it.'

'Not again,' I groaned. We were constantly losing our phones, our bank cards and our house keys. There were black holes in our memories and we got a kick out of piecing the night back together.

Later that afternoon, drinking luminous bottles of Lucozade in our dressing gowns, we logged onto Facebook on her dad's computer, to upload our pictures from the night before. Tara had a flurry of notifications, flashing and pulsing, making our heads sore.

'Oh my god.' She scrolled through her timeline. It was full of pictures of her new nipple piercing, taken from her phone and posted on her wall.

'*This slut was in my taxi last night,*' someone had captioned them. Fifty people had given it a thumbs-up.

'The taxi driver!' Tara shook her head. 'He must have taken my phone! And I was still logged in. What a dick.' I saved a screenshot of the pictures before she deleted them.

'We should have taken his number plate,' I said, but we couldn't even remember what the car looked like.

We downloaded the pictures of our night out from our digital cameras and laughed at them, shrieking at strangers we couldn't remember, our limbs at strange angles in clouds of dry ice. We edited them before uploading them to the internet, cropping out the parts of ourselves that we hated, turning up the exposure so our features were blanked out.

79

We walk up into the hills of Collserola, the air swollen with rosemary and pine, our bodies coated in dust and sweat. My eyes are puffy and my head aches. We stop to catch our breath on a crop of jagged rocks. I throw off my backpack and you lean forward to touch me but I pull away.

'Sorry,' I say. 'Too hot.'

You frown at me but I ignore you, unscrewing the lid from my water bottle and drinking thirstily. I look up at the clear sky, so pure it hurts my eyes. You pull a clump of sage from a bush and sniff it, rubbing it between your fingers.

'What's wrong?' you ask me, impatiently.

'Nothing.' I twist my hair away from my neck and tie it up in an elastic.

'There's obviously something.'

'Sorry. It's just – I found out something horrible. About a friend from school.'

'Oh.' You soften. 'What happened?' I don't know how to explain the white-hot horror of it; the image in my mind of Tara's small hands, a cigarette cocked between her fingers. I don't think you will understand the traces of my teenage self that are still cut through my blood.

'I don't really want to talk about it.'

'Okay.' You slip a silvery leaf into your pocket. 'Shall we keep walking?'

*

We climb higher and you talk about your research, telling me about the people you have been interviewing; collecting their migration stories and then translating them from Spanish to English.

'Are the translations difficult?' I ask you, trying to push Tara to the back of my mind.

'Sometimes. It's hard to get at exactly what the person means, instead of what I think they mean.'

'So how do you know if you're telling it right?'

'Well I don't, not completely.'

'So, what if you're telling it wrong?'

You take your water bottle out of your backpack and drink from it. 'I think it's better to tell the stories and get them a bit wrong, than not to tell them at all,' you say, shielding your eyes from the sun. I consider your words.

'But what if the story you're telling isn't true?'

'It's mostly true. It's just a handful of words that might be wrong. And memory is a kind of fiction anyway.'

'But the right words are important,' I say, thinking of my faltering Spanish and how I cannot always ask for what I need, remembering all of the things I have swallowed and trying to imagine the kinds of words that might set them free. You look at me warily, wiping sweat from your forehead.

'Yeah. They are.'

We are quiet as we walk into a cluster of trees, grateful for the shade. My thoughts drift back to Tara, wondering how she is doing and if she might die, whether I should send her a message, what I could possibly say. We find a clearing and sit down in the scorched grass.

'Shall we have lunch?' you ask and I nod but I am not hungry. You have brought us sandwiches wrapped in foil and I pick at mine, pulling the cheese and tomatoes from inside and discarding the bread.

'Aren't you going to eat that?' you ask me.

'Not that hungry.'

'Maybe you should try?'

'I said I'm not hungry.' I lie back in the grass and close my eyes, the trees casting cool shadows across my face. My stomach has been tight and tense for the past few days and I can feel the old rules closing in on me, squeezing out the light, but I am too tired to push them away.

I keep thinking about Tara. I feel too close to my seventeen-year-old self, as though she has opened her mouth across the years and swallowed all of the women I have been since then. I can see how vulnerable we were in ways we did not understand at the time and I wonder why we did not care for ourselves or feel worthy of being looked after. I feel guilty for being caught up in my own decisions, when Tara no longer has a choice, and it feels right somehow to empty myself, to have something to hold on to.

You lie down beside me, resting your palm on my stomach, tracing my shoulder with your fingertips. You kiss me slowly, your dark hair falling into my eyes, smelling of fresh grass and burnt wood. You press your body close to mine and I give myself over to you but I feel far away from your damp skin and warm breath. I close my eyes and see Tara's name written on the backs of my eyelids in hospital colours, the flash of our teenage bodies in sequin minidresses, her bleached hair strobing in the dark. I want to ask her if she remembers how it felt when we were invincible, when we were almost weightless and the night opened up around us like dark water, when our actions didn't have any consequences because the future was so far away, some distant, grown-up dream. I am afraid that we have ended up in the wrong story, that we took a bad turn somewhere, that we need to go back and start again so that it all might turn out differently. I look up at your face silhouetted against the sky and the weight of all that blue presses down on me, filling my throat.

'Fuck,' you gasp, lying back in the grass, but my body feels numb and your voice too quiet, a lost word spinning in the air between us like an old coin in a dead currency.

80

Louis introduced me to his friends. They hosted sprawling parties in white-walled apartments hung with Matisse prints and clustered with overflowing ashtrays and vases of peonies, records stacked in piles on the wooden floor-boards. I felt clumsy around them in my second-hand dresses with my uncertain syllables but they drew me in, asking my opinions with wine-dark lips, holding their cigarettes too close to my face.

One Saturday night, we were invited to someone's apartment for dinner. Tall black candles dripped onto the table as I pushed fragrant rice around my plate. A woman with long, red hair and dark lipstick sat next to me, topping up my wine without asking, smiling generously when I thanked her.

'Why aren't you eating, *chérie*?' She gestured towards my plate.

Louis intervened from across the table. 'She never eats very much.' I tensed my legs.

'No?' She looked at me, curiously. 'Why not?'

'What do you mean?'

'Why don't you eat much?' I looked at her elegant fingers cocked around her wine glass, the flowers shedding pink petals, the shadows of hands and faces flickering across the walls. No one had ever asked me why, directly, like that. The room was dense with cloves and cinnamon. A scratchy Tom Waits record played in the corner. I looked at the dirty plates pushed carelessly to one side, drops of red wine seeping into the linen tablecloth like blood and I didn't know the answer. In that room, there was no reason why I wouldn't want to take the world inside me, to fill myself up on it, without worry or fear. There was nothing sharp or dangerous, nothing edge-close, no choking, smoky hole for me to throw myself into.

'I don't know,' I said, quietly.

'You don't know?'

I shook my head. The woman shrugged and topped up my wine and I drank all of it and then asked for more.

81

The city sizzles. Exhaust fumes form a rind above the buildings, trapping burnt air in the concrete. The sky feels heavy, pressing into our backs and crushing our lungs. The beaches are packed with sunburnt bodies slick with baby oil, plastic cups and cigarette butts crumpled in the burning sand. Peaches and nectarines rot outside of fruit shops, mangoes melting beneath their skins.

The colours grow sickly and over-saturated. Palm trees spike the relentless blue. We wander around super-markets without buying anything, just to feel the relief of the air-conditioning. We lie on the apartment floor in our underwear, pressing our clammy bodies into the cool tiles. I don't have much of an appetite and the streets swim before me, rippling and viscous. Everyone is weary and fractious, strangers shouting at each other in the street, people revving their mopeds angrily, dogs barking in the night.

You are finding it difficult to work in the heat and you grow snappy and irritable, your heavy mood seeping into the corners of the apartment like a sour smell.

'Do you want to go to the beach?' I ask, pacing the stuffy kitchen and eyeing you cautiously. 'Maybe we should go for a walk.'

'I've got to finish this.' Your face looks tired in the white glare of your screen.

'What about afterwards? We could go for a drink?'

'Sorry.' You snap your laptop shut and take it into the bedroom. 'I just need some space to think.'

I buy a huge watermelon from the fruit shop and carve it into ruby chunks, arranging mozzarella in a flower and drizzling it in oil. You eat silently, scrolling through your phone.

'Are you okay?' I ask you, gently.

'I'm fine,' you snap. 'Stop asking.'

'You don't seem fine.'

'I said I'm fine.'

'Okay.'

It is too hot to sleep and we walk the streets until we find a late-night bar selling cold vermouth. We sit on the kerb with our feet in the gutter, pulling our hair away from our damp faces.

'How do people bear it?' I ask you, looking up at the dark apartments around the square with their shutters tightly closed, imagining people sleeping peacefully behind them.

'They probably have air-con,' you say moodily, shoving your hands in your pockets, clouds gathering behind your eyes.

'Why don't we have air-con?' I sigh.

'Sorry the apartment's not up to your standards.'

'What's that supposed to mean?'

'I don't know. I'm tired. Sorry.'

We sit in silence. Voices echo between buildings, bouncing off the old stone walls. I look at the sliver of crescent moon and try to think about how cold it is in space but I can't imagine it.

'What's the matter with you?' I ask.

'What do you mean?'

'Why are you being like this?'

'Like what?' You exhale and close your eyes. I don't know what is wrong with you and I cannot explain the fear and frustration in my own belly, my thoughts turning rings around Tara and how badly we once wished ourselves away. I don't know how to put my sadness into words; all the ways in which we believed we needed to be smaller in order to have presence in the world. I can see how mistaken we were but I cannot go back and change it or make her better. Your eyes are still closed and I touch your shoulder.

'What are you thinking?'

'Nothing.' You blink at me.

'It's not nothing.'

'Just leave it.' Your voice is taut. We watch a group of teenagers wheel their bikes across the square, laughing and joking. You rub your face and then fumble in your pocket for your tobacco.

'I don't know what's happening to us,' I say, sadly.

You lick your Rizla without looking at me. 'Maybe we should spend a bit of time apart.'

'What?' Fear flickers in my chest. I have been trying to find more space for myself but I don't want to lose you in the process.

'I can't think straight,' you say, looking at the pavement. 'I can't think in the heat, with both of us in the apartment. You make me feel like I've done something wrong all of the time.'

I swallow. 'What do you mean?'

Your words come thick and fast, as though you have been holding them in. 'I know you don't know what you want but I want to be here. It's important for me.' You blow a plume of smoke above our heads and a muscle in your neck twitches. 'Things might be clearer if we have a bit of space for a couple of weeks. So we can both think about what we want.'

'Right.' Panic razes my body like a rash. I opened myself up for you, abandoning the life in London that belonged only to me and now you are pushing me away. I feel rejected, as though I am an inconvenience in your apartment, making me want to pack up and leave. We sit in fraught silence, then you turn to me and your face softens.

'I'm not saying we should break up. It's just so hot and I've got so much work to do. You're obviously not happy and it feels like we're going in circles.' I think about my clothes hanging in your wardrobe and my jackets on the back of your door. I thought it was okay for me to exist here, that I didn't have to make myself smaller or tidy myself away.

'I'll go in the morning, then.' I stand up to leave.

'You don't need to be like that. It's not urgent. I just need a bit of space.'

I am quiet, thinking of all of the space you have here and wondering where I can stay. 'Okay,' I say and then turn and walk away.

You call after me but I move across the square and around the corner, until I am out of your sight, then I sink onto a bench with a sharp, stinging headache. I feel detached from you, careless, as though I could crush everything between us, daring myself to break it, just to see what happens. My thoughts are thick and heavy in the heat and I can't make sense of what you are asking me. I thought we understood each other but I am beginning to wonder if that is true.

I pull my phone from my pocket and think about sending you a message but I look at Tara's Instagram pictures again instead. She has uploaded a photo of a huge bouquet of roses with the caption, *'thankyou x'*. I want to ask her if we were ever really impenetrable or if it was all an illusion, if our bodies were this fragile all along. I press the button that makes a red heart glow beneath her picture, then I quickly press it again and the colour disappears.

82

I came out of my building in Paris one morning to find my bike had been stolen, the cheap lock swinging from its hinges. I swore under my breath and texted the children's mother to let her know I would be late.

'*Dépêchez-vous*,' she replied. '*I have a meeting at 9.*'

Rain lashed the streets with silver as I ran to the metro, stale air and the smell of burning rubber rushing to meet me. It was busy and I clung to the metal rail above my head with one hand, pressed into the thick, shiny hair and heavy perfume of the woman next to me, being careful not to lean on an old man with deep jowls and a dirty raincoat. I counted down the stops impatiently, trying to shake the sleep from my eyes, worrying about how to replace my bike.

I felt something brush against my back and I leaned away from the old man, being careful not to step on his toes. I felt the sensation again and I turned around as the train swung around the corner and the brakes screeched. People winced and covered their ears and the old man fell into me, reaching out both hands and grabbing my breasts.

'What the fuck?' I said in English, pushing him away, but he just looked at me, disgruntled, as if nothing had happened. I tried to move further down the carriage but the train was packed. The woman with the shiny hair shot me a look, sighing and adjusting her handbag, indicating I should stay put. I avoided looking at the man. I didn't feel afraid of him; he was old and almost frail but I couldn't believe his audacity, that he had just reached out and groped my body in a small space full of strangers and no one had said a word.

I was late to the children's house and their mother missed her meeting.

'It's fine,' she said, strapping on her heels and rattling her car keys as I apologised, rushing out of the front door without a second glance.

'You're not pretty,' said Léa sulkily, eyeballing my damp shoes and my rain-soaked jacket.

'I don't care, Léa.' I started clearing away the breakfast bowls.

'*Tu devrais.*' She spun around in her glittery princess dress. Alec laughed and repeated her words in English.

'You *should.*'

83

Carla's flatmate is visiting her family outside Barcelona for a couple of weeks and she says I can stay in her room until she comes back. I take the metro to Sants and climb the stairs to their apartment with my backpack, feeling deflated. I am grateful to have a place to go but I don't want to live like this any more, moving between places, always living in borrowed space. I feel knotted and sore when I think of you, as though I have dropped something small and precious, lost in the infinite sand.

Carla is on her way out when I arrive and she gives me a hug.

'It will be okay, *preciosa.*' She picks up her keys and they jangle. 'Help yourself to anything. There's food in the fridge.'

I hear the front door slam and I look around Carla's apartment at the postcards stuck on the fridge and the bright cotton tablecloth laid neatly over the table, the windowsills crammed with plants in painted pots. Her things are homely and familiar but they do not belong to me. I picture your haphazard pans, your books and papers spilling over the floor and feel a pang, yet those things are not mine, either. I feel dirty and sour, as though I tainted your apartment like a stain.

I listen to the sounds of other people in the building; a baby crying, a television blaring, glasses clinking, laughter caught in the swelter. I don't want to be here alone with my thoughts, so I shove my backpack in the corner of my temporary bedroom, ignoring the wardrobe crammed with someone else's clothes, and I walk to the beach.

It is quiet, groups of teenagers huddled on blankets playing Rosalía from their phones, waving their cigarettes in the dark. Drunk couples kiss in the sand and I slip off my clothes and walk towards the black water, silvered in the trail of the moon. The sea is cold and the waves lap against my bare stomach, making me wince. The water is like mercury in the moonlight, filled with things I cannot see. I swim right out, far away from the shore, trusting my body to carry me. The sky tumbles over me like a reel of dark silk and I am lost in the blackness, unable to tell the difference between land and sea. The city lights glimmer beyond the shore like a distant constellation, far from my grasp.

I imagine you chopping vegetables alone and sadness blooms in me, dragging me down. I feel careless, as though I neglected our goodness and did not hold on tightly enough. I understand your desire for space but it seems unfair when you have your own apartment to stretch out into and I still have nowhere of my own. You want me to move my whole life here for you and you want it seamlessly, without fear or uncertainty, without any of it weighing too heavily on you. Once, I might have accepted that but I am trying to speak more loudly, to voice my needs.

I think about how easy it would be to stop swimming,

to slip beneath the cold water and sink to the sea bed and I am afraid. I don't want to disappear. I want to live in the world without feeling guilty about my needs or wants, to let them move through me in their animal heat. I don't know why there is an impulse in me that chases every good thing with a punishment, but I don't want to feel it any more. I don't want to be punished, denied or debased. I want joy and pleasure, beauty and sensation and I want them without feeling bad about it. I kick my legs hard, splashing and panting, and I make my way back to the shore.

84

I told Louis about the man on the train.

'*Putain*,' he said. 'Paris is full of old men like this. You should not travel on the train when it is busy like that.'

'But my bike got stolen.'

'You should have called me. I would have picked you up.' I didn't want Louis to pick me up and drive me to work. I wanted to make my own way around the city, to go wherever I felt like, without having to rely on anyone else.

The children had a virus and I caught it washing their cups and plates and changing their bedsheets. I stayed in bed for three days, sweating and shivering, coughing until my chest ached.

'*Arrête!*' The old lady who shared my corridor banged on my door. 'I cannot sleep for your coughing. *Un peu de calme s'il vous plait.*' After four days had passed, the children's mother called.

'We need you,' she said. 'Are you well enough to come to work?' My mouth was dry and my muscles were sore. I sat on the edge of my bed and looked around my tiny room at the stack of dishes in the sink, my clothes bursting out of my suitcase on the floor. The attic had seemed romantic in the beginning, but I was starting to wonder if I deserved something more.

'*Je suis désolée.*' I brushed my hair out of my eyes. 'I need to take the rest of the week off.' I heard Alec crying in the background and the children's mother sighed.

'Okay,' she said. 'But we cannot pay you for this week. I hope you understand.'

It was a bright day and sunlight streamed through my little window, illuminating the dust motes like specks of glitter. I pulled on a jumper and went out into the corridor. There was no one around and I propped the ladder up against the wall and climbed up to the trapdoor that opened onto the roof. I had never gone up there before but I had wondered about it often. Some of the buildings in Paris had flat roofs and people sat up there, drinking wine and looking at the city sprawling below them. My body felt weak but I pulled myself up through the opening, feeling warm light on my face.

I inched my way carefully across the flat tiles and sat right on the edge of the roof, with my legs dangling over the city. The purple-grey rooftops stretched into the distance and the traffic flashed below me in the sun. I looked down at the fruit shops, the cafés, people parking their bikes on the pavements and I felt removed from it all.

I wanted to feel the way I did at the party with Louis, talking to the woman with red hair, the way she filled my glass so easily and I drank it, not to escape myself but because the world around us felt safe and I wanted to be part of it. I was so tired of the rules and the secrets, all the running and the lies. I wanted to have a whole life somewhere, to live deeply instead of just grazing the surface. I was insignificant in Paris and I didn't want to be small any more.

My phone vibrated in my pocket and I pulled it out. Rosa had sent me a link to a room that a friend was subletting in London. I zoomed in on it, stroking the white walls, wooden floors and big windows. I wondered if I could learn to be a different person there, to stretch out in the sunlight streaming through the curtains, to hang up my clothes and organise my life.

I stayed up on the roof until the sun bled violet over the city, feeling the familiar yearning in me as I looked at the sprawl of it, the possibility of all the different kinds of people I could be. I remembered how I felt when I first moved to London, as though my life was finally beginning, but I was starting to wonder if there was really such a thing as possibility or if it was all just an unobtainable dream.

I had come to Paris to choose my own life but I couldn't truly choose because there were not many options available to me. I didn't have enough money or a proper place to live or a university degree. I had tried so hard to become another person, but beneath it I was always just me. I had to find a way to live with that girl, to give her what she needed. I thought freedom was the chance to become anyone, but I was beginning to think I had been wrong. I needed to learn how to look at the woman inside me without flinching, learn how to feed her and care for her, to recognise her as me.

85

I have been staying with Carla for a week and I have not heard anything from you. My sadness coils into anger, hard and metallic. I am trying to give you space but it seems unfair that you are making the decisions. I am here because you asked me to come with you, but now you are pushing me away.

'I think he is afraid,' says Carla and I shake my head.

'Afraid of what?'

She shrugs and passes me a beer. 'You don't need him, *guapa*. You can make your own life here.'

All summer, the city erupts in street parties. Every weekend, residents of different barrios twist coloured lights around their balconies and string paper streamers between lampposts, chandeliers made from plastic bottles dangling from the sky. Stages are constructed between apartment blocks and throngs of people spill into the swelter, stamping their feet to reggaeton and pop punk covers. Drag queens blow into saxophones, wearing blonde wigs and leopard-print dresses, pressing the keys with glow-in-the-dark false nails. Karaoke screens are hoisted and DJs hook up their laptops as anarchists dance in hiking boots and older women sit on fold-out chairs beneath their apartments, yellow ribbons calling for the release of political prisoners pinned to their diamanté T-shirts. Toddlers are slung onto shoulders above the crowds, disco lights bouncing off their plastic dummies. Street sellers tout cold beers from the kerbside and people light sparklers in the dark, firecrackers exploding in the gutters.

*

On the afternoon of the Festa Major de Sants, Carla's apartment echoes with the clanging of stages being hammered into place and the low hum of voices as people begin to trickle into the bars along the street. The air is cloying and we open all of the doors and windows to try and coax a breeze. I am looking forward to dancing, unspooling the knot that is twisted inside me. I buy bottles of cava at the supermarket and wedge them in the freezer, filling the ice-cube trays and dripping water onto my bare feet.

My phone bleeps with a message from you.

'*I miss you,*' it says and I am pleased that you want me but my stomach tightens in frustration. I can feel myself sealing up in fear of getting hurt again. You cannot just cut me out and then change your mind. My mouth is dry with anger but I still want to see you, to run my fingers over your summer skin, to feel your bottom lip between my teeth.

'*Going to the Festa Major in Sants tonight,*' I write. '*Do you want to come?*'

You do not reply for a couple of hours and I check my phone anxiously, over and over again.

'*I've got some work to finish,*' you finally send. '*Can I let you know later?*'

My throat clenches in irritation but I reply, '*Okay.*' Spiked energy flickers inside me, barbed and bitter.

Carla and I get ready together, drinking vermouth mixed with fizzy wine and dancing in the tiny kitchen. I pull on a light, short dress, dusting gold glitter across my cheeks and painting my lips red. My hair is static in the humidity and I clip it away from my face, drawing black cat-eyes across my lids and velcroing my sandals. I still have not heard from you and I feel reckless, cresting on the brink of something, looking for trouble, the night rolling in to meet me like a wave.

'Forget him,' says Carla, kissing my cheek and leaving the dark imprint of her lips on my skin. 'We will have a good time tonight.' She sprays her neck with perfume and shoves a twenty-euro note in her bra. She checks the time and grabs my arm. '*Vamos*. Elena is waiting. We are already late.'

The streets are viscous with heat and piss, bodies spilling from doorways, wrapped in sickly tendrils of weed. We wind through the crowd, arm in arm, and find Elena sitting on a stack of plastic crates outside a bar in a pool of yellow light, tattoos curling around her forearms, her nose ring glinting in the dusk.

'*Buenas*,' she purrs in her deep voice, kissing my cheeks. I can smell her bitter sweat and the stale, yeasty hops on her breath. She asks if I have heard from you and I take out my phone and find nothing.

'He said he might meet us later.'

Elena rolls her eyes. 'He will? Or he might?'

'He might.'

'Fuck him,' she snorts. 'Do you want a beer?'

We sit outside the bar and watch the night glitter. Bass hits the pavement and the streets throb with bodies, exposed limbs and damp, flushed faces, voices weaving around us like a song. We finish our beers and pass the bottle of cava between us, our lipstick mingling on the plastic rim. I haven't eaten much all day and there is a tight, fizzy feeling in my head. I can sense a redness building, the lure of abandon, the old pull of danger tugging at my hair.

Elena splits a pill and offers us each a quarter.

'*Salud*,' winks Carla, taking hers eagerly and placing it in the centre of her tongue. I look at the wet prickle of her tastebuds and wish that you were here, then I shake the thought away. I want to make a decision about my body, to prove to myself that it belongs to me. I hold out my hand and then swallow quickly, washing the chalky taste away with a swig of cava.

'Okay.' Elena stands up, stubbing out her cigarette. '*Vamos.*'

We move into the throng of bodies. The music drags us into the centre of the crowd, opening like a wet mouth and swallowing us whole. Bodies pack the streets like a river about to burst and I am pushed up against strangers, writhing and stamping their feet, flashes of tongues and teeth, a gathering storm. I close my eyes and let it rush through me, my gums dry, hands sweating, a dazzle of coloured lights falling around me like rain.

I have been feeling so rigid, caught in the shape of you, but now I am spilling over my own outline, shattering my boundaries like a broken dam. Joy pools in my mouth and I remember how it felt when I was swimming in the black water, how badly I wanted to reach out and touch pleasure. I open my eyes and Carla and Elena are dancing around me, taking me by the hands and spinning in circles. The crowd generates a current and we lean back and let it take us, suspending us above the pavement, swollen with heat.

A man with dark eyes and a smoky, musky feeling dances next to me, his skin copper in the gold streetlights, sweat beading on his bare shoulders, bangles jangling on his wrists. I can smell the ache on him and I want to step into it, to hold it in my lungs. We dance closer, until we are only hips and eyes and lips. I want to put another body between yours and mine, to remember how to be my own person. I don't want to hurt you but I want to assert myself, to remember who I was when the nights glinted with danger and I ran into them, hurtling towards colour and light.

The man leans in to kiss me and I kiss him back, falling into the thick, torrid feeling, letting it pour into my mouth. I am so tired of being shadowy and translucent, of running away from myself, being unable to make myself heard. I move deeper into the acrid heat, wanting to be filled by it, smothered by the hot night and the frantic, slippery beat. I want to claim presence in the world, to reach for things and see ripples around me, evidence that I exist. The man presses his body close to mine and there is a thrill in breaking the boundaries we have built together, remembering the pull of the world before I met you, how it felt to live on adrenaline, precarious and raw. I feel a hand on my shoulder and ignore it, but then it comes again more urgently and I hear Carla and Elena saying your name.

I break away from the man and see you looking straight at me, deep shadows beneath your eyes but still beautiful in your sparkly shirt and silver earring, hurt twisting your mouth like a crushed flower. I look back at you with a jolt and Carla and Elena furrow their brows, caught between dancing and consternation, throwing their arms in the air. You turn to leave and I lunge after you.

'Stay here,' I shout to my friends above the music. 'I'll come back and find you.'

I push my way through the heat and smoke, stumbling over boots and trainers, searching for the flash of your body in the dark. Faces loom red as I reach for you but you move faster, tearing out of my grasp.

'Wait,' I gasp as we reach the edge of a crowd and you spin around to face me. Your eyes flash with something broken I have never seen before.

'What the fuck?' You hold up your hands. 'What the fuck were you doing?' I try to focus but the world is spinning around me, a blur of sound and neon.

'You didn't reply,' I gasp. 'I didn't know if you were coming.' You look wild and vulnerable and I try to reach out and touch you but you pull away, leaving me dizzy and grasping, loose in the world.

'I'm sorry,' I breathe. 'But you asked me to leave.'

'I said I needed space.'

'Well, I'm giving you space.'

You back away from me. 'You're unbelievable.'

'What?'

'All I've done for the past few months is support you, tiptoeing around you, listening to you talk. And then while I'm sitting in the apartment, rushing my work so I can come and meet you, you're—'

'Right. Because it's all about you and your work, isn't it? Making sacrifices for people. Holding everyone up.'

'Fuck off. You just do whatever you want, without thinking about anyone else.' I close my eyes and the world speeds up. I am so tired of the heat and the sting of my skin, the crushing mass of the rules that I am carrying. I am tired of being hungry, holding secrets in my belly, tired of trying to do the right thing. You stare at me and I feel sickly looking at your ashen face.

'I'm sorry that I'm too much for you,' I say, sharply. You shake your head incredulously and I wonder if you really think I just do whatever I want. That is the opposite of how I have lived and I thought you understood that. I wonder if we really know each other at all or if it has just been an illusion, a falsehood, a mistake. I turn and walk away from you and your anger, heading into the night.

'Wait.' You reach out and grab my arm. 'Don't go off alone.' Your voice softens. 'I'm upset but I can't leave you to go off like this. You need to be with someone.'

'Don't worry.' I wrestle out of your grasp as the world lurches around me. 'I can look after myself.'

I walk away from the party, dodging drunk teenagers, bikes locked to lampposts, people congregating outside pizza shops. There is a high-pitched noise in my head and I need to get away from it, the clamour of my thoughts and the echo of your voice, the heat and the noise and the people, everything soaked in red. There is a taxi waiting by the kerb and I open the door and climb into it, resting my head against the leather seat.

'*¿A dónde?*' asks the driver and I tell him to take me to the coach station without thinking about what I am doing.

'*Vale*,' he shrugs and turns the air-conditioning up. The cold air soothes me, a respite from the unrelenting heat. I need to be somewhere cooler and quieter, where I can think clearly. I picture the cabin in the mountains, the wet grass and cold stars.

At the station, I buy a ticket for Tremp and send a garbled message to Maria, asking if the cabin is free. I fall asleep on the bus before she answers, my head pressed against the window, my body jittering and sore. I wake to dawn over the mountains, the rust-coloured hills looming in the distance, the day seeping into the sky like blood in milk.

Part Four

Part Four

86

Maria picks me up from the bus station in her beaten-up truck. Soft rock blares from the crackly radio, rosary beads swinging from the rear-view mirror. She is unfazed by my tired face and the tiny leather backpack slung over my shoulder.

'I'm so sorry for turning up like this,' I say, hardly daring to look at her. 'I'll give you the money as soon as I can. I just need a few days to work some things out.'

'You're lucky the place is free,' she shrugs as I clamber onto the dusty seat beside her. 'I am usually full at this time of year but I took it off the internet for a couple of weeks so I could fix some problems with the water and the electricity.' She holds the steering wheel with one hand, fumbling in the glove compartment for a cigarette. 'You can help me, now you are here. My sons are in Sevilla with their girlfriends.' She shakes her head. 'I could do with, how do you say? *Un par de manos extra.*' She swerves suddenly onto a small side road, swearing as a lorry sounds its horn.

I rub my eyes and wind down the window, feeling queasy as the truck lurches along winding roads, the familiar stone church in the nearby town rising before us. The world is blurry and I am afraid I have put events in motion that are out of my control. I run through the events of last night in my head and feel sick with guilt. I swallow, remembering the man with the musky smell and your pale face in the crowd. I feel angry with you but everything is confusing, my emotions wrought with chemicals and wrung with lack of sleep. I know you will be worried about me and I take out my phone to send you a message but the battery is drained and the screen is black. Maria pulls up outside the cabin.

'*Estamos aquí.*'

'*Muchas gracias, Maria.*' I jump out of the truck onto the soft earth.

'*De nada.* Take whatever you need. I will come in the morning to look at the electricity. There is no light now, but you will be okay.'

Maria drives off across the fields and I open the door of the little cabin. The smell of wood and charcoal curls around my body. I go into the bedroom and flop onto the bed, grateful to be out of the sun. My eyes are blurry and my whole body aches. I bury my face in the thin blanket, remembering our bodies together beneath it, how hungry I felt for the whole of you and how far away that seems now. Regret swells in my chest but I am also relieved to be alone with my own thoughts, in a space that is only mine.

I fall asleep and wake hours later in the blue dusk, my mouth dry and my stomach twisted in hunger. The cabin is stuffy and I open the front door and find a bucket filled with firelighters, a bottle of wine, a baguette and a hunk of soft goat's cheese wrapped in brown paper. Guilt flares in my gut at Maria's kindness. I light a couple of candles and put them on the table outside, watching insects hover around the flames.

I turn on the tap and drink a pint of lukewarm water

standing up, letting the droplets run down my chin and soak into my clothes. My dress smells of smoke and sweat and I pull it over my head and stand on the wooden porch in my underwear, the mountain air soothing my clammy skin.

I sit on the decking and pull chunks from the baguette, smearing them in goat's cheese and eating quickly, the dough and yeast filling me up, softening the spiked edges of my anxious thoughts. I can smell scorched earth and wild rosemary, the heat of the day caught in the wood, smoke from someone's fire drifting over the fields. The stars glitter like broken glass and I remember when we lay beneath the full moon and you said it was an omen. I lick goat's cheese from my fingers, my appetite returning, my body free and wanting, alone beneath the sky. I lie on my back and notice one of Maria's cigarettes, abandoned on the edge of the table. I find a match and light it, lying back and looking up at the mountains, blowing wisps of smoke above my face. I inhale deeply, feeling the tar scorch my lungs, tasting salt on my lips. I run my hands over my stomach and hips, feeling skin, fat and bone beneath my fingertips, part of the world with its trees and tobacco, a person among it, human after all.

87

I left Paris and moved back to London. My sublet room had a wooden floor and a woven rug, left by the previous tenant. It was average-sized but it felt impossibly huge after my tiny attic. I slept with the curtains open, letting the daylight soak into my pillow, taking long, hot showers, delighting in the warm water gushing from the toothpaste-splattered taps.

My new housemates worked in bars, cafés and as bike couriers and we all had different schedules, which meant there was always someone sitting at the kitchen table, making cups of tea or drinking cans of beer. There were boxes of zines stacked in the hallway and flyers from punk gigs tacked to the bathroom walls. There was a row of plants on the kitchen windowsill and I took great care to water them, delighting in their green fronds reaching towards the sunlight, making sure the soil was always moist and they did not get too cold. My housemates liked to cook, simmering vegetable chilis and spicy curries in a big silver pot, leaving notes that read,

'*Help yourself.*'

Someone had carved *Riots not Diets* into the wooden cooking spoon and I traced my fingers over the letters as I spooned rice into a bowl and forced myself to eat it, feeling like a failure, crushed by the weight of everything I was supposed to be pushing against.

London was full of ghosts. Bars and cafés that I used to go to had closed down and been replaced with something new. I saw my younger self everywhere, standing on street corners with bruises on her bare legs, searching for doors that no longer existed, her hair tangled and her eyes blank with hunger. I shrank from her, caught between wanting to take her by the hand and run her a hot bath and being desperate to put as much distance between us as possible, so that her shame and self-loathing didn't rub off on me.

88

I sleep late and wake to muggy air, my head foggy and my skin tight. I find a jar of old coffee granules on the shelf and boil a pan of water on the gas stove. I open the cabin door and find Maria crouched outside it, fiddling with a tangle of wires.

'*Buenos días,*' I say to her in surprise. '*Gracias por el pan y el queso.*' I slip on my dirty dress and go outside, feeling the rough grass between my toes. I watch Maria for a moment, deep in concentration, noticing the swell of her biceps in her paint-stained T-shirt, a rotting friendship bracelet strung around her wrist.

'Can you pass me *los alicates*? The thing to cut the wires?'

'*¿Dónde está?*'

'In the black bag.' I find a dirty black tool bag on the old wooden table and root around in it for the wire cutters. Maria fiddles with something and swears.

'Where did you learn to do all of this?' I ask her.

'All of what?' she replies, without looking at me.

'Electrics. Plumbing. Building your own house.'

She pulls a pencil from behind her ear and jots something down in a crumpled notebook. 'I squatted for some years in Madrid. I learned things there. Can you turn on the light?'

'What?'

'Inside. See if it works.' I press my finger to the switch and the kitchen light flickers on, illuminating layers of dust.

'It works!'

'*Molt bé.*' She begins packing her tools away. 'I had a partner,' she says, without looking at me. 'We came here to build this house together. But things got bad. We finished.'

'Oh. What happened?'

'He went back to France. I was pregnant with my second child when he left. But I decided to stay.' I look around at the grapevines curling around wooden trellises, the over-grown garden, the large sculptures, the red rocks jutting against the sky. I try to imagine how it would feel to sleep beneath a roof that I built myself, to have touched every brick, tile and piece of wood, to know that all of it belongs to me.

'It's beautiful,' I say and Maria laughs.

'It is falling apart. But it is my home.' She looks at me properly for the first time. I am self-conscious of my dirty clothes and smudged make-up, reeking of alcohol and sweat.

'So, where is your boyfriend?'

My throat tenses and I avoid her gaze. 'In Barcelona.'

'Does he know you are here?'

'Not really.'

'What do you mean, not really?'

'No. He doesn't know.' She stares at me. My throat feels tight and my skin is burning before the sun is even high in the sky. Maria shakes her head and throws her tool bag over her shoulder as if it is made of air.

'You are safe here,' she says. 'But you cannot just run away.' She shields her eyes from the light and a sadness passes over her face. I try to smile at her, feeling small and chastened, like a child. She brushes her hair from her eyes.

'Do you want to swim later?' she asks me. 'There is *el barranco* close to here. I go there often with my neighbour. We will drive this afternoon if you want to come.' I picture the cool water and feel weak with longing.

'That would be very nice.'

Maria nods. 'We will pick you up.'

'Thanks for fixing the electricity.'

'*De nada*,' she shrugs and I watch her strong figure cut across the fields.

She seems like she can handle anything, plumbing her toilet and wiring her electricity, defining the parameters of her own world. I wonder what she ran away from and why she decided to stay here, what it was like bringing up two children here alone. I can't imagine her in the city, sitting in a bar or taking the metro. I wonder whether she was always like this or if she grew to fit her surroundings, whether we define our spaces or if they shape us and what that means for me.

I charge my phone and turn it on with a sickness in my stomach. I have fifteen missed calls, three messages from Carla, two from Elena and seven from you. I need to call work and tell them I won't be coming in tomorrow. I scroll through your messages, chewing my lip.

'*Where are you?*'

'*Are you ok?*'

'*Wtf?*'

'*Why aren't you answering?*'

'*Call me.*'

'*Please.*'

'*I'm worried.*'

Elena says, '*¿Preciosa, dónde estas? We are looking for you.*' I rub my eyes. My actions seem melodramatic in the light of a new day and I am embarrassed. I don't know what to say.

'*I'm at Maria's cabin,*' I write to you. '*In the mountains. I'm sorry. I'm ok.*'

You reply immediately. '*Are you serious?*' The dots that mean you are typing flicker on and off for a long time.

'*I'm sorry,*' I type again. '*Can we talk on the phone later?*'

I am still smarting from your words at the fiesta, afraid that I have broken something that cannot be fixed, as if I crumpled all of the goodness between us in my fist like it was nothing, unable to hold on to any of it after all. Yet, I need you to understand that it is important for me to know what I want and to be able to reach out and take it, after years of being unable to answer the question of exactly what it is. I look at your picture while you type a reply, your serious grey eyes and the trees behind you, green and gold falling across your face.

'*Ok,*' you write and I wait for more but nothing comes.

'*Ok,*' I reply. '*Speak soon.*'

89

Rosa had a solo exhibition at a gallery in Peckham. I found her standing by her biggest painting, dripping with a red so bright it was almost painful.

'You're here!' She pressed a cup of warm white wine into my hand. She leaned close to me and her hair smelled of paint and cigarettes. I looked up at her work on the walls. I was always impressed by the way she could twist her feelings into shape and colour so she didn't have to hold them any more. A tall man in a black turtle-neck came over and whisked her away to have her photo taken.

'I'll come and find you,' Rosa mouthed over her shoulder and I nodded. I scanned the crowd in their long leather jackets and neon eyeshadow, looking for someone I knew.

I felt self-conscious and knocked back my wine quickly, trying to find something to do. I bumped into Max, leaning against a wall with his hands in his pockets.

'Want to come for a smoke with me?' he asked, heading for the door and I followed him.

We sat on the street kerb with our feet in the gutter.

'How is it being back in London?' asked Max.

'Yeah, alright. Just finding my feet.'

Someone I didn't recognise came over and asked us for a light. I took in a tangle of dark curls and a torn denim jacket, a tattoo of a fern spilling from the cuff.

'Here.' I passed over Max's lighter and you looked at me and said,

'Thanks.'

90

We drive through tunnels cut straight through the mountains to Mont-rebei, a jade-green gorge carved between jagged cliff faces like a scar, brightly coloured kayaks bobbing on the surface. Maria, her neighbour Diego and I climb a steep path in the hot sun and then scramble down to the water. People dive from a wooden jetty, their bare bodies gleaming in the sun. There is a suspension bridge strung high between the cliffs and teenagers throw themselves off it, their screams caught in the hollows of the rocks.

I am itchy with dust and sweat and I pull off my clothes hurriedly. My stomach tenses as I remember that I don't have a swimming costume but Maria strips naked before me, her tan lines stark against her deep brown arms. I hesitate for a moment and then unclasp my bra, remembering how I felt when I was eating the goat's cheese outside the cabin, as though my body was merely a thing in the world. Diego discards his shirt and lies back on the rocks like a cat, closing his eyes, a cigarette hanging loosely between his fingers.

Maria dives smoothly into the gorge, barely making a ripple. I jump in after her and the cool relief makes me tingle with pleasure. The water is thick and murky, like blue milk, and I propel myself forward, stretching myself out. I aim towards the mountains in the distance and everything is surreal, as though the world has split from its axis and I am swimming through the sky. I float on my back and watch the light coax rainbows from the ends of my eyelashes, resisting the urge to push myself to the border of cruelty, enjoying the sensation of being held by something larger than myself. I wish that you were here and that nothing was broken, your body opalescent in the strange water, drifting together through the blue.

Maria appears beside me, her hair slicked back like a seal.

'¿Es muy bonito, no?' she laughs, her eyes glinting in the light. She turns and we watch as a teenage boy bombs from the bridge, hitting the water with a thud.

'Déu meu.' She wrinkles her nose. 'That will hurt.' The boy bobs up laughing, shaking water from his hair, seemingly unscathed. 'Do you want to try it?'

'What? Jumping from the bridge?'

'Sí,' she smiles. 'Everyone who comes here must try it once. Diego will go with you.'

I climb out of the water and pull on my underwear, wriggling into the elastic as it puckers my damp skin.

'*Vamos*,' says Diego, winking at Maria. I scrape my knees on rough rocks as we climb up to the bridge. Adrenaline throbs in the back of my throat.

'Do you have fear?' Diego smiles at me with brown teeth and I nod. He laughs as we walk to the middle of the bridge and it sways in the wind. A teenage girl appears, her hair wracked with water and her eyes flashing. She swings herself over the railing onto a tiny ledge, then bends her knees and jumps straight into the water like a pencil, disappearing for a second too long, then bobbing up to the daylight again.

'I don't know if I can do it,' I say to Diego and he laughs again.

'It is easy. *Mira*.' I watch his gnarled toes grip the edge of the bridge and then he is off, arms raised in the air like a ballerina, the wind rushing up around his body. He hits the water gracefully, then emerges with long strokes. He waves up at me and I swing myself onto the ledge. My body quivers as I teeter between the cliffs. The water glints like a sheet of metal in the sunlight and I imagine my bones breaking as I hit the surface, my spine snapping and my skull shattering. I can feel Maria watching me, teenagers on the rocks looking up with half-lidded eyes, joints burning softly between their lips. I shiver on the ledge and I know I cannot do it. I am too afraid to step over the edge.

A man with dark, curly hair moves towards me and the bridge rocks beneath his weight.

'*¿Vas a saltar?*' he asks and I swing my legs back over the ledge to safety.

'*No. Lo tienes.*' The man jumps off the bridge and hits the water at an awkward angle, but still comes up laughing, coughing in the spray. I make my way back towards Maria

235

and Diego, feeling pathetic. They laugh and tell me not to worry but I feel like I have let them down. In the past, I would have jumped without thinking about it, relishing the flash of the gorge rushing up to meet me, throwing my whole self to the wind.

I am quiet as we drive back to the village. The clouds begin to darken and the threat of silver flickers in the hills. The air is fraught with electricity and I wonder what has changed, why I am no longer drawn to the outside, stepping away from the edge.

91

'Who was that man you were talking to last night?' I asked Rosa as we eased our hangovers in the café down the road from her flat. I sipped a strong cup of tea and buttered my toast. 'On the street outside. Tall. Black hair. Softly spoken.' Rosa burst the yolk on her fried egg and glanced up at me, stale eyeliner smudged beneath her eyes.

'An old friend from Goldsmiths.' Her lips curled. 'Why?'

'No reason.' I took a bite of toast. 'He just seemed nice.'

'Did you speak to him?'

'Not really.'

Rosa smirked. 'Would you like to?' A headache settled behind my eyes and I took a big drink of water.

'Oh, I don't know.'

'Why not?'

'I haven't been on a date in ages.'

She squirted a dollop of ketchup onto her plate. 'I could give you his phone number, if you like.'

'I can't just text him out of the blue,' I panicked.

Rosa rolled her eyes. 'Come on. It'll be fun. Don't over-think it.'

92

I light a fire in the wood burner and find a knitted jumper in a cupboard. It smells of damp but I pull it on gratefully. Hard beads of rain hit the tin roof and I heat a can of soup on the stove, pouring myself a glass of wine and remembering when we were here together and everything was different. I look at the mugs stacked on the shelf and the pans hanging from nails on the walls and I wonder what it would be like to stay here, to become part of the community, to need less and to live with little. Yet, I have already tried whittling my life down to the bare essentials and it made me too weightless, barely making an impression on the world.

My phone rings, jolting me out of my thoughts. Your name lights up and I swallow and answer your call.

'Hi.' Your voice sounds small and far away.

'Hi.' There is a silence and I listen to the heavy rain and the logs cracking, my soup bubbling in the pan.

'Are you okay?' I ask, tentatively.

'Not really. Are you?'

'No, not really.' There is a pause. 'I'm sorry.' My voice comes out in a whisper.

You exhale heavily and I bite my lip. 'What the fuck?' you say and my body tenses. 'What the fuck were you thinking?' I know I should not have disappeared like that but I felt powerless in your new life, small and rejected, so I pulled away from you and threw myself back into the night.

'I'm sorry,' I say again.

'I was so worried.'

'I know.' There is a silence. 'I'm sorry about what I did.'

'Are you?' Your words are hard.

'Yes.' I take a tiny sip of wine. 'It was stupid. I didn't want to hurt you. But it hurt me when you asked me to leave.'

'I didn't ask you to leave.'

'That's what it felt like.' There is a long silence. I imagine you sitting on the floor of your apartment in a crumpled shirt, biting the skin around your cuticles.

When you finally speak, your voice is strained, as though you are carrying something heavy inside it. 'I'm always worried that you're going to leave.'

'What?'

'I can't live like this. All this uncertainty.'

'What do you mean?' You are quiet and I gnaw at your words. 'Do you mean you don't know if you can live with me?'

'Maybe.'

Anger catches in my throat. I want to make things better, to recapture all the gold I let slip through my fingers and I also want to push you further away, to take us over a cliff just to hear the shatter.

'Okay,' I say bitterly, remembering that you wouldn't give me a straight answer about whether you were coming to the party. 'Maybe it isn't working, then.'

'So, is that it?'

'Is that what you want?' I hold my breath.

'No.' Your voice is hollow. 'I want you to come back.'

238

I look around the small cabin, at the blue shadows of the mountains through the window and my sandals kicked off by the door. I have been searching for a space that feels like mine but I don't know where to find it. I took risks for the right to choose my own life and I can't let you pull that away from me. I have been trying to claw my way back to what is familiar, to let go of all the good things around me because I don't believe that I deserve them, to remember how it feels to be hungry and wild.

'Do you really?' I ask you.

'Yes,' you reply. I am quiet, waiting for you to continue. 'I'm sorry for asking you to go and stay somewhere else,' you say. 'You just got so weird when I asked if you wanted to move in together. I thought that you wanted to leave.' My soup is ready and I stand up and turn off the stove. I look out of the window at the trees blowing in the dark and I realise how it must have looked to you; as if I was rejecting your offer of making a space together, when really, I just needed it to be my own choice.

'Do you really think I just do whatever I want?' I ask you. There is another silence. I press my fingers into the grain on the wooden counter, waiting for your reply.

'No,' you say, sadly. 'But you did at the party.' I pour my soup into a bowl, watching the steam curl in the candlelight.

'Maybe I just had to try it.'

You are quiet for a long time. 'I'm really tired,' you say, eventually. 'Shall we speak again tomorrow?'

'That would be nice.'

We say goodbye and I carry my soup over to the table. My stomach churns and I hesitate for a moment, then I tip the bowl to my mouth and drink it too quickly, burning my lips and tongue.

93

We decided to meet at a pub in Camberwell. I cycled in the rain and my hair hung around my face like damp rope. I spotted you wearing a wrinkled shirt, reading a book with your elbows propped on the table. My stomach contracted and I almost turned around and walked out again but then you looked up and I smiled.

'Do you want a drink?' I asked when I reached your table, hoping that my bank card would work.

'I've got one, thanks.' You closed your book and gestured to the pint of bitter in front of you. 'Shall I get one for you?'

'It's alright, I can get it.'

When I sat down with my glass of wine, I noticed the dirt beneath your fingernails, the small scar above your left eyebrow, the thin silver chain around your neck. You were nervous and cat-like, smelling of smoke and liquorice and I felt a teetering sensation, as though I was standing on a ledge.

94

I wake early and shove on a pair of Maria's old trainers that are one size too small for me, a pair of shorts and a T-shirt I find stuffed in the back of a drawer. I splash my face with cold water and go out into the morning. The air smells moist and fresh before the heat sets in and the grass is wet on my ankles. I walk through the fields and up past the farm, listening to the goat bells ringing, breathing in mud and manure. I reach the dirt path that runs over the hills and remember when we walked along it together, looking at the trees and plants, running our hands through yellow flowers, reaching for things we did not know the names of.

I begin to run, feeling relief as my heart speeds up and my muscles loosen, pounding out the tension that is coiled between my bones. I push myself forward, jumping over rocks and fallen branches, listening to the stones crunch beneath my too-tight trainers, the hot rush of my breath. I think of you pulling prawns from their shells and walking beneath orange trees, your calves stained with bike oil, your face lit up gold in the back of a taxi, your hand beneath my dress on the kitchen counter. I run faster, trying to escape the ache of you, until my lungs burn and sweat runs down my face. I run until I am no longer thinking, until I am only breath and air, leaving muscle and sinew behind.

I trip on a rock and hit the ground hard, grazing my hands as I reach out to steady myself, banging my knee on something sharp. I cry out but there is no one to hear me, just the fizz of insects in the long grass and birds circling overhead. I lie still for a moment, my knee pulsing and my palms stinging, then I sit up and look at the blood running down my leg and I burst into tears. I cry like a child, huge, heaving sobs with my mouth wide open, salt running down my face. I am so tired of contorting myself into small, angular spaces, trying to become an impossible shape.

I brush the grit from my legs and struggle to my feet. My knee is already bruised and swollen. My head pounds as I try to get my bearings and I realise I am miles from the cabin. I take my phone from my pocket but there is no signal. I pull myself together and limp heavily back along the track. I have pushed myself too far again and I wonder if I will ever break this cycle and learn how to sit with who I am.

I think of Tara and remember how it felt when we were younger and the nights were limitless, as though we were invincible, rushing into the unknowable future and maybe now I am here. I am getting older and there are fewer possibilities available to me, or maybe there were never as many possibilities as I once believed, grasping at glimmering cities set in the sky like jewels, blinding and out of my reach. I went to London and Paris to lose myself and they swallowed me whole, but I no longer want to feel inconsequential, throwing myself at impenetrable walls.

I limp past rocks and bushes, hoping I am going in the right direction, trying not to put too much pressure on my knee. I eventually see the goat farm in the distance and I stumble back to the cabin, thirsty and sore, my calves scratched and nettle-stung and my knee sticky with blood. I breathe in the burnt air and feel my heart thudding against my ribs, my hips spilling over the waistband of my shorts. My body is a desperate animal, throbbing with constant need but perhaps I could learn to be unashamed of needing and wanting, to see it as living instead.

I take out my phone and send Tara a message, telling her that I love her and I hope she is okay. My thumb hovers over your name but I do not press it because I don't know what I want to say. I bathe my knee carefully with a pan of warm water, wiping away dust. There is a big chunk of grit trapped beneath the skin and I dig it out carefully with a small twist, like a loose milk tooth wrenched from a gum, and it leaves a tiny wet hole. I roll it between my fingers and wonder how long I might have carried it around, if I had not noticed it. I imagine my skin healing, growing over the stone, sealing it inside me. I wonder if it would get infected, or whether my body would break it down. Maybe I would have just carried it for the rest of my life, without even knowing it was there.

95

I held the thought of you inside me like something delicate, too new and fragile, as if it could easily be broken. Your curling consonants wound around the glass skyscrapers and the streetlights spat your name into the dusk. I pressed my thumb into the letters that would take me to you and wrote,

'*Do you like dancing?*'

You replied straight away with a strobing heart.

96

Maria invites me to a bonfire in her neighbour's garden. People sit on plastic chairs, drinking cups of wine and eating cold black olives, staring into the flames. I sit next to Diego with my knee bandaged beneath my dress, picking at a bowl of salty crisps, my hair thick with smoke. I feel raw, like something peeled open and I let the fire soothe me, half listening to someone playing guitar, wondering where you are and what you are doing, wishing that you were here.

Diego is drunk and he looks at me kindly.

'¿*Todo bien?*' he asks and I smile at him and nod. Maria comes over to offer us both a top-up of wine. She looks older in the firelight as it catches the creases around her eyes, pulling silver strands from her hair. She moves around the circle and Diego offers me a drag of his joint. I shake my head, then he squeezes my knee affectionately, making me wince.

'I was married,' he says to me, unexpectedly. 'Many years ago.'

'Really? What happened?'

'It broke.' He crosses his legs and blows smoke from his nostrils. 'Now there is Maria.' He gestures towards her.

'Are you together?' I ask, surprised.

'*Un poco*,' he smiles. 'We have an arrangement. It suits us both.' He looks into the fire. 'After my marriage broke—' He shakes his head, looking for the right words. 'Maria and me, we love each other. But for how long?' He looks at the fire. 'How long will we love each other? Now I know that love can leave you, like water running down a drain.' He shakes his head slowly and I swallow.

'Where is your ex-wife now?'

'She lives in Galicia. She has a new family.' He starts rolling a cigarette. '¿*Y tu?*' he smiles. 'Why are you here?'

I watch his stained fingers packing tobacco into a brown Rizla. My knee pulses and I turn you over and over in my mind, understanding that you pushed me away because you are afraid of loss, that you mistook my confusion for something else. I think of your hands on my body in the dense, dark night, your lips catching my earlobe as you asked me what I wanted.

I didn't know how to explain to you that I once wanted sensation, beauty and chaos but I had to swallow my basic needs so I could meet my wants because they were bigger than I could afford. I wanted to go beyond the borders of the life that was set out for me, to stand on the threshold and see the world beyond it, but stepping off the edge came with a cost I did not anticipate. I want to inhabit a space with ease, somewhere airy and light with room to grow into. I want to be part of the world instead of just skirting the edges, to feel deserving of love and care. I want to hold on to the good things tightly, to learn what it means to stay.

'I don't know,' I say to Diego, my eyes watering in the smoke.

'¿*No sabes?*' He laughs and I shake my head. I look up at the pearl of the moon, a fluorescent omen, then I take out my phone and find you.

97

I saw you in the dark wearing a silver shirt. You took off your mask and your face was wide open. A strobe of light led me to you through the smoke and I gave myself over to it, letting you pull me to a place I did not recognise, full of trees and clear water, drenched in honeyed gold. We sat outside on wooden crates and watched the sky curdle. You held a flame between your fingers and I wanted to swallow you, but I was afraid of the taste of my own desire, like bleach and petrol, peaches dipped in salt. You knotted your want into a rope and threw it to me. I shivered in the dawn, counting dead stars, then I reached out my hands and took it.

98

Maria drives me back to the station. We leave early, so she can spend the morning fixing a hole in the water tank, in time for new guests arriving in the afternoon. She is tired and distracted, glancing at the clock as I say goodbye to her, kissing me on the cheek and then pulling away. She has been kind to me over the past few days but I am just another temporary person looking for an escape, someone whose bedsheets she must wash and whose bin she must empty, whose hair she will uncurl from the plughole and rinse from her fingers. She looks tired and now I can see that although she has carved a sliver of freedom for herself, her life is hard here, too.

The bus station is small and sleepy. A man lies on a bench, using his rucksack as a pillow. An empty vending machine glints in the sun. There is a ticket booth with the shutters pulled down and an old couple sitting in the shade with a shopping trolley between them. I spot a small bar with tables outside it and I pull out a chair and sit down.

My dress smells of sun and bonfire smoke and my knee aches beneath my grubby bandage. I watch vultures circle red rocks in the distance and I picture you on your way to work, pounding down the stairs with untied laces, your eyes still blurred with sleep.

I fiddle with the menu, tacky with spilled beer and stray grains of salt. The bar sells honeyed aubergine, deep-fried octopus, patatas bravas in chunky salsa. A waiter comes over to my table and I order quickly, before I can change my mind. There is an old man sitting across from me, smoking a cigar. He nods at me and I smile back at him, showing my teeth. The waiter brings me a cold beer and

I drink it thirstily, holding the bitterness on my tongue. I take out my phone and unlock it, and I have a new message from you.

'*What do you want?*' it says and I trace my fingers over the letters. I want to reach out and hold all of the beauty around me, to be unafraid of pleasure. I want love, sticky and painful, fat with desire and mottled with light.

My food arrives, glistening in oil. I chew slowly, tasting batter and sugar, the swell of the sea. It is delicious, even as part of me still worries about my body and what it will cost me. Guilt clogs my throat but I keep eating anyway, taking life in my mouth and choosing to be part of it, even though I am afraid. I want to grow bigger than my shame, to have mass and density, to leave marks and indentations, to prove my own existence. I lick paprika from my fingers as the sun breaks through the clouds and hits the metal table, dazzling me in gold. I pick up my phone and read your message again.

'*What do you want?*'

I wanted not to want anything but you made that impossible. You tore my life wide open and all of my wanting rushed out. I want flavour and abundance, to be full and expansive. I want all of this and I want it with you.

'*I want everything,*' I write and then delete it. '*I want too much,*' I type and then delete it again. '*I want to be able to choose,*' I write and then send it.

You reply quickly. '*But you can.*'

I sit in the warm light until the bus to Barcelona pulls into the station. I gather my few belongings, smelling the sourness of my unwashed hair and skin and not caring. I am loosening, unlocking, opening my mouth and swallowing the world, in all of its butter and salt. The waiter comes over to clear my table. He nods approvingly at my empty plates, shiny with grease and honey. He asks me where I am from and where I am going. He asks me my name and I tell him.

Acknowledgements

Much of this novel was written over various lockdowns during the Covid-19 pandemic when it was easy to lose sight of the importance of making art. Thank you to all of the writers and friends who helped me find my way back to it.

I would like to thank the readers and booksellers who treated my first novel with such generosity. Especially the Portico Library, whose prize validated my identity as a northern writer and whose financial support enabled me to keep going.

A big thank you to Chris Wellbelove, for giving me space to untangle a knot of difficult questions and to everyone at Aitken Alexander, for treating me and my work with care. Huge thanks to all at Sceptre, for their hard work and support. Especially to Francine Toon, for always making me feel as though my ideas are valuable; to Louise Court and Helen Flood, for their brilliance; and to Charlotte Humphery, for her guidance. Thanks to Kamila K Stanley, for letting us use another of her beautiful photographs for the hardback cover.

A special mention to Roisin, who gave me the key to her home in Donegal once again and who passed away during the writing of this book; I will never forget her kindness.

Moltes gràcies to Aida, Tom, Hauke, Aldi, Pedro y todxs

en Garraf for welcoming me into their community during the early stages of this novel. I will always remember the yellow ginesta, heavy thunderstorms and the pink moon rising over the water during those long, strange lockdown days. Un beso especial a Marina, who gave me her house in the rock when I needed a home and who reminded me what dreaming feels like.

Special thanks to Félix and Francesca, for sharing their languages, and to Sarah, Miranda, Cat, Mel, Lee and Colin for being early readers.

Love to my family, for believing in me. Especially to my mam, who has always made me feel as if the world is possible. And to Jack, for all of the lightning.

'A distinctive new voice for fans
of *Fleabag* or Sally Rooney'
Independent

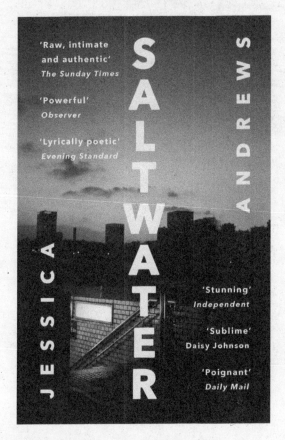

Winner of the Portico Prize

'Raw, intimate and authentic'
Sunday Times

Read an extract from *Saltwater*

Prologue

It begins with our bodies. Skin on skin. My body burst from yours. Safe together in the violet dark and yet already there are spaces beginning to open between us. I am wet and glistening like a beetroot pulsing in soil. Gasping and gulping. There are wounds in your belly and welts around your nipples, puffy and purpling. They came from me, just like I came from you. We are connected through molten rivers like the lava that runs beneath the earth's crust. Shifting. Oil trapped beneath the sea. Precious liquid seeping through cracks. This love is heavy; salty and viscous, stinking of seaweed and yeast. Sweat is nourishing and so is that tangy vagina smell that later men will tell me tastes like battery acid. But there are not any men, not yet. For now our secrets are only ours. You press me to your chest and I am you and I am not you and we will not always belong to each other but for now it is us and here it is quiet. I rise and fall with your breath in this bed. We are safe in the pink together.

I

My first dead body was my grandfather's. My mother and I sat in the funeral home at his wake in Ireland for two days while people I had never met came to pay their respects. I moved to the back of the room because I thought the blue in his eyelids might pierce my skin if I sat too close for too long.

The last time I saw him alive, he was in hospital. I kissed him goodbye and left the imprint of my lips lingering on his cheek. I wore bright red lipstick and it made his skin look grey. I tried to rub it away with my sleeve and he said, 'Oh, leave it. I'll keep it there, 'til you come back.' I reached for his cold hand, fluttering on top of smooth sheets.

2

Before I came to Ireland, I was living in London. I was seduced by coloured lights hitting the river in the middle of the night and throngs of cool girls in chunky sandals who promised a future of tote bags and house plants. I thought that was the kind of life I was supposed to want.

I worked in a bar every night while I figured out how to get there.

3

I never did go back to the hospital.

During my grandfather's wake, I looked for the trace of my kiss on his skin.

I could not find it.

4

London is built on money and ambition and I didn't have enough of either of those things. I felt as though the tangle of wires and telephone lines strung through the city were strings in a fishing net filled with bankers and nondescript creatives, shimmering in banknotes and holographic back-packs. I was something small and weak and undesirable. I was slipping through the holes and down into the deep underbelly of the ocean. I watched these people from my vantage point behind the bar. I noted the colour of their fingernails and the smell of their perfume and how many times they went to the toilet in one night. They did not notice me.

5

I am just another impossibility. Colourless. Unformed. You cannot imagine anything as fiercely small, as fiercely hungry as me. There is a splitting that has not happened yet. This is you before me. You are a daughter and not a mother. Not yet. And yet; there are invisible things drawing us close, even here. Fall into those molten afternoons, his hands all over your body. Spill towards me.

6

My grandfather was born in Glasgow. He and his brothers and sisters were small and soft beneath the tenement buildings. Their father went to the pub one day and never came back. Their mother died soon afterwards, 'Of a broken heart,' people tutted, shaking their heads and supping the tragedy from fingerprinted pint glasses. The children were shipped this way and that by strangers and well-meaning relatives. They ended up in an orphanage, where priests cupped and kissed them in terrible places.

They had an Auntie Kitty who lived in a small fishing port on the west coast of Ireland. She sent for them and they stayed with her and slept in the hay with her animals, warm dung sticking sweetly to their clothes and matting their hair. They walked along the dirt roads to school with bare feet and broke in wild horses while they were light enough to cling to their backs without being thrown off. They raced through long grasses and swam in the rough sea and learned to light fires by rolling oily twists of news-paper and drying out kindling in the sun.

Auntie Kitty rationed the hot water and made anyone who entered the house throw holy sand over their left shoulder, To Keep Away The Devil. Her husband was involved in the IRA and they housed members in their attic. In the springtime she marched around the garden with a pair of scissors, snipping the heads from any flowers that dared to bloom orange.

'Just off out on me horse!' she called as she wheeled her rusty bicycle down the hallway. She was a self-educated woman, and she taught my grandfather how to write and to read constellations in the salty night sky.

As my grandfather grew he worked as a gardener, pruning rhubarb and thatching roofs and occasionally mending leaky plumbing. When he was old enough, he travelled to England on the boat with the rest of the boys, looking for labouring work. He helped to build the Tyne Tunnel, spending his days deep beneath the ocean, installing lights so that strangers could see in the dark.

He found himself in Sunderland, among the crashing and clanking of the shipyards. He lived in a boarding house run by a gentle woman and her sharp and gorgeous daughter. He befriended Toni from Italy, who ate cocaine for breakfast and dreamed of running a café, and he shared a room with Harry from Derry, who played the spoons and had a crucifix tattooed across his chest.

He liked Johnny Cash, horse racing and Jameson's whiskey. He always wore a suit and carried a packet of Fruit Polos in his inside pocket. He was at home by the water with the rust and the metal.

7

I am living in Burtonport, a tiny fishing port in County Donegal, on the north-west coast of Ireland. In order to get here, you have to travel through the Blue Stack Mountains. Time alters as you drive into them. They are brown and reassuring but appear blue in the shifting light, dripping navy and indigo into the valleys.

When I was a child, my mother, brother and I spent dusky Augusts in Donegal. We felt safe when we had passed the mountains, cut off from the tumult of our lives at home. As soon as we arrived, my mother turned off her Nokia and put it in the glove compartment of her car. She didn't switch it on until summer was over and we were back on the motorway.

As a teenager I ran from solidity and stasis and shades of brown. I wanted things that flashed and fizzled. Now that I am here, beneath the peat smoke and the penny-coloured skies, brown seems like a safe place. I can crawl into it and swallow fistfuls of soil.

8

When my grandfather died I called the pub.
  'I'm really sorry, Deborah, but I can't come in today.'
  'You what, babe?'
  'I think I need to go away for a bit.'

'Speak up, will you? Line's breaking up.'

'I have to go to Ireland for a funeral. I don't know when I'll be back.'

'Who is this?'

'I'll come in and see you when I'm back in town.'

I saw a chance and I grasped it. I texted my landlord and told him to keep my deposit. I put my books into boxes and gave all of my clothes away. I took the train north to my mother's house, then we boarded an aeroplane and hired a car and now here I am.

9

I am creeping. The future unspooling. I am forming slowly inside you. Barely even an idea. There are so many ways in which you do not know yourself yet, blue-black and heavy like reams of crushed velvet. All the broken objects of our lives are stretched in front of us, gorgeous and unknowable.

10

My mother and I have inherited my grandfather's small stone cottage, through the Blue Stack Mountains by the sea. It is tucked into a nook crammed with giant rhubarb and purple hydrangeas. There are wild potatoes and mangy kittens and clumps of shamrock clustered in the corners.

The garden is very overgrown but if I climb onto the kitchen roof I can see the sea.

We arrived to find that colonies of mould and specks of damp thrived in my grandfather's absence. They were splattered across the walls and ceilings like a sludgy Pollock painting. Tiny worms and mites had burrowed holes in the wooden furniture. The drawers and cupboards were crusty with rust and the fridge stank of sour milk. The mattresses were crawling with bugs.

In the months before my grandfather's death, something between my mother and me was fractured. Her presence in my life had been solid and gold, then suddenly she was not there any more. I felt her pulling away from me. It hurt inside of my body, my intestines stretched and sore. I felt confused by love; the way it could simultaneously trap you and set you free. How it could bring people impossibly close and then push them far away. How people who loved you could leave you when you needed them most.

We talked about practical things when she called me in London; when the funeral would be and how I would get there. We listened to the radio during the drive from the airport and at the wake we chatted to my grandfather's neighbours and friends. It wasn't until he had been buried and everyone had gone home to their brandies that we were alone together in the silent cottage. The distance glinted between us, sharp and dangerous. We sat on a sheet of newspaper on the floor and looked around.

'What are we going to do?' I asked her.

'Burn it,' she said, blowing on a cup of tea.

'You what?'

'We're going to have to burn everything.'

'Burn it where?' She paused.

'In the garden.'

'Everything?'

'It's the only way.'

She gave me a look. I knew she was trying to teach me something, but I didn't know if I wanted to learn it. I knew she wanted me to let go of things that did not belong to me, but I could not work out which things were mine. I did not know how much of my story I was entitled to take, and how much of the past I was allowed to leave behind.

We lit a bonfire and it burned for three days. We fed it everything: the mattresses, the bed frames, the chairs, the rugs, the chest of drawers, the dishcloths, the wardrobe. Scraps of paper scribbled with his handwriting, pink betting slips, old photographs, boxes of tablets and thick-rimmed glasses, his spare set of teeth. I reread musty letters I had sent him and found forgotten Christmas cards lodged between radiators and walls.

We shuddered as the duvet went up in a flash and took hammers to the dining room table. We emptied bin liners filled with socks and underpants into the flames. I liked watching the sofa best. The upholstery burned in jagged shapes, leaving the wooden skeleton standing on its own for a moment, naked and shy.

Plasticky smoke gathered in the trees.

'Are we allowed to do this?' I asked my mother.

'Probably not,' she replied. 'It feels good though, doesn't it?' She squeezed my hand. Our faces were hot from the flames.

We cleaned the house as the fire razed the garden, clearing the cupboards and scrubbing the sinks. We sang along to the Shangri-Las and the Ronettes, bleaching the kitchen counters until they were bright white and dazzling. I covered my mouth with a scarf, trying not to breathe in black smoke. I didn't want tiny pieces of my granddad's clothes and furniture to settle in the back of my throat.

'Let's get some taties on this fire, eh, Luce?' she joked, stoking the embers with my grandfather's walking stick. I looked at her. She had mud streaked across her forehead. I felt the sharpness between us soften a little, as though the edges had been rubbed smooth. She laughed.

'Don't look at me like that. It's only stuff, you know.'

11

The debris of my grandfather's life landed on our clothes and in our hair. It coated our skin. I learned that the drifting bits of ash are called 'fire angels'. After a house fire, they are considered to be very dangerous because they can re-ignite the blaze. They are small and fragile, but they are still smouldering.

12

When I was a toddler, my mother, my father and I went on holiday to Tenerife. We stayed in a hotel for non-Spanish-speaking tourists, whose name translated to 'Hotel Dead Donkey'. There was a cockroach infestation and they climbed up the walls as we slept, their hard bodies glittering in the moonlight.

Days passed in a haze of hair braids and Mini Milk ice

lollies, cold and smooth against my sunburned lips. I loved the rubbery smell of my inflatable crocodile and the bitter taste of sun on my skin. We went to the beach one day and I paddled in the sea in my white T-shirt, while my mother and father watched from gritty beach towels on the shore. I waded in up to my waist and squinted in the sunlight. I watched the waves dapple my arms and legs and shrieked as the droplets caught the light. I heard an angry noise and turned towards a small motorboat filled with strong, tanned men in fisherman's caps moving steadily towards me. I froze in fear and turned to see my father's arms making big white arcs in the water. He scooped me up.

'My kid!' he shouted at the men. They laughed and waved their arms nonchalantly.

'No problem.' They smiled. 'No problem.' Their teeth were so white against the blue sky. I lay wrapped in the beach towel for the rest of the day, savouring my escape.

13

My mother left Ireland after the burning. Things were still not right between us. I knew she was trying to teach me something important, about how to be in my life, but I was too angry with her to listen.

I am not going back to London. Once I craved the speed and proximity to a centre, the sense that something was always about to happen, just out of reach. The city was a shape that could not be classified, shifting and moving, infinite possibilities hanging from the streets like fruit.

Now, when I think of the city, it is in rectangles and squares; impenetrable shapes with fierce elbows, shutting me out.

I have been dreaming of tube tunnels, smoky and choking. I am feeling my way through them, touching the walls. I am straining my eyes for a glimpse of my father, who is lost somewhere in the darkness, always just out of reach. I am calling for my mother and my voice echoes along the tracks.

14

Redness cracking. Fissures forming. You are falling towards us, rich and syrup-soft. Flesh roiling. Bones shifting. Tongues over bellies and fingers in wet places. Salt stains the mattress; seeps into places where hands cannot reach. Tissues twisting and saline dripping into something new. Sink into the thick of us. The peach pit slick of us.